"山东省高校人文社会科学研究计划"项目

论玛莎·诺曼戏剧中的过去和记忆

王莉 著

Past and Memory in Marsha Norman's Dramatic Works

中国社会科学出版社

图书在版编目（CIP）数据

论玛莎·诺曼戏剧中的过去和记忆：英文/王莉著.—北京：中国社会科学出版社，2014.12

ISBN 978 - 7 - 5161 - 5343 - 7

Ⅰ.①论… Ⅱ.①王… Ⅲ.①诺曼，M.（1947~）戏剧文学—文学研究—英文 Ⅳ.①I712.073

中国版本图书馆 CIP 数据核字（2014）第 304672 号

出 版 人	赵剑英
责任编辑	侯苗苗
责任校对	吴小成
责任印制	戴　宽

出　　版	中国社会科学出版社
社　　址	北京鼓楼西大街甲 158 号（邮编　100720）
网　　址	http：//www.csspw.cn
	中文域名：中国社科网　　010 - 64070619
发 行 部	010 - 84083635
门 市 部	010 - 84029450
经　　销	新华书店及其他书店

印　　刷	北京君升印刷有限公司
装　　订	廊坊市广阳区广增装订厂
版　　次	2014 年 12 月第 1 版
印　　次	2014 年 12 月第 1 次印刷

开　　本	710×1000　1/16
印　　张	11.75
插　　页	2
字　　数	203
定　　价	39.00 元

凡购买中国社会科学出版社图书，如有质量问题请与本社发行部联系调换
电话：010 - 64009791

前　言

　　玛莎·诺曼（Marsha Norman，1947—）是 20 世纪 70 年代末开始闻名于美国剧坛并获得普利策奖和托尼奖等各种不同荣誉的当代剧作家。自创作伊始，她的戏剧作品就体现出浓厚的悲剧色彩以及对人物内心世界的深刻剖析，受到观众和研究者们较为普遍的关注。她的作品不但译有中文，也在中国舞台上多次演出。然而国内外学者更多地关注作者和作品主人公的性别身份的意义。本书在细读诺曼的全部作品的基础上，认定了她作品中的一个普遍而又重要的主题"过去与记忆"，并从戏剧呈现的角度入手，对这一主题做多方位的深入剖析，并比较在不同作品中的不同景象。本书选取诺曼的七部代表剧作，考察了其中三种不同的过去：创伤性过去、让人渴望的过去以及虚构的过去，深刻地剖析了诺曼如何运用各种戏剧手段呈现不同的过去和记忆，以及剧中人物对不同的过去和记忆采取的态度和做出的行动。

　　本书由五部分组成。第一部分为引言。在梳理了国内外已有的研究文献的基础上，阐释了本选题的研究意义，为本书的主体分析奠定了基础。第一章研究了《出狱》（Getting Out）和《黑暗中的行者》（Traveling in the Dark）中的创伤性过去以及主人公对创伤性过去由压抑到和解的过程。在这两部作品中，创伤性过去对主人公心理和情感上造成伤痛，他们试图压抑以便忘记往事。然而他们的压抑行为却造成了生存危机。在朋友和家人的帮助下，主人公能正视创伤性过去，与之取得和解。在诺曼看来，这种和解并非抹杀过去，而是将创伤性过去重置于他们的生活轨迹之中，这有助于主人公重新审视自我与社会之间的关系，对未来的生活怀有希冀。

　　在《出狱》中，诺曼使用了闪回、分裂人格、空间限制以及两个演出场地并置等手段，表现阿林作为儿童性虐受害者以及社会受害者的创伤性记忆。尽管阿林试图压抑她的创伤性记忆，现实中的各种诱因却不断地引起这些闯入性的记忆。最终阿林通过与过去的自我的重新整合与创伤性过去取得和解。

在《黑暗中的行者》中,山姆因压抑母亲去世的创伤性记忆而对其生活造成了严重的后果。诺曼采用具有象征意义的母亲的花园以及房屋外墙所代表的场外空间表现山姆对创伤性记忆的压抑。好朋友的去世激起了他对母亲的去世的创伤性记忆。妻子不懈的帮助和同理心让他走出创伤性记忆的阴影,重新与家人建立情感联系。

第二章分析了《第三和橡树》(*Third and Oak*)、《僵持》(*The Hold-up*)和《爱上丹尼·布恩》(*Loving Daniel Boone*)中让人渴望的过去以及主人公由怀旧到幻灭的过程。三部作品中的主人公均沉迷于对过去的回忆不能自拔,因而他们无法客观地认识过去与现在。事实上,过去并非他们想象的那样美好。他们在认识到怀旧情感的不切实际以及生存现实后,试图走出过去的阴影并接受现实。通过对主人公由怀旧到幻灭的戏剧呈现,诺曼对过度的怀旧情感进行了批判,因为怀旧情感使得主人公无法在现实生活中实施有效的行动。

《第三和橡树》中,诺曼运用不在场人物的物品以及在场人物对不在场人物的语言模仿表达对过去的怀旧情感。两位女主人公在洗衣店的偶然相遇促使她们认识到自己过去的婚姻的现实,进而对自我进行重新认识。台球厅的两位男主人公通过接受舒特的死亡以及乔治即将死去的事实,认识到曾经的美好时光已经过去,从而接受了现实,并消除了二人之间的误解和隔阂。

在《僵持》中,诺曼通过现代牛仔对西部逃犯故事的痴迷以及西部逃犯对现代技术进步的不接受态度来表现对过去的怀旧。但是,现代牛仔的死亡促使西部逃犯反思他所处的时代的暴力性质。现代牛仔的葬礼的舞台呈现是对西部逃犯时代结束的哀悼,而西部逃犯的重生表现了诺曼对人性以及人类的灵活性和适应性的赞扬。

《爱上丹尼·布恩》作为一部时光穿越剧,把弗洛的个人记忆与对丹尼·布恩神话的集体记忆相交织。诺曼通过分割舞台空间将布恩时代和现代博物馆并置。弗洛现代生活中的感情失意让她对布恩时代充满怀旧情感,然而她的时光穿越之旅却让她意识到布恩作为神话人物的虚构性。

第三章探讨了《晚安,母亲》('*night, Mother*)和《特鲁迪·布鲁》(*Trudy Blue*)中虚构的过去以及主人公勇敢面对的过程。两部剧作中主人公的过去是在由他人或自己虚构的世界中度过的。通过对过去的回忆，主人公认识到生活在虚构的世界中让她们的生存毫无意义，无法实现自己的人生价值。她们通过选择摆脱这种虚构的过去，包括做出死亡的选择，展示了自我价值。

《晚安，母亲》通过母女二人的对话展现了女儿的过去是生活在母亲编织的世界中。诺曼采用具有象征意义的阁楼表现杰西过去生活的停滞状态以及生活中的秘密。杰西的自杀是她摆脱过去并实现自我控制的方式。在《特鲁迪·布鲁》中，由于整个剧是金杰的回忆，诺曼采用了空舞台以及插曲式结构。生活在幻想的世界中使得金杰对现实中的人和世界无法正确认识。她逼近的死亡促使她认识到过去幻想世界的虚构性，从而摆脱了幻想人物，回到现实世界中的家庭。

最后一部分为结论。诺曼对过去和记忆的关注实际上是她对人如何生存的哲学性思考。剧中人物对过去和记忆的态度体现了他们的存在焦虑。通过表现人物能够通过解决与过去的关系而获得他们认定的更好的存在方式，诺曼认为人能够通过个人努力改变存在方式并实现自己的人生价值。

Contents

INTRODUCTION

Marsha Norman (1947—) is regarded as a major contemporary American playwright thanks to the acclaim of several major critics concerning her early plays, especially her Pulitzer Prize-winning play 'night, Mother (1982). Robert Brustein, the artistic director of Harvard's American Repertory Theatre (ART), in his well-quoted review, speaks highly of Norman as a universal playwright who addresses general human experiences:

> Nothing reinforces one's faith in the power and importance of the theater more than the emergence of an authentic universal playwright—not a woman playwright, mind you, not a regional playwright, not an ethnic playwright, but one who speaks to the concerns and experiences of all humankind. (162)

Just because of this universality of Norman's concern, he compares Norman to the Russian playwright Anton Chekhov and the father of modern American drama Eugene O'Neill for exploring similar themes (159). Similarly, Frank Rich, The New York Times chief theatre critic, considers it "Marsha Norman's profound achievement that she brings both understanding and dignity to forgotten and tragic American lives" (3). On account of her particular concern over women's issues and her dramatization of women's experiences, Janet Brown, the prominent feminist theater critic, hails Norman as "the most successful author of serious feminist drama working in the U. S. today" (60). The New York Times critic Mel Gussow wrote a long article entitled "Women Playwrights: New Voices in the Theatre" to make a detailed commentary on Norman and 'night, Mother, regarding the playwright as one "at the crest of a wave of adventurous young women playwrights" (22). Besides the topmost honor, the play also earns for its author the Susan Smith Blackburn Prize, Hull-Warriner, and Drama Desk A-wards and four Tony nominations. It has been translated into many languages, included in college drama books and performed all over the world. [1]

Norman's commitment to writing has made it possible for her to author ten original plays, five adaptations (including three musical adaptations [2]), a novel, several television scripts and screenplays. In addition to her own writing, she nurtures upcoming playwrights. She is the co-director, with Christopher Durang, of the Playwrights Program at the prestigious Juilliard School of Drama. She also serves on the board of the Dramatists Guild. Besides, she has won a slew of other honors and awards including grants from the National Endowment for the Arts, the Rockefeller Foundation, the American Academy and Institute of the Arts and Letters, Lifetime Achievement Award for Literary Arts by Guild Hall, and the William Inge Distinguished Achievement in the American Theatre Award.

In light of all these laudatory comments and accolades, some critics believe Norman's works deserve even more critical and scholarly attention than they have been given. Linda Ginter Brown, in the preface of *Marsha Norman: a Casebook* (1996), laments that "contemporary critics give Norman less attention and acclaim than she rightly deserves. As one of America's foremost contemporary playwrights, she merits more" (xi). Matthew Roudané, writing about American plays and playwrights since 1970, also expresses that "[d]espite her important and ongoing contributions to the American stage, Marsha Norman has not been fully embraced by the critics" ("Plays" 378). Christo-

---

① For instance, it was translated into Chinese by Huang Zongjiang and Zhang Quanquan and published in the first issue of *Foreign Theatre* in 1985. It is included in *British and American Drama: Plays and Criticisms*, a course book for Chinese colleges, edited by Liu Haiping and Zhu Xuefeng. It has been put on stage in China several times. It was first performed at China Youth Art Theatre in Beijing in 1993. It was later staged at Oriental Pioneer Theatre in Beijing in 2006, Changqing Arts Theatre in Jinan in 2009 and at Shanghai Dramatic Arts Center in 2011.

② In 1991, Norman's adaptation of Frances Hodgson Burnett's *The Secret Garden*, a Broadway musical, won her the Tony Award for Best Book of a Musical.

pher Bigsby is also disappointed by the fact that Marsha Norman still tends to be regarded as "the author of '*night*, *Mother* and nothing else" (*Contemporary* viii).

In addition, among the critical works on Norman's plays, most of them mainly focus on her two better-known plays, *Getting Out* (1977) and '*night*, *Mother*. The critical reception to Norman's other plays has been less than salutary. To Norman, the reasons for this lack of positive regard is bias: "[t] hey are perceived to be 'girl plays', concerned with loss and death, love and betrayal, friendship and family" rather than "'guy' plays" with guns in them ("Not There Yet" 79). Norman in fact produces a series of plays engaging with the past and memory, profoundly evoking the existential crises through characters that are intertwined in the dynamics between the past, the present and the future. Rather than focusing on a single play, it is most useful to explore her plays as an internally related body of work.

Two books comprehensively encompass almost all of Norman's works to date. Linda Ginter Brown's *Marsha Norman: a Casebook*, published in 1996, is a collection of essays which deals with most of Norman's plays rather than just the more well-known plays. Deeming that Norman's purpose in writing is to "give everyday people, in many instances women, voices to make sure someone, somewhere, is listening" (xi), she hopes that the essays in the book may correct the dearth of scholarship on Norman. However, research on Norman is still far from being adequate. Bigsby devotes one chapter to Norman in *Contemporary American Playwrights* and analyzes her plays from *Getting Out* to *Trudy Blue* (1998). [1] He claims that Norman in plays from *Getting Out* through to '*night*, *Mother* displays a woman playwright's particular concern with women because in these plays she "find [s] in dialogue between women a way of opening up channels to emotional needs and anxieties" (210). However, he also

---

[1] The original version of the play appeared in 1995 Humana Festival in Actors Theatre of Louisville. Bigsby's comments on this play are based on the typescript which is used for a planned off-Broadway production in Feb. 1998. But until Dec. 1999, the final version was performed in MCC Theatre in New York. The ending of the final version is totally different from the early ones. Whereas the early versions end with the suicide of the heroine, the final version ends with the heroine's reconnection with her family.

observes that with men as protagonists, Norman similarly shows the emotional truths and "exposes hidden tensions and anxieties" (210). To him, Norman's dramatization of the emotional truths beneath the banalities of conversations and the desire for connection is Norman's way of examining the isolation of herself, and in extension, of humankind.

Up to now, according to the databases ProQuest, CETD, NDLTD and WorldCat. org, there are thirty-five Ph. D. dissertations and twenty-seven M. A. theses in the United States, one M. A. thesis in Canada, one dissertation in Germany and two M. A. theses in Taiwan which deal mainly with the more famous plays as mentioned above. Among them, only two center on Norman's treatment of the past and the rest approach Norman's plays from diversified perspectives—feminist theories (focusing on female autonomy[1], female self[2] and mother-daughter relationship[3]), family studies[4], aesthetic studies[5], spatial

---

[1] Examples are Linda Louise Rohrer Paige, *The "Other" Side of the Looking Glass: A Feminist Perspective on Female Suicide in Ibsen's "Hedda Gabler", Hellman's "The Children's Hour", and Norman's "'night, Mother"*. Diss. The U of Tennessee, 1989; Karen Kay Keeter Rogers, *Responses to Restriction and Confinement in Selected Plays by Women Dramatists of the English-Speaking Theatre: The Susan Smith Blackburn First-Prize-Winning Plays From 1980—1981 Through 1985—1986*. Diss. The U of Texas at Dallas, 1999.

[2] For example, Linda Ginter Brown, *Toward a More Cohesive Self: Women in Works of Lillian Hellman and Marsha Norman*. Diss. The Ohio State U, 1991.

[3] Examples are Karen K. Foster, *De-Tangling the Web: Mother-Daughter Relationships in the Plays of Marsha Norman, Lillian Hellman, Tina Howe, and Ntozake Shang*, Diss. The U of Nebraska-Lincoln, 1994; Suzanne Elaine Beal, *"Mama Teach Me That French": Mothers and Daughters in Twentieth Century Plays by American Women Playwrights*, Diss. U of Maryland College Park, 1994.

[4] Examples are Gretchen Sarah Cline, *The Psychodrama of the Dysfunctional Family Desire, Subjectivity, and Regression in Twentieth Century American Drama*. Diss. The Ohio State U, 1991; Pamela Powell Monoca, *The Bond that Ties: The Role of the Family in Contemporary American Drama*. Diss. The Catholic U of America, 1995.

[5] Examples are William W. Demastes, *American New Realism in the Theatre of the 80s*, Diss. The U of Wisconsin-Madison, 1986; Carolyn Cope, *The Woman's Aesthetic in Selected Plays Of Maria Irene Fornes, Holly Hughes, Wendy Wasserstein, Marsha Norman and Suzan-Lori Parks* Diss. Southern Illinois U, 2005.

*theory*①, discourse analysis②, reception studies③ and genre studies④. This is also the case for scholarly essays of consequence, some of which have been collected in *Contemporary Literary Criticism* (volume 186). Most of the articles also cover Norman's better-known plays, with only a few of them including comments on Norman's other works.

In China, the name of Marsha Norman was first mentioned in 1983 after she was awarded the Pulitzer Prize for Drama (Fu 265). The next year Huang Zongjiang and Zhang Quanquan translated '*night, Mother* which was published in the first issue of *Foreign Theatre* in 1985. Chen Maiping, in an article on western realistic drama, underlines Norman's realistic mode of writing (30). However, more serious study on Norman's plays began after '*night, Mother*'s first performance at China Youth Art Theatre in Beijing in 1993. Tang Lifeng's study on '*night, Mother* points out that Jessie's committing suicide is a paradoxical way to end the state of living death (44). Shi Jian's article "Reality and Fantasy of Norman's Female Characters" investigates the conflict between reality and fantasy of the female characters in *Getting Out*, *Third and Oak*, *The Hold-up*, and *Traveler in the Dark* (43).

The latest database search for Chinese scholarship on Norman's plays shows both variety and depth. According to the CNKI database, there appeared three Ph. D. dissertations,⑤ two M. A. theses and more than a dozen articles during the last ten years. In addition to reading Norman's plays from a feminist perspective, research on Norman's work extends to the realm of language and exis-

---

① For Example, Huang Shih – yi, *Spatial Repression in Marsha Norman's Plays*. MA thesis. Taiwan Chengchi U. 2002.

② For Example, Alice Spitz, *Power Plays: The Representation of Mother-Daughter Disputes in Contemporary Plays by Women—A Study in Discourse Analysis*, Diss. Universit? t des Saarlandes, 2005.

③ For Example, Jill Dolan, *The Feminist Spectator as Critic: Performance Criticism and Representation*, Diss. New York U, 1988.

④ For Example, Elizabeth Rose Thompson, *Saving the Southern Sister: Tracing the Survivor Narrative in Southern Women's Modern and Contemporary Novels and Plays*. Diss. U of Memphis, 2010.

⑤ The three dissertations are Wu Wenquan's *Cultural Encounter, Dialogue and Confluence: Contemporary American Drama in China*, Diss. Nanjing U, 2004; Zhang Jinliang's *Language as a Perspective: A Study of Three Contemporary American Dramatists*, Diss. Nanjing U, 2007; and Cen Wei's *Lillian Hellman and Marsha Norman: Dramatizing Female Identity*, Diss. Shandong U, 2009.

tentialism. He Anfang and Liu Xiuyu read *'night, Mother* as a play to convey Norman's feminist messages. Zhang Jinliang, reading Norman's plays from the language perspective, takes Norman's characters'silence as an obstacle on their way to become a self (28). Zuo Jin and Han Zhongqian maintain that the person deixis and vocatives show the deep love between the mother and daughter in *'night, Mother* (131) . Cai Xiaoyan considers the play as Norman's concern with modern human beings'existential crisis (47).

Throughout her works, Norman displays a persistent concern over the past and memory of her characters. In her view, her characters'present situation can only be drawn from what they experienced in the past, i. e. — "why the person is the person they are" ("Interview" 150). However, notwithstanding the diversity of perspectives within the known scholarship on the playwright's works, Norman's concern with the past and memory and her dramatic techniques in representing the two have been paid short shrift. Thus, the present study intends to focus on seven of Norman's original plays which display her pervasive concern with the past and memory, including *Getting Out*, *Third and Oak* (1978),①
The Holdup (1979), *'night, Mother*, *Traveler in the Dark* (1984), *Loving Daniel Boone* (1992), and *Trudy Blue*.

There is a small body of criticism which comments on the importance of the past and memory in Norman's plays on various occasions. Most of these critiques, however, merely mention the past and memory in passing and do not delve into it. Other scholars'analyses of the aspect are edifying for a further study. Furthermore, Norman's incorporation of the various dramatic elements in representing the past and memory and the interaction between the past and the present has not been sufficiently tackled.

Among the studies, Jennifer Anne Workman's thesis, *Marsha Norman's Ghosts: The Embodiment of the Past on the Stage*, is the only one which is devoted to examining Norman's representation of the past. To her, the plays not

---

① This play consists of two acts "The Laundromat" and "The Pool Hall" . Because originally Norman allowed the two acts to be produced as separate one-acts, either of the two parts is sometimes discussed as a play without mentioning the other part at all. But Norman says in the preface to the play in *Collected Works* that the two parts are in fact talking about the same thing and should not be treated separately.

only reflect the characters'pasts but also the author's personal past in some way. After an analysis of Norman's personal past which motivates most of Norman's writing, Workman explores Norman's employment of ghost figures as a device to represent the past on the stage, although there is only one play that has real ghost figures on stage. ① Classifying the ghost figures in Norman's plays into three types, "ghosts who are actual characters in the play, ghosts whom the characters represent through imitation and ghosts who are absent characters", Workman argues that Norman's conception of the ghost figure is different from that of the earlier dramatists for its positive aspect—the ghosts "are helpful to the characters they interact with" (72). However, as will be discussed later in this study, the past in Norman's plays is in effect an impediment which causes an existential crisis for the protagonist. In addition, the past is represented in various forms rather than merely through ghost figures.

Through her very first play *Getting Out*, Norman demonstrates her artistic virtuosity in representing the past and memory and the interactions with the present in an innovative way. This is noted by several critics. John Simon, using an ingenious conceit, praises highly the expressionistic technique② used in *Getting Out* to underscore the inextricably linked relationship of the past and present. He writes that "it is one thing just to twine strands together, and another to interweave them artfully, to produce a kind of reweaving. Here the past fills in the aching holes in the present, as seamlessly as if it were the work of a master

① In Norman's musical version of *The Secret Garden*, which is discussed in Workman's thesis, Norman presents real ghosts physically present. In *Getting Out*, the past self of the heroine is put on stage but is only in her memory. Similarly, in *Trudy Blue*, the imaginary characters are in the heroine's mind instead of being real ones.

② Expressionism in drama was a movement in Germany in 1910 and flourished until around 1924. Plays since 1924 written both in Germany and outside it are largely under the influence of the expressionist technique without subscribing to the expressionist philosophy of expressing protest and rebellion. One of the features of expressionist drama is intense subjectivism. The expressionist writer usually shows the world to us as it is seen through the eyes of one character, invariably an alter ego for the writer. Because the world is revealed through one character's vision, it is completely subjective and it becomes deliberately and purposefully distorted. Eugene O'Neill is the first American playwright who made an adept experimentation of the expressionist technique in several of his plays such as *The Emperor Jones* and *The Hairy Ape*. Contemporary American playwrights continue to adopt the technique to explore the subjective mind (John Gassner and Edward Quinn, 256–261). This technique is also used in *Trudy Blue*.

mender" (82). Commenting on the intertwining past and present which is ac-
commodated through the coexistence of the two selves of the heroine, Bigsby observes that "To watch the play is to see a tapestry being sewn, a collage constructed" (*Contemporary* 218). Their remarks show their acclaim of Norman's
dramatic skill in interweaving timescales and events.

In addition to the favorable remarks on Norman's dramatic technique,
scholars' discussions highlight the past as one of the traps for the protagonist to
get out. Nevertheless, because their analyses focus on the theme of "getting out"
or "cutting ties", there is no in-depth discussion of the nature of the past. Mel
Gussow observes that a primary theme of Norman's plays is "as illustrated by the
title of her first work, is 'getting out' — a leave-taking … severing ties of
blood, marriage, and past" ("New Voices" 22). Likewise, Esther Harriott ti-
tles her essay "Marsha Norman: Getting Out" and cites that Norman's chief
concern is about characters "on the point of cutting ties — to the past, to the
present, or even to the future, to their families or friends, or to their former
selves" (129). Summarizing her essay that "Norman's characters are at a critical point, when events of the past intersect with events of the present to bring a-
bout the need for a change in direction for the future" (147), she suggests that
Norman's characters are driven by the passion to disentangle themselves from
entrapped situations and try to achieve a kind of redemption.

Andrea J. Nouryeh, in the essay "Flashing back: Dramatizing the Trauma
of Incest and Child Sexual Abuse", maintains that both *Getting Out* and Paula
Vogel's *How I Learned to Drive* "disclose the effects of trauma on their central
characters and force audiences to confront the difficulties of the characters' healing process" (49). Because of her focus on the devastating effects of child sexual abuse in *Getting Out*, she overlooks the traumatic experiences of social victimization that the protagonist underwent in her past life. However, her study
enlightens a reading of the play through the perspective of trauma studies. As
the story of a survivor of abuse who is tormented by intrusion of traumatic memories once repressed, and who heals through finally releasing those memories,
Getting Out stands up well to such an analysis.

Although the characters' immersion in the past and memory in *Third and*

Oak: The Laundromat and The Pool Hall is a prominent feature, it has been largely overlooked by scholars. One of the reasons is that most of the scholarly focus is on *The Laundromat*[1] and its feminist issues. Jennifer Anne Workman's research stands out as it regards that Norman in this play represents the past through two types of ghosts: "ghosts that the characters imitate and ghosts that the characters describe" (79). Although she detects the phenomenon of the characters' imitation of the dialogues and mannerisms of the absent characters, she does not give an in-depth study of the causes and motivations behind the characters' behaviors. In fact, the characters' nostalgia for the past, which is represented by the absent characters, is the driving motivation.

Among the studies on *The Holdup*, Robert Cooperman's essay discusses the topic of mythological past in Norman's play. In the essay entitled " 'I Don't Know What's Going to Happen in the Morning' —Visions of the Past, Present, and Future in *The Holdup*," he points out that in the play Norman dramatizes the battle between the present and the past, and "the past, even a mythological past, becomes a respected advisor, not a hindrance to be dismissed in the name of progress, and women become active as nurturers and nation-builders" (106). In fact, it is argued in the present study that Norman has a futurist outlook which considers the violent and life-negating past as unproductive and the present and future, with promise and prosperity, as productive. Different from Cooperman, Konstantinos Blatanis in his book *Popular Culture Icons in Contemporary American Drama* approaches *The Holdup* through the perspective of cultural studies. Comparing Norman with Arthur Kopit and Sam Shepard, he argues that Norman invites her audience to "turn critically toward its own celluloid nostalgia" (164) through displacing and deconstructing pop images of the American West and presenting a picture of the promising, expansive, and polysemous West. His opinion on the outlaw as a western icon and Norman's critique on nostalgia is inspiring for the present study. However, his study lacks the discussion of Norman's usage of dramatic elements in representing the nostalgia for the

---

[1] Examples are Esther Harriott's "Marsha Norman: Getting Out", Jenny S. Spencer's "Marsha Norman's She – tragedies" and Cen Wei's *Lillian Hellman and Marsha Norman: Dramatizing Female Identity*.

past and the transforming process of the protagonist.

Scholars have insightfully explored Norman's concern with the past and memory in '*night*, *Mother*. Vivian M. Patraka in "Staging Memory: Contemporary Plays By Women" remarks that the play is "in part the struggle of memories between a mother and a daughter concerning their concept of and relationship to the deceased father, a struggle that culminated in an overtly Freudian suicide by the daughter with her father's gun" (290). Bigsby also points out the absent father's prominence in the contested memories of both mother and daughter (*Contemporary* 236). C. Casey Craig in *Family Ties and Family Ties* illustrates that the family's past lies are what causes the mother and daughter to be the most intimate strangers (333). Their comments are illuminating for a further exploration of the past and memory and the aim of the heroine to make sense of the past, which is replete with misrepresentations.

Despite that the religious element in *Traveler in the Dark* has attracted critics' attention, the effects of the past and memory on the protagonist are touched upon. In "The Way Out, the Way In: Paths to Self in the Plays of Marsha Norman," Leslie Kane comments on Norman's use of the symbolic setting in embodying the effects of the past and memory on the present (270). To her, the protagonist's present crisis originates from his unresolved past crisis, i. e. the death of his mother. Scott Hinson in "The 'Other' Funeral" explores the protagonist as a narcissist because of his unresolved feelings over the death of his mother (111). His essay concludes that with his philosophical crisis being resolved, the protagonist still does not face the truth of his mother's death (119). Although his essay sheds light on understanding Norman's protagonist as one with the psychology of a narcissist, he fails to notice the therapeutic function of an empathic family in helping the protagonist resolve the traumatic past.

Studies on *Loving Daniel Boone* mainly focus on Norman's technique in alternating the past and present and the play as a time-travel play. Marya Bednezik, in "Writing the Other," makes a comment that in *Loving Daniel Boone*, with Norman's fabulist skill in portraying time traveling, " [t] his frequent alteration of scenes past with scenes present causes the audience to examine and, perhaps, reformulate some of their assumptions about the historical event, the formation of gender categories, the act of marriage, and the value of family" (155). Edward Martin Dee includes *Loving Daniel Boone* in his doctoral dissertation of time travel plays. According to his study, backward time-travel plays possess a pair of common characteristics: the coexistence of two time frames and the romantic element. There is a frame story set in the present that anchors the temporal fantasy and a romantic/sexual triangle that forces the time traveler to choose between remaining in the past or facing a difficult present. Although time travelers are generally men, Norman's atypical woman-focused time traveling play follows the traditional paradigm of time travel plays. Because of present disappointments, the protagonists' time travel to the past is perceived as romantic and fulfilling. After returning to the present, they have a renewed sense of self and the present (147). Dee concludes that the plays are cathartic in nature in alleviating fears of the future (252).

Trudy Blue, Norman's most autobiographical play, receives less attention than it deserves. The only comments on this play are from Bigsby. However, his comments are based on the 1998 typescript, rather than on the 1999 performance, the ending of which is different from the earlier one. Nonetheless, Bigsby points out the dynamics of the past and memory with the present in the play. He opines that the play contains "a wealth of memories, a kaleidoscope of fantasies and future projections... The past is not finished business" (*Modern* 333). This aspect of Norman's plays warrants an in-depth analysis of the imaginary past's function and the heroine's intentions in recalling those memories.

From the above studies, it is obvious that Norman's concern with the past and memory need further study both in scope and in depth. Thus, the present study intends to examine in what way the past and memory functions on characters and how Norman dramatizes them in her plays. My approach to this topic is interdisciplinary, drawing upon the methods of theatre history, theatre semiotics, memory studies, psychoanalysis and American history.

Norman expresses her opinion about what the past means to her characters as well as to us in the following manner:

When we talk about our pasts casually, we can present whatever we choose. But *our* version of the past—as we feel it, as we are haunted by it, as we are held back by it, or in some way defined by it — is our own to escape or make sense of, or to triumph over, or to carry with us. And nobody that can possibly come into that kind of drama and resolve it... it is still ultimately the person who owns the past who says what can be done with it. (qtd. in Stone 58; italics original)

From Norman's view, each one has his or her own past which is filtered through memories. Therefore, people represent the past in their variegated ways. That is the reason why she uses the plural form of the word. In a sense, Norman's words illustrate the ways in which the memory of the past affects the present and future and, in her dramas, the coping strategies of the protagonists in her plays. According to Norman, there are three different pasts which the protagonists feel. There are pasts which haunt us, which hold us back, and which define us. In Norman's plays, the protagonists have the different pasts which exert a powerful impact upon the present filtered through the characters' memories.

For the purpose of this study, the traumatic past, the wistful past and the fictional past are used to refer to the different pasts. In Norman's plays, the protagonists with a traumatic past are haunted by the unpleasant memories; the protagonists who cannot bear the stark truth of the present harbor nostalgia for the wistful past and are stagnant; and the protagonists who are shielded from the real past are defined by the fictional past which are concocted by others or themselves. Because of the different natures of the past, there are different ways to deal with it. However, whatever the nature of the past, Norman emphasizes that it is only the person in question that can solve the present dilemma which is entangled with the memory of the past. Complicating her characters in psychological and emotional dimensions through their interaction with the past, Norman expresses her concern about the ontological questions related to human existence and strives to show human beings' capability in understanding and disentangling the past.

Since it examines the past and memory in Norman's plays, it is necessary to define those and related terms as they are taken up in this study. Past, as

Webster's Encyclopedic Unabridged Dictionary of the English Language defines, denotes "the time gone by; the history of a person, nation, etc. ; what has existed or has happened at some earlier time; the events, phenomena, conditions, etc. that characterize an earlier historical period" (1055). In other words, the past has always been regarded as objective facts which have taken place at an earlier time.

Nevertheless, memory refers to "the mental capacity or faculty of retaining and reviving impressions, or of recalling or recognizing previous experiences...act or fact of retaining mental impressions; remembrance; recollections" (895). This definition points out the metaphor of memory as inscription which is considered by Anne Whitehead as one of three motifs discussed in her book *Memory*. In her view, the notion of the mind as a writing surface is consistent in the Western tradition form Plato's description of wax tablet, to John Locke's metaphor of the child's mind of tabula rasa, to Freud's 'Mystic Writing Pad', and to Cathy Caruth's image of trauma indelibly engraved on the mind (10). To a great extent, Norman adopts this aspect of memory as inscription from the perspective of the individual subject. Of course, Norman is not oblivious to the importance of the collective memory functioning on the state of mind of individuals. As will be shown in the discussions of *The Holdup* and *Loving Daniel Boone* in Chapter Two, the individual's nostalgia for the historical past is intersected with the collective memory that has been passed down in a mythic form. Although the content of the collective memory is not an experience in the individual's past, Norman's plays embody an interest in the dynamics of collective memory, in how it weaves itself into the intimate texture of the individual lives.

In Norman's plays, the past is impressed on the mind and is retrieved as a response to the surrounding environment. The characters in Norman's plays adopt three different ways in retrieving and recollecting the past with regard to the nature of the past, namely, reminding, reminiscing and remembering. ① Remin-

---

① These categories related to the discussion of memory in Norman's plays are drawn from Garrett A. Sullivan, Jr. and Edward S. Casey. Sullivan regards memoria, recollection, and remembering as three components of memory in his book *Memory and Forgetting in English Renaissance Drama: Shakespeare, Marlowe, Webster* (6 – 12). Casey subcategorizes remembering into three mnemonic modes: reminding, reminiscing and recognizing (88 – 141).

ding implies the passivity of the subject in recollecting the unpleasant and traumatic past experiences. Reminiscing, on the contrary, connotes the active posture of the subject to get in touch with the wistful past. The third term, remembering, indicates the imperative to recall the past in order to attain a purpose for the present. Despite the definitions, the terms are not rigidly differentiated since they overlap one another in some cases.

Of course, Norman is not the first to focus on the past and memory of the characters in the history of western drama. From ancient Greek Drama to contemporary American drama, dramatists have deployed various techniques to incorporate the past within the present action of the drama. For example, in *Oedipus Rex*, Sophocles dramatizes the play in such a way that the past of the eponymous protagonist's whole life is like a riddle for him to solve. In Henrik Ibsen and Arthur Miller's plays, the protagonists' past actions cause dire consequences for them to confront in the present. Eugene O'Neill's characters are deeply immersed within and cannot divest themselves from their memories of the past so that they are totally inactive in the present. Tennessee Williams' plays usually present the protagonists' nostalgia for the irrevocable past from which they are not able to walk away.

As a matter of fact, Norman expresses her indebtedness to some of the predecessors. She notes the influence of the classical plays on her writing on several occasions. ① In John L. DiGaetani's interview with her, Norman states succinctly that, having studied the dramas of the Greeks and Shakespeare, she "was greatly influenced by those great tragic pieces that present one person trying to figure out what sense it all makes, why it happened this way, and what one is supposed to do about the situation" (245). Nevertheless, unlike the elevated classic tragic heroes who agonize because of something wrong they have done in the past, Norman's are the invisible and marginalized (and in most cases, women) who suffer because of their familial estrangement, marital crisis

---

① On one occasion, Norman specifies that the three plays *Oedipus*, *Antigone* and *King Lear* have a great impact on her writing ("Marsha Norman" in *A Search* 245). On another one, she underlines that there is the particular tragic sense in her plays similar to that in *Oedipus*, *Medea* and *King Lear* ("Conversation with Brustein" 190) .

and social alienation which motivate them to act toward the past in their respective ways. Tennessee Williams is another playwright who Norman admits has influenced her writing. She says that Williams'"portraits of women living in isolation—people not really at home in the world" (245) impress her most. Similar to Williams in presenting the nostalgic, Norman also presents characters that indulge in nostalgia. But different from Williams who has a fear of personal disintegration with his nostalgia for the Old South, Norman marshals her critique on the nostalgic point of view. Norman also mentions that the theatricality of the British playwright Peter Shaffer's plays, such as *The Royal Hunt of the Sun* and *Equus*, both of which employ a memory frame, have an impact on her playwriting ("Marsha Norman" in *A Search* 246). However, Norman never patterns her plays on Shaffer's but makes an eclectic use of his dramatic techniques and incorporates with her own innovation. [①] Following the footsteps of dramatists beginning from ancient Greek dramatists and concurring with contemporary playwrights, Norman consistently underscores the great magnitude of the past and memory elements in the present action of her plays.

The past in Norman's plays performs a triple function: complicating the characters, contextualizing the present existential dilemma and initiating the characters' actions toward the past. It should be noted that Norman's characters are compelling ones. The reason for that is Norman's creative pattern of arriving at character first in her play crafting. In one of her interviews, Norman stresses this point: "[I]t's almost always a question of character. I know that other people write from different motivations, but I almost always write with a desire to understand the action of one person" ("Marsha Norman" 188). However, to achieve an understanding of the action of the person, it is very important to "select the two hours from that person's life or the collected moments that add up to two hours from which the whole life is visible" ("Marsha Norman" 189). In other words, her unique technique in making those compelling characters is giving them atypical pasts. The characters' entanglement with the past accords

---

[①] In the two plays, Shaffer features the protagonists as narrators who reflect on the past. While Shaffer's plays demonstrate a high degree of diegetic narrativity, Norman's plays, such as *Getting Out* and *Trudy Blue*, display a high degree of mimetic narrativity without employing a narrator.

them psychological complexity.

Norman's plays are investigations into the past in the characters' life to explain the present crisis. The reason that the characters are in a predicament is just because they are reduced to inaction for their entrapment in the past. It is noteworthy that, abiding by her creative pattern of portraying active central characters, Norman pens her characters as active ones who refuse to merely react to the past passively. Usually focusing on "a person representing a particular life who has to make a particular decision" ("Marsha Norman," *In Their* 189), she asserts that a theme of her plays is "survival—what it takes to survive. I find people very compelling who are at that moment of choice. 'Will they die or go on? If they go on, in what direction or for what purpose?'" ("An Interview" 17). Envisaging the present existential dilemma of the protagonists through the lens of the past, Norman provides a humane understanding of the protagonists who show courage and determination in critical decision-making. Despite the impact of the past and memory on the present, Norman is persistent in providing a possibility for the transformation of the self and restructuring of affective relationships and social surroundings at the resolution of her plays.

The present study explores the past in Norman's plays which is embodied through individual memories, and sometimes, intersecting with the collective memory. Norman employs dramaturgical techniques to display the past and the dynamics of memory of the past in relation to the present. In plays such as *Getting Out* and *Trudy Blue*, Norman employs a mimetic mode in representing the past and memory through direct scenic enactment. In others, Norman makes use of a diegetic mode to present the past events and memories related to absent characters through narrative. In either mimetic or diegetic mode of representation, Norman incorporates multifarious resources, such as lighting, setting, the auditory element, stage props and virtual props, stage space and extrascenic space to represent the different past and memories of the characters and the dynamics of the past with the present. Whatever nature the past has, traumatic, wistful or fictional, Norman renders them in such a way that they are considered to have shaped the protagonists' lives to a large degree. However, with a kind of Kierkegaardian hope, [1] she directs her protagonists to the future and accords them epiphanic self-transformation.

The present study is divided into three parts. Chapter One is an exploration of Norman's dramatization of the traumatic past and the protagonists' progression from repression of the unpleasant memories to reconciliation with the traumatic past in the two plays *Getting Out* and *Traveler in the Dark*. It reveals that the protagonists' traumatic past has a catastrophic impact on their lives and leaves psychological and emotional scars on them. However, the repression of the traumatic past renders them incapable of dealing with the present crisis. The present environment causes their being reminded of the traumatic past. Reconciling themselves with the traumatic past with the presence of an empathic community makes it possible for the protagonists to heal and face the future with hope. To Norman, the reconciliation is not a purging of the traumatic past, but the integration of it into the protagonists' life which is of crucial importance for them to reconsider themselves in relationship to the society and the world.

The first section of Chapter One makes an in-depth analysis of Norman's theatrical debut *Getting Out*, which is critically commended for its blend of expressionism and realism. In the play, Norman uses flashback, split selves, spatial confinement and juxtaposition of two performance areas to represent the traumatic memory of childhood abuse and victimization. The intrusive traumatic memories are triggered by present cues despite the protagonist's efforts to repress and dissociate them. The heroine achieves her self-reintegration through reconciling herself with the traumatic past. *Traveler in the Dark*, the focus of the second section, endeavors to elaborate on the ramifications of the traumatic memory of the death of the protagonist's mother. Norman employs a symbolic setting—the dilapidated mother's garden studded with various objects and the extrascenic space represented by the house façade to reveal the past of the protagonist's interdependence with his mother and the repression of his traumatic memories. The traumatic death of his mother results in his aversion to the fairy tales, nurs-

---

① Norman once remarked: "Kierkegaard says there are two primary forms of illusion — recollection and hope. My work, I think, reflects a sense that you hope in spite of what you know" (Stone 58).

ery rhymes and the *Bible*, which play a prominent role in forming and shaping his mindset in his early life. The death of his best friend due to the failure of his medical operation makes it an occasion for him to come back to the mother's garden and to look back on his past life. With the sustained support and empathy of his wife, he is able to come to terms with the traumatic death of both his mother and his lifelong friend and reach mutual forgiveness and reconciliation with his father.

Chapter Two examines Norman's dramatization of the wistful past and the protagonists' change from nostalgia to reevaluation of both the past and the present in the three plays *Third and Oak*, *The Holdup* and *Loving Daniel Boone*. The protagonists are ensnared in their nostalgia for a past way of life to which they have no way to return. However, reminiscing the past in preference to the present prevents them from reflecting on the past and the present in an objective manner. The reappraisal of their obsessions with the wistful past compels them to realize the impracticality of their nostalgia and their disillusionment with the past which resituates them in the present condition and reorients them to the future with an awakening. Through dramatizing the protagonists' change from nostalgia for to disillusionment with the past, Norman shows her critique of the nostalgic point of view because indulgence in the past leads to unproductive engagements with the present.

The first part focuses on *Third and Oak* which consists of two acts, "The Laundromat" and "The Pool Hall", but the two acts have always been regarded as two separate one-acts. In the play, Norman employs objects which are closely related to the absent characters to represent the onstage characters' nostalgia for the past. The women's chance encounter at the laundromat provides them a time and space for them to narrate their different stories of their past of loss. Norman utilizes the clothes of the absent husbands and gifts from and to their spouses to indicate the past and the women's nostalgic feeling toward the past. Their empathy and encouragement toward each other make both reevaluate their past relationship with their husbands. The pool hall in the second act is a reminder of the good old days of the pool players. The imitation of the absent characters' words and gestures indicates the onstage characters' loss of selfhood for their nostalgia for the wistful past. The realization of the pastness of the old days makes it possible for the two African American men in the pool hall to patch up the former ruptures and clear up the misunderstandings resulting from the death of their respective beloveds, friend to one, father to the other.

The second section examines Norman's critique of the nostalgia for the western outlaw era in *The Holdup*. The nostalgia for the past is presented through the modern cowboy's obsession with the western outlaws' stories and the Outlaw's unwillingness to accept the technological advancements. But the nostalgia for the western outlaw era is disrupted by the death of the modern cowboy, which causes the Outlaw to reflect upon the violent nature of the past era. The metaphorical funeral on stage mourns the passing of the western outlaw era. Nevertheless, the ritual of rebirth which strips the Outlaw of his former identity reflects Norman's praise of humanity and the flexibility and adaptability of humankind. The focus of the third part is on *Loving Daniel Boone*, a time traveling play. In the play, the individual memory of the heroine is interlinked with the collective memory of the Daniel Boone myth. Dividing the stage into two parts, Norman uses them to stand for the different settings in the space-time continuum, partly in a modern-day museum and partly in Boone's time. Norman posits the heroine within the nostalgic framework of romance. The heroine cherishes nostalgia for Boone's time because of her loneliness in the modern time as a result of failures of romantic relationships. The time traveling to Boone's time demystifies the heroine's memory of Boone as the archetypal hero. Getting out of the insular life with the dead Boone due to the courageous efforts made by the modern hero in fetching her back to the modern time, the heroine forms a renewed sense of self which is crucial for her prospective marriage with the modern hero.

Chapter Three examines how Norman dramatizes the fictional past and the protagonists' transformation from avoidance to confrontation in '*night, Mother* and *Trudy Blue*. The past of the protagonists is based on a fictional one concocted by others or themselves. The protagonists' purposeful remembering of the past unlocks the truth of their past. The realization that their past life of avoidance has not rendered their life to be a meaningful one prompts them to confront the past.

Through the confrontation with the past, the heroines display their self-determination and power in controlling their own lives.

The first section makes an exploration of how the past is remembered in their duologue by the mother and the daughter in *'night, Mother*. The announcement of the intended self-destruction of the daughter initiates a revelation of their past life. The past life of the daughter is lived through a fabricated reality made by the mother. The daughter's suicide is a way to confront her past of powerlessness and a means to achieve self-control. The active choice of the daughter proves the significance of her existence paradoxically through non-existence. The second part examines Norman's most experimental play *Trudy Blue*, which reaches its present form after five years' revision. The fictionality of the protagonist's past is reflected through her memory of what happened to her during the past twenty four hours which contains a mobile hodgepodge of earlier memories and fantasies. To accommodate the memory frame, Norman makes use of the pliability of the minimalist stage and adopts an episodic structure. Totally immersed in her inner world with imaginary selves, the heroine has maintained a distorted vision toward the real world and the surrounding people. The realization of the unreality of her inner world triggered by her imminent death propels her to walk out of her fictional world and establish connection with her family.

Chapter One

REPRESSION TO RECONCILIATION:
COMING TO TERMS WITH THE TRAUMATIC PAST

Concern with the past is an essential element of Norman's sensibility. From her very first play, she mines her own experience and those of others to create characters on whom the traumatic past has made a catastrophic and indelible impact. This chapter is to give an in-depth analysis of the dramatic representation of the traumatic past in Norman's two plays *Getting Out* and *Traveler in the Dark*.

Trauma, as a term which was used to describe a surgical wound, came to be applied to psychology in the late nineteenth century. Sigmund Freud defines the "traumatic" as "any excitations from outside which are powerful enough to break through the protective shield" (*Beyond* 23). I. Lisa McCann and Laurie Anne in their book on psychological trauma defines an experience as traumatic which " (1) is sudden, unexpected, or non-normative, (2) exceeds the individual's perceived ability to meet its demands, and (3) disrupts the individual's frame of reference and other central psychological needs and related schemas" (10). Their definitions of trauma point out the devastating nature and the severe and wide-ranging consequences of trauma. In other words, traumatic events are unpredictable and uncontrollable which result in panic, frailty and vulnerability and violates the victims'beliefs and assumptions that promote safety and stability.

Writing on the concept of "trauma", Tao Jiajun opines that "trauma is the symptom of the violent essence of modern civilization" and "trauma theory has undergone four phases of development from Freudian psychological trauma theory, Post-Freudian psychological trauma theory, race/gender trauma theory to trauma culture theory" (117). In this study, trauma refers to trauma of psychological and psychosexual origin instead of trauma associated with war, race or terrorism.

In *Getting Out*, the heroine suffered from child sexual abuse and social victimization; and in *Traveler in the Dark*, the protagonist's traumatic loss of his mother when he was a child causes his psyche scarred. Because of the disruptiveness or unintelligibility of the traumatic events, they are intentionally blocked out incompletely and temporarily from the consciousness and inhibited and suppressed in the unconscious. However, the protagonists' repression of their traumatic past, rather than help them work through the trauma, results in their present dilemma. The present environment reminds them of the traumatic past which has been deeply repressed. As Christina Wald argues, "the traumatic event ... itself possesses the subject, which can only belatedly, in its psychic returns, experience trauma" (96). To represent the complexity of their traumatic memories, Norman employs expressionistic and symbolic dramatic techniques. The theatrical representation of the traumatic past accords the protagonists a profound psychological complexity.

However, Norman's plays invite the audience to witness the recovery of the protagonists from the traumatic past through their recounting of the traumatic experience. Both Judith Herman and Dominich Lacapra maintain that verbalization of the traumatic experience can help the survivors work over and through the trauma (Herman 175; Lacapra 90). The narrating of the traumatic experience to an empathic community[1] enables the protagonists to move a step towards detraumatization and to reconcile with the past. Only after they come to terms with the traumatic past can they gain a renewed sense of self which is propitious to their future survival. To Norman, the reconciliation is not a purging of the traumatic past, but the integration of it into the protagonists' life which is of crucial importance for them to reconsider themselves in relationship to society and the

---

[1] To some extent, the audience performs a similar role as the empathic community in that they are listeners to the protagonists' traumatic past. Dori Laub writes that "the listener to trauma ...partakes of the struggle of the victim with the memories and residues of his or her traumatic past" (57 – 58).

world.

1. Embodying the Traumatic Memory of
Victimization in *Getting Out*

Getting Out,① Norman's debut in the theatrical world, typically reflects Norman's use of memory to represent the lingering effects of the traumatic past on the heroine's self-definition. It is a harrowing play about a newly reformed ex-convict Arlene who on her first day out of prison adjusts painfully to the new life with her blighted past impinging agonizingly on the present. The play takes place during the twenty-four hours after Arlene returns to her hometown apartment which is formerly rented by her sister. While the present action moves forward with Arlene to adapt to the new environment, the traumatic memories of her past are enacted by Arlie, her former violent self, who lived a bitter life as a result of child sexual abuse, prostitution, social ostracism and penal incarceration. After she comes back to her hometown accompanied by her former guard Bennie, she encounters her mother's coldness and refusal to accept her. In front of her, there are two life paths. One is her former way of life, which is enticed by Carl, her former pimp boyfriend, a dangerous but possibly profitable existence on the streets; the other one is a meager living working in the kitchen of a local café as her upstairs neighbor Ruby recommends. With Ruby's empathic understanding and encouragement, Arlene determines to gain self-autonomy through shaking off those who have exploited and persecuted her in the past and reconciling with and incorporating her past self.

The inner tensions between past and present, memory and reality of the heroine strike an emotional chord in the hearts of the audience of *Getting Out*.

---

① It had its premiere in November 1977 by Actors Theatre of Louisville, Kentucky, under the direction of Jon Jory. It was later produced at the Mark Taper Forum in Los Angeles and at the Phoenix Theatre, New York in 1978 and off-Broadway at Lucille Lortel Theatre in 1979. Co-winner of the Great American Play Contest, it also won the John Gassner New Playwrights Medallion awarded by the Outer Critics Circle and George Oppenheimer/Newsday Award and the American Theatre Critics Association Citation.

John Simon considered it "such a good play...for its remarkable insights, truthfulness and untearful compassion" (172). Regarding the play with "before-and-after diptychs", Jack Kroll hailed it as "exhilarating with the energy of truth, of compassion, of empathy, of a sincerity that becomes luminous and exciting" ("Before and After" 103). Comparing with '*night, Mother*, Christopher Bigsby deemed it more "original and compelling" (*Modern* 326). Sacvan Bercovitch also considered it as "powerfully original in its stagecraft and as relentless in its emotional force" (92).

Juxtaposing the past and present selves on the stage, Norman makes it possible for the audience to have a full knowledge of the traumatic past of the protagonist. Arlie's enactment of the traumatic memories speaks much of the patriarchal oppression, exploitation and persecution of the heroine. Arlene's attempts at repressing the traumatic past result in her present split condition. With the nurturance of the female community, Arlene reconciles her two selves and realizes her self-integration which is of crucial importance for her future survival.

The most prominent feature of *Getting Out* in presenting the past of the heroine is the employment of the technique of split character as two actresses play the main role at different stages in her lifetime. William Gruber argues that in narrative rather than on stage, "widely separated personal or historic times can easily be juxtaposed or made to overlap in ways" (Gruber 138). Yet, in the play, Norman incorporates this split self to make the play "temporally 'stratified'" (Gruber 138). Of course, Norman is not the first to utilize this technique. Nevertheless, her employment of the technique moves a step further than that of the earlier practitioners. Positing the play in the tradition of the split character in dramatic writing, Albert Wertheim argues that *Getting Out* "marries the psychological, spiritual and philosophical divisions explored by [Alice] Gerstenberg, O'Neill and [Adrienne] Kennedy with the chronological divisions presented by [Hugh] Leonard and [Peter] Nichols" (8). The technique proves to be successful in juxtaposition of the past and present selves on the same stage.

The play opens with an exposition seemingly in the tradition of realistic plays of Henrik Ibsen and George Bernard Shaw, with Arlene sketched in outline though not by secondary characters, but through a warden's voice for her to step into her role when she comes on stage. However, the serene appearance of Arlene is put in sharp contrast with the vicious Arlie with her monologue on her mischief about the neighbor's frogs. Arlie's presence undermines the expectations formed initially and prepares the audience for a play with the past and present selves of the main character occupying the same stage.

By placing both the past and the present selves on the same stage and by featuring their physical closeness but emotional discrepancy, Norman exploits the gap between the different conditions of a person before and after rehabilitation. As Norman puts it, "I would have to put them both on stage—Arlie, the girl she had been, and Arlene, the woman she had become in captivity—and the play would uncover the relationship between them" (*Collected Works* 3). While Arlie represents the childhood personality: "vital, aggressive, streetwise, foulmouthed, angry, vindictive, resistant", Arlene is the consciousness: "suspicious, guarded, potentially withdrawn, vulnerable, indecisive" (Bigsby, *Modern* 327). Thus the polyphonous split character technique[①] helps Norman solve the problem which proves to be a fruitful synergy between expressionism and the realistic frame. In the performance, Arlene and Arlie are performed by two actresses who are supposed to be unaware of the existence of each other until the last moment of their unison. Susan Kingsley and Pamela Reed, the two actresses staging Arlene and Arlie respectively in the initial performance, are highly praised by Richard Eder, in his review for The *New York Times*, for their "power and suppleness" in portraying the contrasting roles of the heroine like "two sides in a stereopticon" (C19).

Although the two selves have no communication until the last moment, Norman utilizes lighting to shuffle back and forth between the two to indicate the intrusive nature of the traumatic memories. Any time Arlene is triggered by the slightest outer stimulus, the light shifts to her other self which in effect embodies her memory. The stage direction indicates: "Arlie, in a sense, is Arlene's

---

① Helen Keyssar considers the play script as a powerful invention because it is a "dramatic embodiment of a particularly female form of schizophrenia" (162).

memory of herself, called up by fears, needs, and even simple word cues. The memory haunts, attacks, and warns. But mainly the memory will not go away" (*Collected Works* 3). Bars on the window of the apartment remind her of her once failed burglar attempt. Lighting a cigarette reminds her of lighting a fire in the cell in an escape attempt. Checking the stove and refrigerator summons up images of Arlie battling with the guards for forcing food on her. Mother's voice immediately calls to her mind of the pain and fear caused by her rapist father. The presence of Carl conjures up images of repulsive johns whom she was forced to serve. Bennie's regret about having no children elicits Arlene's mournful memory of planning and warning for her unborn child. Even Ruby's displaying care for her revives her memory of the inmate who tried to seek sexual favors from her. With the enactment of the memories by Arlie, the linear time sequence is broken. The audience is invited to observe the complex psychological activities of Arlene behind the seemingly calm façade.

To make the presence of the past, Norman makes the stage space a dynamic element of her entire dramaturgical conception. Commenting on Norman's spatial conception for the play, Darryll Grantley opines that in the play Norman "makes most varied and fluid use of the stage as an acting and signifying space" (146). The setting contains several areas including the apartment and the prison cell. The stage direction designates: "A catwalk stretches above the apartment and a prison cell, stage right, connects to it by stairways. An area downstage and another stage left complete the enclosure for the apartment by playing areas for the past. The apartment must seem imprisoned" (*Collected Works* 5). The catwalk presents a spatial nexus joining the prison and the apartment. Such an arrangement of the performing areas for the past and present selves enhances our visualization of the mixture of the present and the memories. According to Norman, the joining catwalk is to show that the jail is real close, as if to say, "I've got one foot out of it, it's just not gone. It's right there with me" (qtd. in Thompson 105). But metaphorically, it signifies the specter of the past from which she is struggling to disentangle.

Celia Wren, in her review of the 2007 performance of the play by Journeymen Theater Ensemble, "A Bleak Prison Break, 'Getting Out' Explores a

Haunted Past", credits the set designer with the artful use of wire mesh as the fence of the prison for setting the chilling tone of the play even before it begins (C04). Similar to the literal prison, "a barbed no-man's land" (Simon, "Out of" 98), the apartment is a metaphorical one with the bars on the window which at once reminds Arlene of her former incarcerated life. A sense of physical entrapment pervades. The statement that "the apartment must seem imprisoned" (*Collected Works* 5) makes it clear of the protagonist's restrained living condition and the haunting presence of the past. Although Patsy Hammontree calls Norman's plays as modern gothic without considering the settings as gothic as those in earlier gothic literature (31), the theatrical design, physically and psychologically threatening, adds volume to the burden of the past. Although the 1994 movie version of the play "is indeed a good many notches above the average television movie" (O'Connor C14), the effect of simultaneity of the past and the present cannot be represented as well as in the theatre. The space of the stage gives Norman the opportunity to present two perspectives at the same time. From one perspective, the audience finds sequentiality; and from another, it experiences multiple sequences playing themselves out simultaneously.

As one who has undergone many traumatic events in the past, Arlene cannot lay the memories of the past to rest despite her efforts in repressing them. On the contrary, the past is intrusions taking the form of sensory images which are experienced as if they were happening in the present. Believing that certain memories are not evanescent, French psychiatrist Pierre Janet wrote that "certain happenings would leave indelible and distressing memories—memories to which the sufferer was continually returning, and by which he was tormented by day and by night" (589). The traumatic memories of Arlene, enacted by Arlie, who is "called up by fears, needs, and even simple word cues" (*Collected Works* 3), have made her suffer a lot. The reawakening of traumatic experiences by all sorts of stimuli and stressors is the most predominant feature of Post Traumatic Stress Disorder (PTSD). Arlene suffers all the symptoms of the disorder such as "flashbacks, nightmares and other reexperiences, emotional numbing, depression, guilt, autonomic arousal, explosive violence or tendency to hypervigilance" (Leys 2). The haunted past which has caused intense pain and deep shame always pops up unexpectedly and afflicts her badly. Having a "compulsion to repeat" (Freud, *Beyond* 26) the "unclaimed experience", to use Cathy Caruth's term, Arlene releases the early traumatic experiences from the repressed state.

The sharp contrast between the present and past selves, one jittery and timid and the other violent and incorrigible makes it hard for the audience to regard one as the continuity of the other. However, during the process of the play, the audience is increasingly given access to Arlene's past through the virtually simultaneous scenes of present Arlene and past Arlie. Through Arlie's enactment, the audience witnesses Arlene's "history of dehumanization" (Harriott 131) which includes childhood abuse by her father who never appears on stage, negligence by her mother, sexual exploitation by her pimp-boyfriend Carl, maltreatment and molestation by the prison guards, her child being taken away from her while herself being in prison, and emotional manipulation by the prison chaplain. To use Lynda Hart's words, "society's institutions—the school, the family, the rehabilitation center and the prison—have all proven oppressive rather than redemptive" (73).

As a victim of childhood sexual abuse, Arlene is severely affected by the "unconscious memories" (Freud, "Aetiology" 212) of the repeated violations of her father. With the compulsion to repeat, Arlene is always haunted by the traumatic memories despite her efforts to repress them. The knocking at the door of the apartment by her mother triggers Arlene's traumatic memory of being violated by her abusive and alcoholic cabdriver father who never appears on stage. The hurt done to her is immediately enacted by Arlie: "I can't git up, Mama. (*Hands between her legs.*) My legs is hurt" (*Collected Works* 14). Admitting her mother who has brought cleaning instruments to the apartment, Arlene feels more intense pain upon hearing the mother's following utterances:

> MOTHER: Shoulda beat you like your daddy said. Make you eat.
>
> ARLIE: Nobody done this to me, Mama. (*Protesting, in pain*) No! No!
>
> MOTHER: He weren't a mean man, your daddy.

ARLIE: Was … (*Quickly*) my bike. My bike hurt me. The seat bumped me. (*Collected Works* 14)

The mother's words immediately bring to our mind the vivid scenes of Arlie being beaten frequently by her father because of her refusal to eat. What appears in Arlene's memory is the lingering fear of being battered. Arlie's words to cover her hurt and lies to her mother about the causes of her pain testify that, contrary to her mother's claim, her father was a mean man who had abused her.

As a matter of fact, Arlie's traumatic life begins in her family in which her sexual vulnerability was exploited by her own father. Her family, rather than giving her a sense of warmth and being loved, reminds her of the battering, fears and anxieties in her childhood caused by her rapist father and negligent mother. Living in a dysfunctional family with both parents working as cabdrivers, Arlie had not received proper care, with only basic needs met. In some senses, Arlie is the scapegoat of the poor family which is struggling for existence at the bottom of society.

Arlie's father's violation shatters her fundamental assumptions about the world and her safety in it. "The generation of feelings of trust in others, as the deepest-lying element of the basic security system," Anthony Giddens argues, "depends substantially upon predictable and caring routines established by parental figures" (50). However, with the unpredictable violence done to her, Arlie lost trust in her immediate surrounding. In the book *The Body Bears the Burden: Trauma, Dissociation, and Disease*, Robert C. Scaer writes about the loss of the sense of safety as a result of violence done by family members in the following:

The most devastating form of traumatic stress therefore clearly occurs when caregivers, the intrinsic safe haven, the providers of our basic sense of boundaries, become the existential threat. When the maternal caregiver at times is also the raging and alcoholic abuser, when the loving father is also the source of incest, molestation, or physical abuse, there is no safe haven and no safe boundary between the child and his or her outside world.

The child's perception of self is constricted and shrunken, with little resid-
ual buffer between what is perceived as a safe, bounded space and the un-
knowable threats of the external environment. (5)

For him, those who have undergone such traumatic experiences cannot
build trust toward others and have a healthy sense of self. Indeed, Arlie's subjectivity was rendered useless and viewed as worthless since she was reduced to
a mere object for her father's will. Intimidated by her father and losing trust in
others, Arlie did not dare to tell her mother about the truth of her father's rape
by inventing excuses and concealing her injuries. Rather than providing a haven
for emotional intimacy, Arlie's family only institute and regulate "emotional restrictions" (Cline, "Impossibility" 3).

Notwithstanding the fact that she is also a victim of the dysfunctional family
whose several children have gone astray, Arlene's mother was complicit in Arlie's
tragedy. In sharp contrast to the upstairs neighbor Ruby who shows empathy toward the perplexed Arlene, her mother did not provide any emotional support
and rather ignored her by deliberately blinding herself to the fact of violation and
the hurt done to her daughter. Ignoring her child's plight, Arlie's mother chose
to remain in the dysfunctional relationship with her husband.

Never literally confined in a prison, Arlene's mother was always enduring
the prisons of gender and class, and never freed from these metaphorical mana-
cles. Taking up the burden of supporting the whole family because of her husband's ineffectuality, she is still unwilling to regard her husband as the main
reason which made the family dysfunctional and Arlene's disarrayed life. As
Sally Burke argues, Arlene's mother could not "open her eyes to the sexual violence her husband inflicted upon Arlie and see what was truly hiding in her own
bed all those years ago" (109). Instead, she blamed herself and her children.
Although she comes to visit Arlene seemingly to celebrate her release from prison, her aloofness, discouragement and criticism make Arlene more depressed.
Unsatisfactory with her daughter's appearance, especially her hair and body
form, she expresses her belief in the female beauty myth which, according to
Naomi Wolf, is a perpetuating trick that encourages women to participate in their

own oppression (10). Arlene's mother not only remarks overcritically upon her daughter's appearance, but also imputes her trouble to her homeliness: "I always thought if you'd looked better you wouldn't have got in so much trouble" (*Collected Works* 18). Her reproving tone has depleted Arlene psychologically who becomes more dejected even after she tries to look better by putting on lipstick. Never finding a clue about what causes her children's failures, Arlene's mother asks self-reproachfully, "I ain't hateful, how come I got so many hateful kids?" (*Collected Works* 20). Her depreciating attitude toward herself to a great extent affects her children. Adrienne Rich writes in the following words: "The mother's self-hatred and low expectations are the binding rags for the psyche of the daughter" (201).

Psychically split by the incestuous rape by her father, Arlie experienced all of the emotions of hate, fear, revenge and shame. To protest against her overbearing father and ignoring mother, Arlie made bologna and toothpaste sandwiches for her alcoholic father which almost choked him and peed in her mother's shoes, the memory of both enjoyed by Arlene. Refusing to eat is another strategy to show her rebellion against her father. This refusal to allow a foreign object into her body is an indication of her attempt to gain control over her own body which is not considered to belong to herself. But this strategy is ineffectual for what waited for her was more battering. In effect, her father's attempts to force her to eat have similar connotations with that of the prison guards for their voyeuristic intrusion.

Arlene's memory of Arlie's dreadful treatment of her neighbor boy's pet frogs suggests not only her irrational aggression to elicit pleasure but also Arlie's aspiration for paternal love and care which she was not able to feel in her own disjunctive family. Unlike her own abusive father and indifferent mother, the parents of the boy show love toward and provide protection for him. Having stolen the frogs which were brought back by the boy's father after fishing, Arlie threw them onto the street to be hit by car windshields or squashed. The splat and splash of the frogs and the hurt done to the boy gave Arlie great satisfaction as she tells enjoyably that "I never had so much fun in one day in my whole life" (*Collected Works* 6). This kind of aggression toward others is explained in the entry "acting out" in *The Encyclopedia of Child Abuse* as a consequence of being physical-ly abused. In fact, stripped of power and control, Arlie displayed envy and ag-gressive behavior toward others. Defenseless against her rapist father, she "be-come [s] abusive toward other children as a way of acting out aggressive feel-ings that cannot be expressed safely in the presence of the abuser" (Clark and Clark 13).

In addition to this particular incident from which Arlie gained satisfaction, there are other undesirable behaviors such as fighting with others, playing truan-cy and scrawling on the bathroom walls, as related by the school Principal who finally dismissed Arlie. According to Rosine Jozef Perelberg's review of litera-ture on aggression, many American psychologists maintain that aggression is re-active to a frustrating or depriving environment and discharging aggression to-ward others can be a source of pleasure (24). Feeling ignored, unloved and helpless, she refused to eat and resorted to angry outbursts and vicious attacks which drove people further away from her. Despite the violent behaviors dis-played toward others, Arlie was "caught in a real schism. There is the 'you' that's out in the 'real' world, and then there's the child inside who is still a frightened victim" (qtd. in Burke 111). These self-defeating coping mecha-nisms are, to a great extent, only because of her distrust and anxiety toward oth-ers despite her need for companionship and acceptance.

The feeling of shame and embarrassment as a victim of child sexual abuse was elicited in response to her mother's refusal for her to go to her house. The memory scene of Arlie chasing Ronnie for the necklace which her father had giv-en her reveals much of Arlene's shame of her incestual relationship being ex-posed.

The habitual violation by her father in exchange for some money and small gifts made Arlie sexually precocious and led her to adolescent prostitution. Jan Heney and Connie M. Kristiansen note that "A sexually abused child may de-velop misconceptions about sexual behavior, aggression and morality, and a child who is rewarded for complying with the abuse may come to believe that her sexuality is her only value" (31). Lynda Hart also opines that Arlie must have learned that "her body was a commodity to be bought, sold, manipulated and controlled, that it belonged to others and gave them a certain power over her" (70). Due to the lack of care and love in a dysfunctional family where most children have led a deviant life, Arlie, like many others who have endured sexual abuse in their childhood, was not able to grow emotionally. For her undeveloped ability to make accurate judgments about people, she was unable to protect herself from future victimization. Misplacing her trust on Carl, her pimp lover, Arlie, after her "familial scapegoating", was involved in the process of "social scapegoating" (Cline, "Impossibility" 3) starting with prostitution.

As a victim of child sexual abuse in her family home, Arlie became a prostituted woman. Thus doing, Arlie perpetuated her sexual vulnerability and victimization she suffered in childhood. Regarding prostitution as another form of sexual slavery, Sheila Jeffreys argues that "Prostitution is a form of male sexual violence against women, consistent in its effects upon the abused women with other forms of violence, particularly child sexual abuse" (6). From Jenny Spencer's point of view, it is "Arlie's sex [that] determines the particular forms of abuse she suffers" ("She-Tragedies" 154).

The presence of Carl, who has broken out of prison for his "sweetheart", in the apartment triggers Arlene's memory of being a prostitute. Exploiting Arlie sexually to make a living, Carl never regarded Arlie as a full person who had her own feelings or showed concern for whatever risks Arlie would face. As the haunted memories of the never dissipating fear of physical hurt from her father, the "fearful memories of life-threatening episodes" (Hart 72) of working for Carl hanged on Arlene:

> Carl, I ain't goin' with that dude, he's weird…I don't need you pimping for me. You always sendin' me to them ol' droolers…They tyin' me to the bed! … (*Now creaming, gets further away from him.*) I could git killed working for you. Some sicko, some crazy drunk…. (*Collected Works* 28)

These are the images of the dangerous and repulsive encounters with the men that Carl had forced her to serve. Used and abused by Carl, Arlie was denied her sovereignty over her body. Like Arlie's father who had violated her and threatened and beaten her for her disobedience, Carl not only owned her body but even lambasted her into prostitution because she was regarded as "his meal ticket" (Harriott 133).

From the flashbacks enacted by Arlie, other powerful cultural agents like the school principal, the doctor, the prison guards and even the prison chaplain are on behalf of the disciplinary institutions which exert restraining forces to people in society. Internalizing the disciplinary imperatives, what they do is just to discipline in a Foucauldian sense. To young people with antisocial behaviors like Arlie who had experienced traumatic events unknown to others, they did not give any concern about the psychological motivations for doing so.

As a disciplinary organization which is "mobilized within the dialectic of control", the school draws its power and authority from "the more or less continuous compliance of those who are its 'subjects'" (Giddens 136). However, because of her indocile behaviors, Arlie was deemed as an intractable pupil who was incapable of integrating smoothly into the institutionally established framework of the school. Listening to Arlie's mother's negative view of Arlie being not suitable for a regular school, the school principal expelled Arlie from the school for her unwanted behaviors. As she[1] says in anger, "You've made your choice. You *want* out of regular school and you're going to *get* out of regular school... I'm not making you go. You've earned it. You've worked hard for this" (*Collected Works* 18). Isolation and final rejection as punishment made Arlie a victim of the educational system.

Like the school principal, the doctor represents the medical system which helps produce docile bodies for the patriarchal society. Seemingly to provide some psychiatric counseling for Arlie, the doctor did nothing constructive for Ar-

---

[1]　In the characters list, Norman intentionally gendered the principal as female to indicate the role of the principal as agent of the institution (Norman 3). Leslie Kane indiscreetly mistakes the principal as one of the male figures who are symbols of abuse and authority (260). In the play, the characterization of so many "mean, nasty men" causes people's doubt of Norman as a misandrist. Norman responds, "People keep asking me that ... because all these guys are such creeps. No, it is simply just the selection of the day, the soup du jour. You get all these creeps, and you get this nasty mother... This is not my vision of the world. All mothers are not nasty, all men are not rapists" (Judy Klemesrud D4).

lie's healthy development but bore partial opinion against her. When Arlie refused to go camp, he reiterated in an intimidating tone that she had to go. The
counseling resulted in nothing but unit cleanup as punishment. Likewise, without investigating the cause of the conflict between Arlie and Ronnie, the boy
who teased Arlie with a sexual innuendo, the doctor gave her three weeks of isolation as punishment for physical assault. From what the doctor says to Ronnie,
"You should've known" (*Collected Works* 26), we see that Arlie was always
considered the troublemaker because of her violent behavior and profanity despite the fact that Ronnie was the instigator of the fight.

The memory of Arlie's setting fire to her room in the juvenile institution
makes clear the doctor's role of subjugating indocile bodies for the institution.
Although the doctor saved Arlie's life, what he did was more for the safety of the
juvenile institution than for Arlie. As he blamed the guard Evans for his negligence of duty, "You going to let her burn this place down before you start pay-
in' attention up there?" (*Collected Works* 11) To ensure that Arlie would not
cause further trouble, he gave Arlie an injection to tranquilize her.

Arlene's memories of her incarceration involve many aspects which range
from lack of privacy, sexual harassment (physically and verbally), the use of
force, to confinement. The prison system contributes to her revictimization by
perpetuating her feelings of powerlessness and vulnerability which had followed
her since her traumatic childhood. A young woman at her late twenties, Arlene
has been incarcerated for the past eleven years—three years at Lakewood State
Prison for forgery and prostitution and eight years at Pine Ridge Correctional institute for the second–degree murder in conjunction with a filling station robbery.
In *Discipline and Punish: The Birth of a Prison* (1977), Michel Foucault takes
penal imprisonment as one of the three distinctive historically existent ways of organizing the power to punish the criminals (130–131). In this prison institution, "punishment was seen as a technique for the coercion of individuals; it
operated methods of training the body—not signs—by the traces it leaves, in the
form of habits, in behavior; and it presupposed the setting up of a specific power for the administration of the penalty" (131). In such an environment of surveillance, the body is "object and target of power", "is manipulated, shaped,

trained, which obeys, responds, becomes skillful and increases its forces" (136).

The prologues preceding both acts speak much of the managing process of the bodies of the prisoners to make them rehabilitated in order to be productive. The prologues, as indicated in the stage direction, are transmitted by a disembodied voice in a "droning tone" (*Collected Works* 4). Jindřich Honzl, in "Dynamics of the Sign in the Theatre", regards such a voice as an "acoustic actor" (270). However, the authoritative imperative sentences underscore the power of the acoustic actor. Moreover, as in other plays which Norman deploys the off-stage characters, Norman exploits the dialectic between invisibility and potency. That is to say, the absence of the source of authority, however, strengthens rather than decreases the power of the institution. Timothy Murray asserts that the voice "is always demanding production and reiterating subjection, always construing orders and making judgments" (379). Patricia R. Schroeder notes that the voice-over announcements just represent the invisible, disembodied but potentially ubiquitous presence of the control over the prisoners (145). Commanding Arlie to eat, the guard Caldwell tries to terrify and daunt Arlie resorting to the absent authority behind him. The following dialogue shows the omnipresent authority behind the physical agents:

GUARD (CALDWELL): You gotta eat, Arlie.

ARLIE: Says who?

GUARD (CALDWELL): Says me. Says the warden. Says the Department of Corrections. (*Collected Works* 13)

Although the guards and wardens are agents of the specific power of the prison system to coerce the prisoners and train their bodies to make them productive, they always abuse the power to attain personal ends. Arlene's memory of the scene being forced to eat specifies this kind of abuse of the administering power of the prison system. Reminiscent of her father's forcing her to eat, the guards'coercing her to eat is not for the health of Arlie but for their voyeuristic looking. In the shower room, there is a two-way mirror which functions as a tool for both panoptic gaze and sexual fantasy. Unprotected and constantly observed, Arlie has no privacy at all because of the ever-present surveillance. The existence and even encouragement of such privacy-invading sexual harassment speaks volume of the imbalance of power between the guards and the prisoners.

The guards'degrading language and threats made against Arlie are traumatic for Arlene who has dropped her old way of speaking and become discreet in choice of words. In the prison, Arlie is always referred to as "slut", "bitch", "wildcat", "cutie pie", "honey", "my girl", and "dollie", words related to "animal metaphors" and "highly sexually-charged insults" (Zhang 87). These "derogatory, demeaning speech and sexist language [which] are used in patriarchal societies to allocate to women a place marked by muteness and degradation" can hurt "psychologically and emotionally" (Zhang 86). While the words are dehumanizing and disempowering to women, they are empowering to men.

To the insults and sexually-loaded words, Arlie was defiant and rebellious. As have been mentioned above, refusing to eat is a form of rebellion Arlie resorted to against the imposition of power. Although the rebellion gives Arlie a sense of control over her own body, it is ineffectual in such an environment where she has been deprived of freedom and individual identity. What is worse, her rebellion only invites more severe punishment—isolation " in a maximum-security cell" (*Collected Works* 36).

The unbearable conditions and loneliness of solitary confinement is a painful memory for Arlene. Living in the adjustment room with no light or toilet and full of bugs, Arlie was deprived of talking with other inmates and correspondences with the outside world. Rather than being treated like a human being, she was caged like an animal because she was totally dependent on the guards for supply of food and removal of waste. The segregation was inhumane in that it tried to submit the prisoners to total obedience. Arlie's conversation with the Warden testifies to this fact,

ARLIE: I don't even remember what I done to git this lockup.

WARDEN: Well, I do. And if you ever do it again, or anything like it again, you'll be right back in lockup where you will stay until you forget how to do it. (*Collected Works* 39)

As a result of the solitary confinement, Arlene suffers loss of memory. The consequence is comparable to the numbing effect of lobotomy which had been operated on her inmate Frankie Hill. As Arlie and Bennie's dialogue shows:

> ARLIE: They done somethin' to her. Took out her nerves or some-
> thin' . She...
> BENNIE: She jus' got better, that's all. (*Collected Works* 46)

Only if the prisoners become "better" —silent and obedient— the agents of the prison system will resort to whatever means to achieve that aim.

Bennie, whom Arlene considers as the "nicest" guard, is in fact more insidious. As Gretchen Cline points out perceptively, Bennie "represents her most important connection to her institutionalized scapegoating: institutionalized rape" (14). He treated her in a condescending and humiliating way. Seeing that the other guards found Arlie difficult to handle with, he told them that the "correct" way to tame the inmates is to satisfy their needs in exchange for favor for himself. As he said to them:

> Outta a little thing like her? Gotta do her like all the rest. You got
> shorts washed by givin' Betty Ricky Milky Ways. You git your chairs fixed
> givin' Frankie Hill extra time in the shower with Lucille Smith. An you git
> ol' Arlie girl to behave herself with a stick of gum. Gotta have her brand,
> though. (*Collected Works* 37)

Regarding her as "a little thing", Bennie reduced Arlie to an object which he could manipulate according to his own will. Furthermore, what he gave Arlie was a piece of gum which had already been chewed by him: "Well, (*Feigning disappointment.*) I guess I already chewed it" (*Collected Works* 38). Notwithstanding its physiological and psychological functions for Arlie's temporary "mental tranquility," the chewing gum is utilized with a "political dimension" by Bennie, "as a strategy and a tool to tantalize the girl, make her behave herself and quiet down" (Zhang 91). Albeit the chewing gum is not put to use to fatten her up for the sexual fantasy of the guards, Bennie's pacifying strategy is to seek for sexual fulfillment from Arlie/Arlene.

Arlene's memory of the prison chaplain indicates that he is also the agent of the religious institution which ensures the obedience of faith of human beings including the prisoners. It is the prison chaplain who triggered Arlie's transformation into Arlene. The presence of the picture of Jesus Christ indicates Arlene's conversion to Christianity. Unlike the guards who always employed derogatory words on her, the chaplain, with "kindness and respect" (Bigsby *Modern* 328), addressed her Arlene which she later takes as her new name. Nevertheless, the new naming itself demonstrates the authority and power on the chaplain's side and the powerlessness on Arlie's side. Giving her a picture of Jesus Christ and inculcating her with the belief in God, the chaplain made Arlene believe that Arlie was her hateful self which had to be gotten rid of. As Arlene recollects and relates to her upstairs neighbor Ruby hysterically,

> This chaplain said I had... said Arlie was my hateful self and she was hurtin' me and God would find some way to take her away... and it was God's will so I could be the meek... the meek, them that's quiet and good an git whatever they want... I forgit that word... they git the earth. (*Collected Works* 54)

Splitting her ego into two with the soul perceiving the body as a separate but dangerous object, Arlie was imbued with a sense of self-hatred. Traditionally regarded as humanity in the correctional setting, the chaplain proved the power of word. However, the chaplain's words are a simplification and even distortion of Jesus'beatitude to the meek (Zhang 98). The chaplain's twisted interpretation of "inherit the earth" as "git whatever they want" is just another patriarchal strategy to produce obedient subjects.

Notwithstanding that Bigsby's opinion that Arlie's attachment to the chaplain is the "single relationship which had brought meaning into her life" (*Mod-*

ern 327), it is this relationship that resulted in the most violent activity done to Arlie. Without saying goodbye to Arlie/Arlene who had converted to Christianity, the chaplain transferred to another prison. Feeling again deserted, Arlie/Arlene raised hell in the prison. Using the fork which her inmate Doris had stolen from the kitchen, Arlie performed a sacrifice which almost killed her. It is ironic that the life-sustaining tool is transformed into a self-destructive weapon. However, because of the chaplain's inculcation, in Arlene's mind, killing the alien object which is represented by her own body is an act of self preservation. In Gretchen Cline's words, the chaplain commits "a metaphorical rape that split her psyche" (22).

After symbolically "killing" her Other Arlie, Arlene led almost an anesthetized life through numbing herself to the environment "jus'done my work an knit ... an I don't think about it, what happened" (*Collected Works* 55). Arlene took up the traditional, gender-stereotyped roles prescribed by the patriarchal society. Rejecting Arlie's destructive tendency, Arlene became a model prisoner who has grasped several skills, such as knitting and hairdressing which were considered as musts for traditional women. Nevertheless, ironically, the skills can not be put into practice out of prison because of the restrictions imposed upon ex-convicts by the local legislation.

Arlene's past as embodied by Arlie is a history of female victimization. Defined in gender specific terms and sexually exploited, Arlie displayed antisocial behaviors. However, the resistant attitude only made her life worse. To survive in such a sexist social order, she had to eradicate her 'evil' self and adopt the culturally prescribed roles for women, which render them passive, voiceless, and most importantly, obedient. Notwithstanding that she intends to repress the memories of the past which are enacted by her past self, the traumatic past keeps coming out, thus causing her split position. The tension between the past and the present is the tension between the savage self and the conforming one. Accepting and integrating the past self into the present one is of paramount importance for her future life outside the prison.

Nevertheless, the play's ambiguous title causes heated controversy among scholars and critics. Despite Arlene's getting out of the literal prison, many deem it impossible for Arlene to get out of her tough situation. Regarding Arlene 's rehabilitation in the reforming school "as a kind of self-destructive feminiza-tion" (154), Jenny S. Spencer maintains the impossibility of the title's hopeful declaration because Arlene's socially constructed identity "assigns her perma-nently to a powerless, passive position, to a female 'self' she hardly recogni-zes" ("She-Tragedies" 156). Entitling her article "The Impossibility of Getting Out", Gretchen Cline argues that in ending the play with the disguises of Ruby's assurance and Arlene's integrated psyche, Norman "converts complex psycho-drama to normative idealism" (23).

However, others concur with Norman's optimism in Arlene's unity of self and the power of sisterhood. Bigsby not only considers that the play has a-chieved much for presenting "Arlene's struggle for possession of herself, a battle waged externally with society and internally with her own destructiveness (*Mod-ern* 328)", but also argues that the reconciliation between Arlie and Arlene at the end of the play signals the getting out of the reconstructed Arlene who has transcended the sensibilities of her former self (*Contemporary* 220). Timothy Murray writes in his article from the perspective of Foucauldian panopticism that it is "a play not only concerning memories of the father, of violence, and of prison, but also offering hope in an innocent sisterhood, Arlene's promising re-lationship with Ruby, who has gotten out" (383). Leslie Kane maintains that in making autonomous Arlene accept Arlie and her past, Norman is "betting on Arlie/Arlene's survival" (261). Despite her claim that the interpenetration of Arlene and Arlie would have deepened the play further, Esther Harriott does not consider the play a depressing one (135). Regarding the play as one that re-flects Norman's feminist aesthetic, Janet Brown and Catherine Barnes Stevenson contend that women like Arlene who have been moved to center stage "resist their marginalization, transform lifelong silence into speech, and try to find a way to control their individual destinies while maintaining close bonds with oth-ers" (193). Norman herself reveals her optimism about Arlene's future autono-mous life by expressing her belief in Arlene's capability to get her son back (Thompson 118). The author of the study shares the optimistic view in the sur-vival of Arlene. The following part gives an analysis about how Arlene achieves her integration after breaking apart with those people who had shaped her in the past.

Arlene's memories of her traumatic past indicate that her past self is shaped and defined by others who have, more or less, attributed to her victimization, physically, spiritually, linguistically, institutionally and etc. Arlene's rehabilitation is in effect at the expense of repressing the deplorable past. Norman once remarked that "Our writing is absolutely linked to this problem of how do you change when the perceptions of the people around you don't change. How do you know who you are when you are made up of these people that you *despise*?" (*In Their* 183). *Getting Out* must be in Norman's mind when she talked about this creative intention. Arlene faces the same problem when she is paroled out of prison. Despite Arlene's determination to obliterate her past and begin a renewed life with an expectation to take back her son, the people around, her mother, her pimp lover and the prison guard still regard her as what she was before. For Arlene who has become anesthetized as a result of the normalization experienced in the prison system, the society is no better than before. The presence of her mother, Carl and Bennie elicits her traumatic memories of Arlene's past experience which causes overwhelming pain to her. Moreover, they still want to continue to treat her as they did in the past. Therefore, it is of crucial importance for Arlene to cut ties to them.

Having never showed real concern toward her in the past, Arlene's mother is the first tie to for her to confront. Leslie Kane maintains that the mother figure in Norman's early plays "provides neither protection nor guidance..., do [es] not nourish with food or love..., [and] is an "archetypal 'bad' mother, cold and rejecting" (158). Having brought some daily necessities and cleaning supplies to the empty and dirty apartment of which she had notified the prison officials, Arlene's mother makes her obligatory visit to Arlene with whom she had completely no correspondence during her imprisonment. For Arlene/Arlie's past, she still shows distrust toward her daughter. Despite Arlene's insistence of her being called Arlene instead of her childhood name Arlie, her mother does not pay attention to this demand. Her great vigor in cleaning the apartment is an implication of "her desires to sanitize Arlene" (Kane 159) in a metaphorical way. ① Doubting Arlene's competence as a mother and despairing at herself as a failure in mothering, she is reluctant to give information about Arlene's son Joey of whom she only had a glimpse two years before. Only at the incessant request of Arlene, she talks about him callously. Feeling the coldness of her mother, Arlene still tries to have some conversation with her. But the efforts either meet with disapproval or are just ignored. Arlene's last request to be allowed back to the family for a Sunday dinner is bluntly refused by her mother by saying "Sunday... is my day to clean house now" and "I still got two kids at home, don't want not bad example" (*Collected Works* 21). When Arlene says that she can "tell them some things" (*Collected Works* 21) which means that she may warn them of making similar mistakes like herself, her mother blurts out viciously "Like about the cab driver" (*Collected Works* 21) whom Arlie had killed unintentionally. Arlene's last request for nurturance from her mother who never really provided any in the past comes to nothing. When she sees a hat which Arlene explains belongs to Bennie, Arlene's mother considers her daughter as the "same hateful brat (*Collected Works* 25)" as ever. Hearing her mother's last words "Don't you touch me (*Collected Works* 25)" after she takes back her gift bedspread, Arlene realizes that her hope for a rapprochement with her mother totally fails.

Arlene's claim that "I wanna work, now, make somethin' of myself" (*Collected Works* 21) is her declaration to begin a new life and construct a new self. Nevertheless, her mother is oblivious to her efforts in her self-redefinition: "I'm your mother. I know what you'll do" (*Collected Works* 24). Notwithstanding Arlene's breakup with her mother is depressing for her, "if she is to re-invent herself, become the protagonist of another drama of her own construction," Bigsby argues, "she has to free herself of her author, the mother who seems effectively to have written her life for her, determining, by her disregard,

---

① In an interview with L. Elisabeth Beattie, Norman mentions that her mother is the prototype for the mother in *Getting Out*, especially the scene of the mother walking in with a basket full of cleaning supplies. To her, what the mother did was always cleaning, "it's a religious activity... Sort of trying to get the dirt out, get rid of the sin and the evil, that's masquerading as the dirt on the floor" (285).

her denial, her self-absorption, the direction she was to take" (*Contemporary* 216). Craig concurs with Bigsby in observing that "for Arlene to change her life and survive outside, she must detach herself from her mother and find other nurturing from within and without" (*Family Ties* 313 – 14).

As she has to break from her mother, Arlene also has to gain sovereignty over her body through exiting sex work for Carl. Carl still regards her as the one who was absolutely at his mercy. Despite Arlene's intention to renounce prostitution, Carl tries to persuade her to accompany him to New York and go back to the streets to make easy money. His glibness in asserting that the money gained for one night's work as a prostitute can amount to a week's salary for washing dishes is very effective for Arlene who is in the dim hope of finding a decent job. Showing tenderness toward Arlene, Carl tries to use "Joey as a tool for manipulation and emotional blackmail" (Bitonti 169). He envisions for Arlene about their son being proud of a rich mother working in New York sending various stuff back:

> You come with me, you kin send him big orange bears an Sting Ray bikes with his name wrote on the fenders. He'll like that.... Joey be tellin' all his friends ' bout his mom livin' up in New York City an bein' so rich an sendin' him stuff all the time. (*Collected Works* 50)

Nevertheless, what Arlene cares about is not money itself, but a normal life with her son Joey. Having never been allowed to stay with him in the prison, Arlene considers having a reunion with her son outside the prison. As she tells Carl, "I want to be with him" (*Collected Works* 50). Her own deplorable childhood and the ensuing chaotic life make Arlie/Arlene pessimistic of growing up. Never had an intimate relationship with her mother who had turned a blind eye to what she had undergone, Arlie expressed her wish to be a protective mother to her own child. Carl's rude way in handling the baby sweaters, booties and caps which Arlene has spent a great time and efforts in knitting hardly prove his capability in helping Arlene achieve this aim. Eating Arlene's cookies in a voracious way further proves that he regards Arlene as his meal ticket. As she has to sever her ties with her mother for her self-redefinition, she has also to cut loose from Carl who had regarded her none other than a sexual slave.

Her former prison guard Bennie, who had always tried to seek sexual favors from her to no avail, wants to extend their guard-prisoner relationship to the outside world. As he says to Arlene when she asks him to go, "I'd be happy to stay here with you tonight. Make sure you'll be all right. You ain't spent a night by yourself for a long time" (*Collected Works* 32). He conceals his sexual intention by claiming that he wants to take his first trip to Louisville. Not as violent as other guards in the prison, he is no better than them. He tries to gain favor from Arlene by buying chicken for her as he had done in prison by giving her a piece of already chewed gum to appease her. Bigsby argues that Bennie "is motivated by confused feelings of sexual aggression and romantic need" (*Contemporary* 218), but he is ill-suited to perform the romantic role. Feigning to help her relax by rubbing her back, he unmasks his true colors when he "tries to wear down her resistance by half-whining and half-shoving Arlene into bed" (54).

Like other sleazy prison guards who force food upon Arlie in order to fatten her up for their pleasure of looking, Bennie still considers Arlene as Arlie—the "screeching wildcat (*Collected Works* 46)", on whose figure his male gaze projects its voyeuristic fantasy. In fact, the attempted rape is a result of the collusion between the projection of the male gaze and the eroticization of the female. As a result of her normalization, Arlene has lost much of the strength Arlie owned which had caused much trouble for the prison guards. However, Arlene resorts to the power of language which proves to be effective. By calling Bennie a rapist which stings his self-dignity, she stops Bennie's physical coercion toward her. Bennie's next-day efforts to patch up their relationship by bringing pots of flowers for the barred window is no different from his offering the chewing gum to Arlie in expectation for sexual favors. Furthermore, the violent way which Bennie treats the broken flower pot not only reminds us of the brutality and violence done to Arlie but also predicts his future treatment to Arlene if he is to keep track of her. As she has to walk out of the path that her mother has put her in, Arlene has also to cast off the shadow of the persecuting system represented by Bennie.

Jenny Spencer notes that Arlene's rehabilitation is realized through managing her sexual behavior and assuming a "presentable feminine demeanor" ("She-Tragedies" 154). Although the rehabilitated self meets the standard of the prison system for her to get out of the real prison as stated through the warden's voice at the beginning of Act I: "Subject now considered completely rehabilitated" (*Collected Works* 5), it is at the expense of splitting her self, however. In order to survive, it is of utmost importance for Arlene to incorporate her past self to ensure a unified autonomous self. Harriott notes, "If Arlene is to survive, Arlie is to survive, Arlie's vitality must survive as well" (134). Laurin Porter expresses a similar view that "[Arlene's] ability to invent herself, to discover who she is and who she wants to become, depends on her own inner resources, her integration of Arlie's energy and strength, and her newly forged bond with Ruby" (203).

Arlene's recovery from the traumatic past roughly echoes the three stages Judith Herman puts forward in her book *Trauma and Recovery*. She states that recovery unfolds in three stages: establishment of safety, remembrance and mourning and reconnection with ordinary life (155). The establishment of safety is achieved with the presence of her upstairs neighbor, Ruby, an autonomous self who has gotten out of prison and "is making a painful adjustment to a bottom-rung existence" (Eder C19). Arlene's reconciliation with the past self is facilitated by the female community formed with Ruby. Initially, she distances herself from Ruby who comes to offer help and regard because of her distrust toward others as a result of her former prison experience of the woman who tried to expect sexual favors from her. When she finds Ruby's empathy toward and real concern over her, she loosens increasingly her vigilance toward her.

It is noteworthy to point out the fact that it is with Ruby's presence that Arlene breaks off with Bennie and Carl. According to Herman, "Establishing a safe environment requires not only the mobilization of caring people but also the development of a plan for future protection" (164). Ruby not only presents herself as an empathic listener, but also recommends Arlene to have a life free of the continuation of exploitation from her earlier abusers. Hearing the confessions of Ruby, who was also formerly imprisoned, hoaxed by a seemingly pitiable guy, Arlene resolutely tears up the brightly colored matchbook and the piece of paper on which Carl and Bennie have written their numbers respectively. With only the barest necessities for survival, Arlene's "hunger for power, freedom and control ... takes precedence over the beguiling ease and false security" (Hart 71). Arlene's rejection of the temptations is a measure of her profound courage and self-determination. Shaking off the shackles of Carl and Bennie, Arlene decides to live an honest life on her own resources without any interventions from those who have exploited or ignored her in the past.

Recounting the traumatic past is the second stage of Arlene's recovery. Entrusting herself to Ruby, she is able to recount her traumatic suicidal attempt in which she stabbed herself repeatedly with the fork and was covered by blood without feeling any physical pain. Feeling split into two selves, she is mentally satisfied that "Arlie is dead an it's God's will. (*Collected Works* 54)" Becoming trancelike, she reexperiences the traumatic incident unconsciously. As the stage direction indicates, Arlene "[c] lenches one hand now, the other hand fumbling with the front of her dress as if she's going to show Ruby" (*Collected Works* 54). Unlike the other memories which are performed by Arlie in the stage area set for the past or in the cell, this memory of the bloody violence done to herself is narrated by Arlene to Ruby. It is presumed that Norman does not let Arlie enact the scene is maybe because of the bloodiness of such a scene. However, it can also be argued that Norman has another intention in substituting telling for showing. Indeed, Arlene's narration of this scene is in effect a releasing of her repression of the traumatic memories. Dominich Lacapra opines that through verbalization of the traumatic experience

> one has begun the arduous process of working over and through the trauma ... which may enable processes of judgment and at least limited liability and ethically responsible agency. These processes are crucial for laying ghosts to rest, distancing oneself from haunting revenants, renewing an interest in life, and being able to engage memory in more critically tested senses. " (90)

In other words, narration rather than compulsively acting out the traumatic experiences involves some measure of distance from the traumatic past and it initiates a working through of the trauma. It is worth noting that after Arlene's speaking out the traumatic memory, Arlie only appears the last time toward the end of the play where her laugh evokes the smile on Arlene's face. With Ruby as an empathic presence and as a witness to this re-telling, Arlene's recollection retroactively reconstitutes the meaning of the past event and is to bring about a change in future conduct.

Ruby performs two roles at once: both a surrogate mother and a sisterly confidante, representing emotional succor and intimacy. Calming and holding Arlene "tenderly, rocking as with a baby" (*Collected Works* 55), Ruby gives Arlene the kind of care and love which she had never been able to gain from her own mother. Like a sister, she offers herself as a listener to Arlene's suffering and comforts her empathically and unjudgmentally. With Ruby's female nourishment and nurture, Arlene is able to unite the two selves. Without the vitality of her former self, Arlene feels a profound loss regretting what she has done to herself telling Ruby "I didn't mean to do it, what I done…" (*Collected Works* 55). With Ruby's assurance that "You can still…you can still love people that's gone" (*Collected Works* 55), Arlene begins to "realize that she can handle herself properly and even live with the vestiges of Arlie that still cry within her" (Bordman and Hischak 259). Roudané also opines that Arlene "learns to accept her former self, to grant Arlie her presence, and to push beyond the emotional wreckage of her past. And such an insight becomes the master key to her existing and existence" (*American Drama* 126). Thus, Arlene achieves her psychological rebirth reconciling her two selves for her future survival.

Having orchestrated the two voices with a powerful strength, Norman ends the play with the unification of the two selves of Arlene and Arlie when both simultaneously simulate her mother's gesture with one hand on her hip and imitate her mother's questioning Arlie who was locked inside her closet "Arlie, what you doin' in there? (*Collected Works* 58)" A smiling Arlene shows that she has totally accepted the former self as an integral part of her life's story. No longer obsessed with the traumatic past, she begins to face the future life with self-determination and a reintegrated self.

2. Recalling the Traumatic Memory of Maternal Loss in *Traveler in the Dark*

Traveler in the Dark, ① Norman's sixth play, takes the traumatic memory of the death of the protagonist's mother as its subject. The play is, to a great extent, a homecoming play. Having never come to the house since his mother's death, Sam, with his wife Glory and their twelve-year-old son Stephen, comes back to his childhood house where his father Everett lives by himself for the funeral of Mavis, his lifelong friend, head nurse and cancer patient. This coming back to his childhood environment makes Sam recall the memory of the past, especially his mother who died when he himself was twelve years old. The death of his mother caused him to lose his faith in Christianity and fostered a belief instead in his own intelligence. However, the death of Mavis makes him realize his limitations as a human being. For fear of further pain, he wants to divorce Glory and bring his son with him to a place which he believes can be insulated from the world of pain. However, with Glory's empathy, he is persuaded to believe in the mystery of the world. The protagonist progresses from a sense of confusion about his life and crises of faith to a comprehensive vision of the world through coming to terms with the death of his mother. After he exorcizes the pain of his childhood trauma, he finally reestablishes connections with his family.

Shadowed by the earlier plays which mostly center on women's dilemmas, especially *'night, Mother*, this play receives a lot of negative views. Considering it as "less an effective drama than a didactic argument between opposing points of view", Hilary DeVries deems the play as a failure for "it loses, in fact never finds, its way in a fog of intellectual speechifying" ("Traveler" 19).

---

① It was premiered at the ART in February, 1984, a year after Norman won the Pulitzer Prize for *'night, Mother*. Shadowed by the success of the former play and also because it touched the topic of religion, *Traveler in the Dark* met with scathing reviews which caused Norman to stop writing for the theatre for four years.

Bigsby not only opines that Norman has "less assurance" "in choosing to focus on the relationship between men" (*Modern* 332), but also argues that the play lacks all the distinguished qualities of her early plays— "an acute ear for colloquial speech, a credible and moving sensitivity to family relationships, an ability to engage profound issues obliquely but powerfully, a sense of the rhythms not only of speech but of emotions and thought" (*Contemporary* 243). Despite her praise of the play for its "passages of fluent and engrossing dialogue, lively characters... and moments of high drama leavened by humor", Esther Harriott considers that "Norman would have served her art better by focusing, as she has in the past, on the personal dilemma rather than the philosophical issue" (146). It is obvious that those critics did not expect Norman to write plays concerning philosophic debate which involves rationality and intelligence.

However, the critics' attack on the play for its lack of emotion and focus on the philosophical issue is unfair. The play is in fact about the personal dilemma of the protagonist facing the serious issues of life and death, rationality and emotion. This is noted by Gerald Weales who claims that the play is both "an intriguing character study and a fascinating philosophical/theological debate ("A Long Way" 117). He imputes the play's delayed production in New York in 1990, six years after its first performance to the audience's taste for spectacular entertainment. He writes in a critical tone: "New York theatergoers have no great taste for ideational confrontation, their intellectual perceptions having been dimmed by too much moving scenery" (*Collected Works* 117). In effect, the seeming cynicism of the protagonist is a façade to cover his stifled love-hate emotion toward his parents, both of whom he considers have betrayed him.

Considering that the play has "the most gorgeous writing" (*In Their* 192), Norman thinks "[i] t's a complex piece, and a real step for me in terms of risk. I wrote the play to find out whether it was possible to write a sympathetic smart person for the American stage" (*Interviews* 326). Unlike her earlier characters who are always underdogs at the periphery of the society, the protagonist as a successful surgeon is among the topdogs. However, "intelligence is not always useful" (Norman, "Interview" 153). Despite his remarkable accomplishments, the protagonist deserves sympathy because of his entrapment in the traumatic past of his childhood. In presenting such a figure, Norman "demonstrates her ability to extend insight into men that parallels her previously demonstrated insight into women" (Kane 268).

In the play, Norman presents the catastrophic effect of the traumatic death of the mother on the self-development of a child who can become rigidly rational as a result of loss. The repression of the traumatic memory causes the protagonist to become a narcissist who restrains emotion toward others. But with love and empathy from the family members, the protagonist comes to terms with the traumatic past.

The play is in fact Sam's working through the traumatic memory of the death of his mother in his childhood. Although he has painstakingly avoided coming back to his parents'house, which speaks much of his unwillingness and inability to come to terms with his mother's death, the death of his lifelong friend Mavis prompts him to do so. His life, which is now "a mess" like the mother's garden for lack of maintenance, is because of disastrous effect of the childhood trauma.

It is noteworthy that Norman uses the mother's garden to suggest the repressed traumatic past. Hilary DeVries considers the set in its world premiere at the ART as "pleasantly atmospheric" with "a leaf-strewn garden with ceramic animals in front of a shadowy house" ("Traveler" 19). The various scattering objects in the garden and the overgrown bushes show that it has been in such a dilapidated state for a long time. The imbedded toys in the crumbling stone wall suggest clearly that Sam had spent much of his childhood life in the garden. Grantley holds the view that Norman exploits the symbolic meaning of the garden in several ways. It not only signifies Sam's childhood past and his disordered present life, but also takes on the cultural association of "the *hortus conclusus*, particularly to do with lost innocence" (161). The messy garden is in sharp contrast to the garden in his childhood which has its Edenic connotations, indicating the condition of innocence and carefree existence.

Norman's use of the symbolic stage is similar to that of Tennessee Williams in evoking emotions. In Williams' memory plays, which impressed Norman in her adolescence① and more or less influenced her writing, the symbolic stage with its various objects is deployed to express the emotional value. As he asserts such an intention in the stage direction to *The Glass Menagerie*:

> The scene is memory and is therefore nonrealistic. Memory takes a lot of poetic license. It omits some details, others are exaggerated, according to the emotional value of the articles it touches, for memory is seated predominantly in the heart. " (Williams 1)

Similarly, Norman also intends the symbolic stage to be evocative of the inner emotions. Norman explains her reason that she does not want to put the objects on the stage in a prominent position in the stage direction, "it is not important that these objects be seen by the audience. The less impressive the garden appears, the better. It is Sam's connection to the garden is important" (*Collected Works* 224).

The garden and the objects provide an immediate spur to memory. Symbolically speaking, the objects in his mother's garden are traces of the unresolved past which have been carried into the present. Sam's unearthing those small stone figures and brushing away the leaves initiates a course of unfolding the long – buried memories of the traumatic past which has been painstakingly repressed and deliberately avoided. However, Sam's tidying the garden in a seemingly casual way is a token of the potential for the garden to transform from its chaotic status into an orderly one. Retracing the path from rupture back (or forward) to rapture, Sam comes to terms with the death of his mother. Indeed, it initiates a process of Sam's redeeming humanity and restoration of peace as he transforms from isolation and antagonism to reconciliation and connection to his family members.

The death of his mother when he was twelve was traumatic to Sam and he felt a keen sense of loss. Trying vainly to wake her up from unconsciousness

---

① In many cases, Norman mentions her experience of watching *The Glass Menagerie* at the Actors Theatre of Louisville (Harriott 148) .

through reading his mother's favorite *Mother Goose* story, Sam was left with a sense of guilt and insufficiency which resulted in a psychic scar to the core of his personality. With his mother becoming irretrievably lost, his whole inner world was devastated. He recalls this feeling expressly: "It was awful. I took it, well, like it happened to me instead of to her. I couldn't eat. I broke things. But now, well, if she hadn't died, I'd be the biggest momma's boy you ever saw" (*Collected Works* 234). To Sam who had always been possessively and passionately attached to his mother, the sudden disruption of the narcissistic bond between his mother and himself made him despondent, rageful, cold and aloof.

Just as Scott Hinson points out, Sam's ambivalent view toward his mother is a symptom of one who loses the love object (111). On the one hand, he cherishes a nostalgic memory of her, but on the other hand, he also shows bitterness toward her. At one point in his memory, the mother was a loving figure. As he remembers, his mother is "the gingerbread lady. Curly red hair and shiny round eyes and a big checked apron. Fat, pink fingers, a sweet vanilla smell, and all the time in the world. Sing to you, dance with you, write your name on the top of a cake" (*Collected Works* 234). From Sam's description of his mother, it is easy for us to recognize those motherly images in fairy tales which he and his mother had enjoyed reading together. Furthermore, just like Laura in *The Glass Menagerie* who likes collecting glass animals, Sam's mother had a habit of collecting stone animals and various objects from the ground to share with him. The various objects in the garden are overt indications of Sam's mother's emotional input to him. They immediately remind Sam of his blissful childhood with the company of his mother and he still clings to his childhood memory of his empathic mother. The stage direction indicates his cheerfulness upon seeing the garden again: "He smiles and nods, happy to see it again" (*Collected Works* 224). His mother offered love and ministrations which made him feel special, powerful and outstanding. Sam remembers clearly and tells his son Stephen:

> Every day when I came home from school, here she'd be, with a glass of milk for me and a pile of things she'd found in the ground that day, like dragons' teeth, witches' fingers, and fallen stars. I would sit,

there, where you are, and she would work. (*Collected Works* 234)

Like Laura who visualizes an imaginary world through adding life to the glass animals, Sam also brings his imagination into play describing those stones as articles in a magic world. As a child, he experienced all his needs as being gratified instantaneously and completely by the nurturing mother. Perceiving his mother as an extension of his own being, he had been organized unconsciously on the basis of a powerful self-object fantasy of merger with the idealized maternal presence. With her mother's encouragement and admiration, he had a sense of greatness and omnipotence.

However, the death of his mother also left in him the sense of betrayal. Brought up believing in the fairy tales and nursery rhymes in which frogs can turn into princes, or eggs can become man, he was imbued with a sense of omnipotence. Superficially commenting on Humpty Dumpty in *Mother Goose*, he was speaking about his feeling of grandiosity and invincibility filled by his own mother: "She told him he was a man. See? She dressed him up in a little man's suit. He didn't know he could fall. He didn't know he could break. He didn't know he was an egg" (*Collected Works* 227). Emphasizing that it is the mother that made Humpty Dumpty believe that he can be a man, he imputes his own mother to the instillation of such a sense of grandiosity which renders him unaware of the real world of loss and death. Unable to save his mother, he realized his impotency and was unable to continue to live in the imaginary world concocted by his mother.

What was more infuriating for Sam was his sense of abandonment by God. Influenced by his father's Christian belief, he believed in God as savior who can respond to people's prayer. However, his repeating the beloved nursery rhyme as a kind of prayer to awaken his mother from unconsciousness fell on deaf ears. The loss of his mother deprived him of his earlier belief in God as savior indoctrinated by his father's sermons. To his disappointment, God was indifferent: "He just let her die. He took her back. He was only kidding. She wasn't mine. She was His" (*Collected Works* 246). If faith in God cannot prevent death and suffering, "there is no reason to believe" (*Collected Works* 263).

The death of his mother initiates his rivalry with God whom he considers is only a restless and irresponsible tester indifferent to people's lives.

His father Everett's failure in showing sorrow for the death of his mother and consoling him in his suffering sowed the seeds of antagonism between father and son, God and himself. In Sam's memory, Everett did not seem to feel any sorrow for his dead wife and was still devoted to his fire-breathing preaching. What Sam still remembers to this day is his father's obsessive talking on the Sunday when he preached the sermon after his mother's death. Because of his piety to God, Everett was oblivious to Sam's mother's feelings and needs. Idealizing his mother, Sam thinks that his father is not suited to his mother. As Sam blames his father for his lack of concern for his mother, "She was nothing to you. Nothing at all. You never paid any attention to her. You spent all your time tending the flock" (*Collected Works* 256). To Sam, his father is nothing than the agent of the specious Christianity in which he ceases to believe.

The traumatic death of his mother precipitated him into a crisis of faith in the magical world which is represented by the fairy tales, nursery rhymes and the *Bible*. They are all in the house represented through the façade of a house on stage. It should be noted that during the two acts of the play, while the other three characters go into the house several times, Sam never enters the house. In effect, the extrascenic interior of the house also constitutes Norman's way of exploring the buried traumatic memory. Remarking about offstage space generally, Henri Lefebvre posits the scene against the obscene:

> [W]alls, enclosures and facades serve to define both a *scene* (where something takes place) and an *obscene* area to which everything that cannot or may not happen on the scene is relegated: whatever is inadmissible, be it malefic or forbidden, thus has its own hidden space on the near or the far side of a frontier. (36)

In other words, what happens before and behind the façade are of contrasting natures. As in ancient Greek plays which uses the skene facade to house scenes which are psychically dangerous and must be kept out of sight, Norman uses the façade of the house to imply that what lies immediately in the extrascenic house also arouses Sam's psychical pain. According to Stephen's report, inside the house, there is "a whole room of books…Like a forest of books growing up out of the floor. Just books and a rocking chair" (*Collected Works* 226). Not allowing a brief glimpse of the inside of the house through the window, the audience is asked to resort to their imagination to visualize such a room. In this sense, the books and the chair are a kind of virtual prop. But they are given depth and weight. The books which Stephen finds contain fairy tales, nursery rhymes and the *Bible* stories which he had been forbidden to read. However, they are the books that exactly formed Sam's worldview as a child. The rocking chair is a symbol of enjoyment and indulgence in reading the books. However, his disingenuous denial of having read those books speaks much of the pain caused by the devastating death of his mother and the ensuing crisis of faith.

However, out of the belief in the magical world, he fosters a belief in his own rational way of understanding of the situation. But it is this belief in himself that makes him a narcissist and renders him incapable of conveying emotion toward others.

The death of his mother causes Sam to have humiliating feelings of powerlessness and helplessness. In order to prevent further injury to his sense of importance, Sam repressed the traumatic memory which resulted in a narcissistic life as reflected in his "self-serving" (Kane 271) relationships with Everett, Mavis, Glory and Stephen. Never forgiving his father for not being able to save his mother, and responding to his sorrow, he harbored anger and antagonism for Everett for the past thirty years. Abusing Mavis's loyalty to him, he only regarded her as a source of admiration to augment his own sense of grandiosity which his mother had instilled in him. Oblivious to Glory's love and care for him, he even blames her for the death of Mavis. Taking away what he considered as lies and illusions of the world from Stephen's life, he deprived his son of his own rights to make his own choices for his life.

The sense of betrayal by his father for his incompetence to save his mother caused an unbridgeable emotional gulf between father and son. Sam's perception that his father did not love him was reciprocated by his feeling that he did not love his father, either. In response to the powerlessness that he felt deeply as a result of his mother's death, he attempted to restore the lost unity by making himself the center of the world, "With the exception of a mother who died and left me with the preacher, my mind is all I ever had" (*Collected Works* 240). Renouncing his Christian belief, Sam had a feeling of being Godlike and responsible for all the other people. When Glory finds out one of his number jackets with which he ran around the town every morning before, he is reminded of the scenes which he saw and his sense of being responsible for the whole world during his morning jogging in his school years:

> I liked that run before school every morning. Out of the house... down the street... Everybody asleep but me and the milkman. I got to feeling real useful, you know, like I was supposed to check out the town before everybody got up. Mile after mile, so far, so good, I'd think. No fires, no stray dogs, and no lights on, so nobody's sick. We did okay. We made through another night. (*Collected Works* 258)

The words immediately remind us of God who is the creator of the world and claims to be responsible for all human beings.

His choice to become a surgeon suggests not only his intention to rival his father, but also his resistance against death. His devotion to the profession enabled him to achieve outstanding accomplishments in the medical world. Being a world famous surgeon who thinks that he is always combating with death, which in his mind is God, he has been proud of himself in pulling a lot of people away from death: "Day after day I've been proud of myself 'cause I won more round" (*Collected Works* 256). William M. Czander explains that a person's occupational choice and the satisfaction obtained within one's occupation are associated with two needs: gratification of the search for the fulfillment of a wish and the need to experience a sense of safety and comfort (76). This applies to Sam's case. Saving people's lives, to some extent, makes up the feeling of insufficiency toward his mother's death. Although Everett considers Sam's becoming a doctor as God's plan because it is God who let his mother die, it is in fact Sam's search for empathic response which underlies his choice.

It seems that Sam had rejected his father's belief, but in worshipping his own reasoning, he had practiced his father's religion but not worshipped his father's god. Commenting on Sam's rebellion against his father's belief, Norman speaks that "it is not possible to live your life in total rebellion against a parental stance, without somehow incorporating that stance. The parent's beliefs are the foundation of the child's new religion, rebellious though it may seem" (*Interviews* 331).

His antagonism against his father also manifests in his marrying Glory instead of Mavis. Although his father thought Mavis and him to be a perfect couple, Sam did not take her into consideration as a marriage partner. Since they were only ten years old, Mavis had begun to love him for his undauntedness to probe into the reality of things. Exposing Everett's magic trick to amuse Mavis, Sam showed her that there was no magic. Mavis and Sam were "two of a kind" (*Collected Works* 260), as Glory says perceptively. To use Sam's words, Mavis was "Somebody exactly like me. Somebody who believed in hard work, who couldn't wait to be an adult. Somebody who never read "Sleeping Beauty" and never said a prayer except, 'God let me stay awake long enough to get everything finished'" (*Collected Works* 260). The presence of Mavis made Sam feel safe and secure. Alice Miller, in her study about the relationship between the narcissist and his narcissistically cathected partners, writes that a narcissist must constantly find those who can be made to admire and esteem him and is powerfully dependent upon those whose admiration and esteem he can compel (39). Despite Sam's deliberate indifference to her, Mavis was persistent in following him, propelled by her admiration for him. She finally managed to become Sam's head nurse. However, Sam did not show his needs for her because in so doing he would have to admit the fact of his needfulness and vulnerability at the heart of his defective personality. In spite of their physical closeness, there was an emotional distance between them. Sam admits to Glory about his lack of empathy toward Mavis: "I didn't love her, I used her. And then... when she really needed me... she was counting on me to see it, Glory, only I wasn't looking. And I wasn't looking because I didn't want to see it" (*Collected Works* 262). Unwilling to commit himself to a close relationship with Mavis, he did not understand her as a person, just as he failed to find the mysteries of the human body when he performed a medical operation to save her.

Just as Mavis's presence makes him feel a sense of security, his marriage with Glory gratified his narcissistic vanity. Thinking himself to be special, he deserved to be married to someone unusual. Sam made great efforts in winning the hand of Glory who was the most beautiful girl in ten counties and is still regarded by Everett as so. However, having always carried around the trauma of his mother's death and the hurt and anger caused by his father, Sam brought this emotional burden to his adult relationships. Norman describes his temperament in the stage direction: "He can seem preoccupied, impatient, and condescending" (*Collected Works* 223). Despite his inner sense of worthlessness and lack of self-esteem, his grandiose self prevented him from seeing himself in an objective light. He is badly in need of others to show admiration toward him. He comments on the story of *The Princess and the Frog* in light of his relationship with Glory, "The frog believed that the beauty could turn him into a prince. One kiss from her and he would be handsome, and play tennis, and mix martinis, and tell jokes at parties, just like all her other boyfriends" (*Collected Works* 228).

Self-centered and egoistic, he is blinded to see his abusive attitude toward Glory. To a great extent, his married life is similar to that of his parents. Although he blames his father for his neglect of his mother, he is no different from his father in this aspect. Absorbed in his life-saving profession as his father is engrossed with his Christian duties, he has no intention of taking notice of his wife's innermost feelings and needs. Because "his work has been his mistress," he formed with Glory a relationship "of habit rather than affection" (Kane 272). It is fortunate that he married a wife like Glory, who, in Norman's introductory notes to the characters, "is blessed with a rare grace, an elegant of spirit, and nobody understands how on earth she has stayed married to Sam for all these years" (*Collected Works* 223). Just like Sam's own mother, Glory is both an understanding wife and a loving mother. Leslie Kane rightly points out that disparate from her earlier plays in which there are only supportive and understanding surrogate mothers, Norman, for the first time in this play, has presented "loving and supportive wives who are warm, affectionate mothers" (269).

Sam was always in a brusque and abrasive manner but he is unaware of the fact. Glory's words confirm the fact: "You just don't notice it, because this is how you always are" (*Collected Works* 240). Seldom taking any time off, he expected to be waited on hand and foot when he came home from work, and always believed that the demands of his work were given top priority. Seeing himself as a prominent figure who must confront urgent issues and make complex decisions which affect a lot of persons' lives, he was displeased with his wife whom he considered enjoyed herself (*Collected Works* 262) rather than took care of him as his mother used to. Although Glory is perceptive enough to feel his depression and his need for empathic resonance, Sam is still not satisfied. He tells Glory that "I want you to be the woman I want" (*Collected Works* 240). According to Freud, a man with a strong mother fixation has an irreplaceable unconscious image of his mother, his ideal of womanhood, and is always trying to find in every woman his mother, a quest which inevitably results in disappointment for his unwillingness to give up the his unconscious mother fixation. In fact, setting up Glory as a fantasized replacement for his dead mother, Sam unconsciously fantasized that his wife would serve in the same self-object capacity as his mother had prior to her death. Coming back to his mother's garden which symbolically represents the sheltering mother, he is unwilling for Glory to touch any object in the garden. His mind is still occupied by an unconscious image which fuses himself and his mother. When he hears that Glory's words that "I want a way in", he responds resolutely that "There isn't any way in. There never was. You never had a chance. I married you to spite my father" (*Collected Works* 241). Although he later admits that what he said to Glory was purposely hurtful, the words reveal some truths about his unconscious state of mind.

Narcissistically possessive, Sam regarded his son as a tabula rasa for him to mould according to his own will. Initially not wanting to have a child, he was afraid of losing his wife's exclusive attention to and admiration for him. However, after Stephen's birth, he regarded him as his possession and attempted to mold

Stephen as he desired which, in his mind, was for Stephen's good. Taking away the television from him, he also directed his son to read books like *The Call of the Wild*, *Lord of the Flies* and *Donner Pass* in which survival instincts are displayed at the forefront instead of the nursery rhymes and fairy tales which he had read in his childhood but was disillusioned with. Leslie Kane is right in noting that "Sam has taken away Stephen's youth and dreams and replaced them with his own" (217). For fear of Stephen being influenced by his father's Christian belief, he even tries to prevent them from being together alone. As his father had done instilling the Christian belief in his mind, he inculcates his son with his "suspect philosophy" (Bigsby, *Contemporary* 242). He speaks eloquently about his doctrine of self-reliance in the following:

> God is not in control. We are. There is no heaven, there is no hell. There is this life [. . .] Life on earth, which we make better through careful thought and hard work. But we make the progress, and we make the mistakes. Not God. God has nothing to do with this, so there is no point in believing in Him. He's just another fairy-tale king, as far as I'm concerned. If you want to believe, believe in yourself. In your power, in your mind, in your life. This life. Because that's all there is. (*Collected Works* 248)

At the expense of Stephen's rights to choose and his curiosity toward the world, he is tyrannical in instilling in him the belief that he is special and he should be confident in himself rather than believing in God's almighty power.

Having a sense of godlike omnipotence, Sam always put himself in a position to protect and save others. However, Sam is in despair and feels guilty for his failure to save Mavis: "I was showing off! I could fix it. I could pull her through. I could make it disappear" (*Collected Works* 263). His sense of omnipotence vanished as he recognized this defeat and his limited capacity as a human being. His grandiose attempt to save Mavis from cancer through operation resulted in her death. Feelings of humiliation and emptiness ensued.

Although Darryll Grantley thinks that Norman should not consign Mavis to silence and invisibility because of her far more potential dramatic power, it is argued that Mavis's death, in Norman's dramatic design, functions merely as a catalyst for Sam to come to terms with his mother's death, the memory of which has been long repressed. The death of Mavis reactivated the painful feeling that Sam had felt ensuing the death of his mother but had been deeply repressed. Although he never forgave his father for his unresponsiveness to him, the injury this time made his pain sharper than before. Suffering the old traumatic rejection from the empathic environment and dreading further injury which will be caused by the death of Glory in the future, he responds with withdrawal rather than fighting back like the former time. Feeling shamed and guilty for his inability to save Mavis, he desires to escape from his current life—his profession and his wife. Thinking little about the pain that Stephen will experience being ripped way from Glory, he wants to take his son with him to "someplace wonderful. Northern California, maybe, with the ocean out the front door, and the redwoods out the back" (*Collected Works* 252), or even South America or Africa (*Collected Works* 253). Ironically, his defensive withdrawal is unrealistic. Always a person who structures his life around receiving admiration and support from others, it is impossible for him to live with Stephen by himself. On the contrary, as Glory says, Stephen will be the one who takes care of him.

Thinking that he has finally arrived at the state of being free of faith, he claims that he does not believe in anything because

all the faith in the world… [w] on't save any of us. Won't do a thing except make fools of us. Give us tests we cannot pass. Bring us to our knees, but not in prayer— in absolute submission to accident, to the arbitrary assignment of unbearable pain, and the everyday occurrence of meaningless death. Only then can we believe… that dreams, like deadly whirlpools, drown us in their frenzy… that love blazes across a black sky like a comet but never returns… and that time, like a desert wind, blows while I sleep, and erases the path I walked to here, and erases the path that leads on. (*Collected Works* 263)

Confused at the absurdity of life and death in the world, he becomes atheistic. However, as Bigsby argues, "this, too, is a kind of faith, a belief which has taken over his life as profoundly as his earlier conversion had briefly done. It is, however, in the context of the play, a destructive faith and the play, essentially, is concerned with bringing him back if not to a faith in God then to an acceptance of mystery" (*Contemporary* 243).

In ending the play with Sam's family staying at his childhood home for some time, Norman suggests that Sam has removed his guilty preoccupation with the past and has a renewed self in connection with his family members. To a great extent, Sam's remembrance of the past is a means to liberate him from the traumatic memory, to be forgiven and to forgive. As he tells his son, what he saw after he cut Mavis open in the operation room was "forgiveness" (*Collected Works* 268). Leslie Kane observes that "Sam must be able to accept his past and the present crisis and move beyond it or... he will be unable to go on" (271). Coming to terms with the death of his mother in his childhood and the death of Mavis, he is able to attain self-reflection and self-awareness which is of vital importance for his future relationships with his father, his wife and his son.

Relinquishing his former sense of omnipotence which he believed could protect and save others, he accepts the limitations of being human which is critical for his renewed sense of self and his future life. As he says thoughtfully, "When I am out here, on this wall, in this garden, looking up at the sky, I think, yes, there is something out there. I actually want there to be something out there. I want there to be a God, and I don't want it to be me" (*Collected Works* 252). Recognizing the world of mystery, he is able to shed his sense of guilt for his incapability to protect and save others. Commenting on the issue of protection in this play, Norman expresses her idea that "[o] ne of the things that is critical for survival is to understand that you cannot protect the people you love. As soon as you understand that, you can begin to figure out what you *can* do" (*Interviews* 331). Realizing the human limitation and working through the losses, Sam determines to come out of his isolated world into the intertwined familial relationships and attains his inner transformation.

With the sustained love and support of Glory, Sam reaches out to Glory, abandoning his aloof and condescending attitude toward her. Despite Sam's abusive attitude with her in their marriage, Glory is insistent in helping Sam to get through his crisis of faith. To some extent, Sam and Glory establishes a relationship just like that between patient and therapist. Despite Sam's lack of empathy toward her, Glory has accepted the status quo and put up with Sam for years because she regards him as a genius who needs her: "I have no idea why you need me but you do. I can feel it. I see it all the time. I don't understand at all, but I have no doubt whatsoever" (*Collected Works* 240). Although Sam is disillusioned and intends to leave her, Glory, like an empathic therapist, listens to Sam's confession of his guilt and rage and tries to direct him to maintain a realistic self-assessment and judgment of others. Her persistence in providing a supportive milieu is necessary for Sam to achieve his psychic structural completeness which had been fragmented by the traumatic loss and disappointment in childhood. Commenting on the altruistic function of empathy, Marion F. Solomon remarks that

[p] roviding a sustaining echo of empathic resonance to someone who has lacked it in earlier relationships is a reparative experience that unlocks the gates and releases the interrupted maturational push thwarted in childhood, enabling the developmental process to begin to reassert itself. (292)

Through his talking with Glory, Sam begins to have a more realistic view of himself and his whole perspective on the world is transformed.

His transformation also is reflected in his forgiveness toward his father. Through forgiving the old wrongs, he regains peace and his relationship with Everett is mended. Forgoing his antagonism toward his father which has lasted for the past thirty years, he forgives his father for his negligence toward his mother and unresponsiveness toward his sorrow. For the first time, both father and son talks about their real feelings toward the death of the mother. Blinded by his deep grief for his dead mother, Sam was unjust in blaming his father for his mother's death. Himself being a father who needs to be forgiven by his own son whose real feelings had been neglected for his own purpose, Sam realizes the sadness of his father who is profoundly hurt by Sam's words that "you don't get the boy you want, you get the boy you get" (*Collected Works* 257). The hear-trending sentence immediately reminds us of what Jessie has said to her mother: "I am what became of your child" (*'night, Mother* 76). Expressing his love—the essence of forgiveness—for his father, he is again connected to his father as he was in his early childhood.

After reliving and working through his unresolved childhood feelings, Sam is able to construct a renewed relationship with Glory, Stephen and Everett. Bigsby notes that Sam "eventually finds himself led back to a belief if not in the ineffable then in the intangible and irrational fact of human relationships and of a need which can finally not be satisfied by a pragmatic struggle with the conse-quences of fate" (*Contemporary* 244). Having always been fighting against fate, Sam did not cherish his family life. The crisis of faith enables him to re-flect on his past narcissism and come out of the isolated world which he formed around himself. Forsaking his arrogant attitude toward his wife, he admits his need and love for Glory. Accepting the mystery of the world, Sam stops his son from breaking the geode which his mother had left to him and he passes on to his son. The joint recalling of the verse of the twinkle star by Sam and Everett sig-nals a rapprochement between father and son. Attacked for its lack of emotion, the last scene is nothing but laden with emotion. Ending the play with the choru-sing of the nursery rhyme, Norman mixes gestures of reconciliation, forgiveness and understanding to produce an image of family unity and love.

Through her portrayal of a protagonist whose self-development has met se-vere problems because of the traumatic loss in childhood, Norman posits that fa-milial love can be a positive catalyst for self-transformation. Thanks to empathy and compassion of the family, Norman's protagonist transforms from his initial estrangement and indifference to willingness to engage in the connection with the family. An earlier rage yields to a sense of renewal and hope.

Chapter Two

NOSTALGIA TO DISILLUSIONMENT: MOURNING THE WISTFUL PAST

While Chapter One examines the repressed traumatic past and the protagonists' reconciliation with the traumatic past with the support of an empathic community, this chapter focuses on the wistful past and the protagonists' change from nostalgia to disillusionment with it in *Third and Oak*, *The Holdup* and *Loving Daniel Boone*.

Nostalgia, a term originally referring to a medical condition which resulted from displacement from home, has come to be regarded as an emotion— "an emotion of wistful longing for the past" (Wilson 22). However, the word "wistful" embodies the paradoxical bitter sweetness of the nature of nostalgia. The paradox of the word is pointed out by Elihu Howland when he explains its meaning. He observes: "When we examine the meaning of the word 'wistful', we find the same puzzling combination of eagerness, expectancy and mournfulness" (qtd. in Wilson 24). Kimberly Smith similarly remarks that "Remembering the past should instead be seen as a way to express valid desires and concerns about the present—in particular, about its relationship (lack of relationship) to the past (qtd. in Wilson 26). From what they observe, two aspects of nostalgia are indicated. On the one hand, nostalgia denotes a longing for the past which people believe can give them a sense of comfort and security. On the other hand, the fact of the pastness produces the feeling of loss and pain for the nostalgic.

Some scholars consider nostalgia as a positive way in interpreting one's immediate surroundings. In the book *The Future of Nostalgia*, Svetlana Boym remarks that nostalgia is a yearning for a different time…a rebellion against the modern idea of time, the time of history and progress. The nostalgic desires to obliterate history and turn it into private or collective mythology, to revisit time like space, refusing to surrender to the irreversibility of time that plagues the human condition. (xv)

According to Boym, indulgence in nostalgia represents "the conscious decision to reject the logic of modernity" and "an existential life choice for individuals who admire ideals associated with premodern societies" (Su 4). Contrary to his opinion, Norman presents a critique of nostalgia in her plays through dramatizing the protagonists' change from nostalgia for the past to progression towards the future. Although nostalgia can temporarily enable the nostalgic to evade disappointing circumstances, it leads to unproductive engagements with the present in the long run.

In the plays that will be discussed in this chapter, the protagonists harbor a nostalgic feeling for the past when things were supposedly better than the present. The tendency to nostalgia represents an unwillingness to face the unbearable reality. But reality shatters their illusion and facilitates them to reflect on the past and regard the present in a way untainted by illusions of memory. The disillusionment with the past resituates them in the present condition and reorients them to the future with an awakening.

1. Lamenting Loss of Marriage and Friendship in *Third and Oak*

Third and Oak, [①] Norman's second play, consists of two acts, with each

---

[①] It was premiered in 1978 at Actors Theatre of Louisville where she had been named playwright-in-residence, under the direction of Jon Jory. Later each of the two acts, *Third and Oak: The Laundromat* and *Third and Oak: The Pool Hall* is frequently performed as two one-acts. Although they did not receive the raves of *Getting Out*, response to these plays were generally favorable. Both were later adapted into films, well-received by the critics.

one being an extended duologue between a parentlike figure and a child figure at three o'clock in the morning. The first act takes place at a laundromat where two white women, Alberta and Deedee encounter and narrate their different stories. Recently widowed, Alberta still cannot accept the death of her husband Herb. Although she comes to the laundromat at midnight intending to wash Herb's clothes, she has difficulty in washing the shirt in which he died accidentally. Living in a marriage dominated and betrayed by her husband Joe, Deedee comes to wash his clothes to avoid her loneliness. The two women's conversations provide both an occasion to reflect on their past life, especially their relationship with their husbands. The second act transpires at a pool hall next door to the laundromat where two black men, the pool hall owner Willie, and Gary Wayne,① the son of his best friend Shooter, the former best pool player who committed suicide, come to reconciliation after they accept the truth of their lives. Overcome by the death of Shooter and the increasing physical deterioration of another friend George, Willie has a bias against Gary Wayne, who regards himself with his father's name Shooter. The frankness and sincerity in their conversations make them open heart to each other and lead to their ensuing reconciliation. The two acts are connected by the child figures, who, to some extent, also act as intruders for the parent-child scenes of each act.

Because it seems that the two acts of the play are not in any way connected, it causes critics such as Darryll Grantley to speak unfavorably. He complains that "the play might be seen as attempting to engage too many issues and knitting together two episodes which are not sufficiently connected, thus compromising its unity and focus" (148). Nevertheless, Norman herself prefers the two parts to be seen together "like the right foot following the left" (*Collected Works* 60) because they are about the same thing, i. e. , "why we lie to protect ourselves when we could tell the truth and be saved" (*Collected Works* 60) .

As a complex play of character portrayal, *Third and Oak* presents the nostalgic desire of the characters for the wistful past ensuing the loss of their

---

① In the play, because Gary Wayne uses his father's name Shooter to address himself to others, Norman uses the name Shooter in the character list and throughout the play to indicate him.

marriage and friendship. Different from the mimetic representation of the traumatic past in *Getting Out*, the diegetic presentation of the wistful past in this play demonstrates the anachronous potency of the absent characters who continue to occupy a palpable emotional space in the present life of onstage characters. Nevertheless, the characters' midnight reminiscence of their past exposes the illusions which make them bogged down and unable to continue their lives with personal wholeness. Through the reminiscences of the characters, the play initiates a process of working through the loss. Out of their memory of the past losses, the characters are able to look at their present lives in a more honest way.

The central dramatic action of the first act is the interaction of the two lonely women as they reminisce nostalgically about their husbands while washing their husbands' clothes. By portraying the encounter of two women at midnight in a laundromat, Norman dramatizes the sense of loneliness and longing for jointure with their husbands to fulfill their need for intimate human contact.

The first act of the play presents before us two women in sharp contrast with each other. At the unusual hour of 3: 00 A. M. , Alberta Johnson, a reserved and refined woman in her fifties, comes to the all-night laundromat to wash her husband's clothes, but we do not know that her husband has died until quite late in the act. Willing to prefer her privacy, she is relieved finding the male attendant of the laundromat asleep. However, her temporary tranquility is broken by Deedee Johnson, a restless, jittery and compulsively talkative woman in her twenties who has the same aim of washing her husband's clothes. Despite their same family name, they are in sharp contrast with each other. While Alberta is quiet and does not show any willingness to have a conversation with Deedee but is obliged to do so out of decorum during much of the act, Deedee seems to have a lot of words to pour out of her lips. While Alberta is neatly-dressed and a retired teacher, Deedee is "a wreck" and does not have much confidence even in naming seven presidents of the United States. Being punctilious, Alberta checks the cleanliness of the washer before she puts the clothes in. Deedee, however, bundles up all the clothes in one of her husband's shirt and because of her carelessness she sprawls herself and the clothes all over the floor which makes for the dramatic movement of the scene. While Deedee tries to cover her loneliness through compulsive talking, Alberta suppresses her emotional pain through a-voidance.

Despite their different dispositions and patterns of behavior, Alberta and Deedee bear similarities in that both display a nostalgic desire for their lost marriage. The death of Albert's husband Herb disrupts her ordinary life as a wife. Deedee's husband Joe's betrayal of her causes her disorientation. Actually, both women have identified themselves with their husbands and never have an independent identity. Jean Baker Miller points out that one central feature of women's development is that

> women stay with, build on, and develop in a context of attachment and affiliation with others. Indeed, women's sense of self becomes very much organized around being able to make and then to maintain affiliations and relationships. Eventually, for many women the threat of disruption of an affiliation is perceived not as just a loss of a relationship but as something closer to a total loss of self. (326)

Always organizing their life around their husbands, the women feel devastated for the absence of their husbands in their present life and they refuse to accept the absence and attempt to preserve them by incorporating them into themselves.

In Kierkegaard's *Sickness onto Death*, there is a parable about a young girl who has lost her lover, which resembles the situation of the two women in the play. It is quoted at length in the following:

> A young girl despairs of love, that is, she despairs over the loss of her beloved, over his death or his unfaithfulness to her. This is not declared despair; no, she despairs over herself. This self of hers, which she would have been rid of or would have lost in the most blissful manner had it become "his" beloved, this self becomes a torment to her if it has to be a self

without "him" . This self, which would have become her treasure (although, in another sense, it would have been just as despairing), has now become to her an abominable void since "he" died, or it has become to her a nauseating reminder that she has been deceived. (20)

Similar to Miller's argument that the women have lost their selves, Kierkegaard also points out the lack of boundaries between the women's selves and their beloveds. For the two characters in the play, coming to the laundromat to wash the clothes of their husbands "becomes a metaphor for them to work through their separate disjointed life" (Cen 208) .

The neutral territory of the laundromat and washing process of their clothes provide a space and time for the two women, who met coincidentally, to tell their different stories of loss, which Bigsby considers as the theme of the first act (*Contemporary* 221). Applying Helene Cixous' feminist ethics which locates "the site of political action between *women* who are able to recuperate for one another their appropriated selves and bodies through the metaphorical act of support and love from another woman", Grace Epstein maintains that " [i] n the midst of their own unmediated losses, each woman mothers the other across the chasm of economic, social, and perhaps even spiritual disparities" (27 – 28). In fact, the play not only reveals their "disappointments and disillusionments of their lives" (Bigsby, *Contemporary* 222), but also presents their struggle to disencumber themselves out of the shadow of their past life. Facilitating the women to reveal their sorrows and fears through their midnight encounter, Norman provides a possibility that both women are going to face the truth of their past life, and get out of their different traps in memories or lies which are all-consuming and incapacitating. Thus, the laundromat goes beyond its physical function of purification, and "becomes a symbol for purging and redemption" (Harriott 138) .

Both women are absorbed in their own memory of the old days which they spend with their husbands who exert a great deal of power over themselves. Adeptly incorporating music, one of the important dramatic signals to "guide and extend an audience's feeling and imagination" (Styan 47), Norman sets the mood for the act. The song "Stand by Your Man"[1] at the beginning of the play, which "exhibits something of Tennessee Williams's sense of the lyricism of setting (Grantley 150), speaks much of the living status of the two women. Put in Bigsby's words, "men had been the key to the meaning of their lives" (*Modern* 329). One restrained and the other talkative, Alberta and Deedee display disparate ways to show their nostalgia for their lost marriage.

Esther Harriott considers that the substantiality of the first act is due to Norman's humorous and compassionate portrayal of Deedee (135). In dramatizing Deedee's first appearance on stage, Norman employs a comic technique which is the stock-in-trade of comedy playwrights. Her coming on stage with a fall can make the audience laugh. This is similar to the situation of the man who stumbles and falls while running along the street because of his absentmindedness which is described in Henri Bergson's *Laughter* (8 – 9). Robert Leach takes is-

---

[1]   "Stand by Your Man" is a song co – written by Tammy Wynette and Billy Sherill and originally recorded by Tammy Wynette, released as a single in Sept. 1968. The lyrics of the song are as follows:

Sometimes its hard to be a woman

Giving all your love to just one man

You'll have bad times

And he'll have good times

Doing things that you don't understand

But if you love him you'll forgive him

Even though he's hard to understand

And if you love him

Oh be proud of him

'Cause after all he's just a man

Stand by your man

Give him two arms to cling to

And something warm to come to

When nights are cold and lonely

Stand by your man

And tell the world you love him

Keep giving all the love you can

Stand by your man

Stand by your man

And show the world you love him

Keep giving all the love you can

Stand by your man

Web. 15 Sept. 2011 < http: //www. stlyrics. com/lyrics/sleeplessinseattle/standbyourman. htm >

sue with this kind of response to people's misfortune since it seems to reflect people's cruelty, viciousness and indifference toward those who suffer the misfortunes of life (46). As a matter of fact, while the audience may laugh at Deedee for her carelessness at the beginning, it is increasingly to show compassion for her for her situation revealed through her insistent communicativeness. On the one hand, Deedee's words show her nostalgia for the past; on the other hand, her words disclose the reality of her marriage in which she has not been able to maintain her subjectivity.

As Anton Chekhov in *The Three Sisters* uses "memories and dreaming of the future" (Szondi 18) to present the sense of loneliness and meaninglessness of his characters, Norman employs nostalgia and illusion to function as a sign of impotence for Deedee. Deedee's nostalgia for the romantic feelings and physical intimacy in her marriage is expressed manifestly. She reminisces: "I like how he comes in the door. Picks me up, swings me around in the air..." (*Collected Works* 80). What's more, she cherishes the hope that "he's gonna be a famous race car driver someday and I want to be there" (*Collected Works* 80). Consequently, she does not think her present life to be of any significance. Moreover, she treasures the blue light with a stalk of blueberries which Joe sent her as a gift and puts it beside the window of her apartment. Despite the fact that she does not like the color of blue, she is unwilling to admit it. This is indicated when she later explains to Gary Wayne when she goes to the next door pool hall to bring his clothes to him: "I mean, I like blue, it's not my favorite color, but I like it a lot, and somebody gave it to me ..." (*Collected Works* 103). The blue light, instead of merely functioning as a light, is rather a demonstration of Deedee's nostalgic desire for the romantic feelings that she once had in her marriage life in the past.

As a matter of fact, Deedee's marriage life is not good at all. While Deedee's compulsive talkativeness discloses much information about her nostalgic desire for the past, it also shows clearly her loneliness and her desire for connection as a result of the reality of her miserable married life.

Deedee's first words after she gets up from the floor immediately reveal much about her marriage life. She has been married to Joe for two years. However, despite her unwillingness to talk bad about Joe, it is easy for the audience to see from Deedee's words that Joe does not seem to be the kind of man one can depend on. Joe is lazy, slovenly, uncouth and short-tempered. Because "[h] e hates to run out for beer late" (*Collected Works* 64), Joe chooses to live in an apartment over the Old Mexico Taco Tavern. Always a man waiting to be served, he seldom cooks. As Deedee says, "The only time he ever even fried an egg, he flipped it over and it landed in the sink. It was the last egg, so he grabbed it up and ate it in one bite" (*Collected Works* 80). Having lived in the apartment for two years, Joe "still ain't found the closets" and never puts his clothes on hangers because "[h] e thinks hangers are for when you lock your keys in your car. (*Collected Works* 62)" His hot temper is best disclosed when Deedee tells Alberta about the incident of Joe's bowling shirt being damaged by her mother's washer: "Whoo – ee! Was he hot. Kicked the chest of drawers, broke his toe. (*No response from Alberta.*) And the chest of drawers too" (*Collected Works* 64). Working at the Ford plant, Joe has not come home till the middle of the night.

In effect, Deedee's compulsiveness to talk is her strategy to get over her feeling of loneliness. Unable to tolerate the torment of waiting up for her husband to come home, Deedee picks up the clothes which Joe has scattered on the floor and comes to the laundromat wishing to meet somebody who can talk to her to distract her from her feeling of loneliness. As she later admits to Alberta because she has realized that Alberta seems to be forced into conversation with her, "I'd talk to somebody else, but there ain't nobody else" (*Collected Works* 65). Just like Ginger in *Trudy Blue* who talks to herself because she feels isolated from the other people, Deedee talks in her sleep sometimes or even "find [s] somethin' to say to a head of cabbage" (*Collected Works* 103). Jenny S. Spencer is right in commenting that Deedee's unthinking chatter "indicates the depth of her unhappiness and her inability to face it" ("She-Tragedies" 149).

Through her talk with Alberta, we can see that Deedee's marriage life with Joe is not a satisfying one. In her world, there is not the word "happiness" as she cannot name Happy among the seven dwarfs in *Snow White and the Seven Dwarfs*, despite her great efforts in recalling. But she has no courage to break away from him. Being a male chauvinist, Joe does not permit Deedee to work. Largely dependent on Joe economically, Deedee has hardly any power. In order to decrease her boredom and loneliness, Deedee takes a job of writing names on envelops for a New Jersey company without telling Joe. However, this furtive job does not alleviate her loneliness at all. As she tells Alberta, "Sometimes I bring in a little stand-up mirror to the coffee table while I'm watching TV. It's my face over there when I look, but it's a face just the same" (*Collected Works* 82). What's more, the money she earns cannot be spent without being noticed by Joe, so she has to hide it in her mother's house. Because she sometimes goes to her mother's house to do the laundry, her mother usually takes the money as the water charge. Although Joe squanders all his money in a 1964 Chevy for drag racing, Deedee is cajoled into believing that after winning a big race they can have kids.

Deedee's recounting of the scene which she gave Joe a doll with an image of her own face as an anniversary present not only indicates her loss of self but also her husband's indifference to and emotional torture of her. Trying every way to please her husband, Deedee painted her face on a doll which would be an anniversary present to Joe. But unfortunately, Joe thought it ridiculous and laughed so hard that he fell on the radiator and broke his head. To make matters worse, he even sent the doll to a totally strange sick girl met in the hospital. Like Nora in Henrik Ibsen's *The Doll's House*, to whom the doll is allusive, Deedee is subject to the sudden caprices and moods of her husband. Treated as "an object, fair game for male advances and insults" since she was in high school, Esther Harriott argues that

> [n]ow she [Deedee] plays that role for her husband. Deedee is like the pre-Arlene Arlie, who was a pushover for Carl, and her name—not short for anything else, she tells Alberta—has the same connotations as Arlie's. It is not a full-fledged name and its bearer is not treated as a full-fledged person. (136)

Dependent and a mere plaything of her husband, she is not allowed to develop any individuality of her own.

What makes Deedee really broken-hearted is Joe's extramarital affair with the woman whom Deedee has seen the night before in the bowling alley. Even when she hears that Alberta's husband is in Akron, Deedee imagines that "Akron, he could be sittin' at the bar in some all – night bowling alley polishing some big blonde's ball" (*Collected Works* 68). The words are very offensive to the genteel Alberta who abides by the principles of social decorum and is prudent in choice of words. However, when Alberta later realizes that Deedee is really talking about her own husband who messes around with another woman, the emotionally sensitive Alberta shows sympathy toward Deedee. Nevertheless, for all the shortcomings and inconsiderateness of Joe, Deedee has tolerated him. Never living on her own before, she dare not leave Joe.

Despite her unhappiness in her marriage life, it is not possible for her to seek advice, not to say comfort, from her mother. Actually, in Norman's plays, lack of communication between mother and daughter is a motif. Commenting on parent-child relationship in Norman's plays, Craig observes that "characters connected by blood are the ones most separated by beliefs" (*Family Ties* 314). Like Arlene and her mother in *Getting Out* and Jessie and Thelma in *'night, Mother* who hold disparate views about life, Deedee and her mother have different opinions about marriage. Deedee married Joe against the will of her mother. Thinking that "Joe's a bum" (*Collected Works* 67), Deedee's mother always wants them to break apart. She even tries to match Deedee with a guy working at Walgreen's who she thinks will become manager of the drugstore. Worldlier than Deedee who believes in the feeling of love, Deedee's mother considers economic condition as the prerequisite of a marriage. Therefore, Deedee does not want to tell her mother about the truth about her marriage life. Even though sometimes she goes to her mother's house for laundry after she married, there is not much to talk about between mother and daughter. This is confirmed by Deedee's words: "Course she don't ever say how she likes seeing me, but she holds back, you know. I mean, there's stuff you don't have to say when it's family" (*Collected Works* 63). What Deedee and her mother do is just sit there, watch TV and wait for the washing and drying to be over. In addition, the mother's distrust of Deedee's ability in doing things appropriately deepens the estrangement between mother and daughter. Wishing her mother to be more like Alberta, Deedee thinks that her own mother is "the *last* person I'm tellin'" (*Collected Works* 80; italics original). Deedee is really angry about Joe's infidelity as her mother has anticipated that it is the "itch" year of her marriage. Deedee explains her mother's idea of itch, "When guys get the itch, you know, to fool around with other women. Stayin' out late, comin' in with stories about goin' drinkin' with the boys or workin' overtime or ... somethin'" (*Collected Works* 68). In fact, Grace Epstein maintains that the "itch" is "a convenient, if not characteristic excuse for the patriarchal privilege that underwrites and supports female dependency and male betrayal" (38) .

The appearance of Gary Wayne who regards himself as Shooter, the black DJ whom Deedee listens to every night, gives her a possibility of betraying her husband. However, even though Deedee does have such a thought, she only wants to make Joe jealous rather than for her own happiness. As she says, "Yeah, that would teach him to run out on me. A little dose of his own medicine. Watch him gag on it" (*Collected Works* 76). Still denying the fact of Joe running out on her to Alberta, she pours out all her rage against Joe on Alberta but at the same time reveals the truth about her life. She says to Alberta,

> And you don't believe me. You think he just didn't come home, is that it? You think I was over there waitin' and waitin' in my new nightgown and when the late show went off I turned on the radio and ate a whole pint of chocolate ice cream, and when the radio went off I couldn't stand it anymore so I grabbed up all there clothes, dirty or not, and go out there so he wouldn't come in and find me cryin' . Well, (*Firmly.*) I wasn't crying. (*Collected Works* 77)

Having never told or dared to tell Joe about her real feelings for fear of him leaving her, Deedee is desperate to find Joe's betrayal against her. Deedee is so discomfited that she curses in a flood of invective: "I hope he gets his shirt caught in his zipper. I hope he wore socks with holes in ' em. I hope his Right

Guard gives out. I hope his baseball cap falls in the toilet. I hope she kills him" (*Collected Works* 79). Deedee splutters her irrational feelings with rage due to a strong sense of abandonment. Leslie Kane makes a comment on Deedee's expressing her pent-up animosity toward Joe. She observes that Deedee has "verbalize [d] the unsayable in her own vernacular" and "the outpouring of suppressed emotion releases her from the deception she has been living" (263) .

Alberta's words are illuminating for Deedee who not only has a renewed sense of self but begins to reflect on her own life. Deedee always regards herself not as a subject who can and should have one's own rights but as an object whose life is totally dependent on men. Despite Joe's unfaithfulness, she tries to be a woman who always "Stand [s] By Your Man" as the song on the radio at the beginning of the act plays. In her life, there is never a relationship which provides reassurance of her worth and the ramification of such a lack results in a sense of anxiety and vulnerability. Never thinking of herself as being able to do anything by herself and accepting other people's opinion of her being dumb, Deedee always has a sense of worthlessness. Her situation is much like that of those women described by Jean Baker Miller who, without the presence of another person, lack the "ability to really value and credit their own thoughts, feelings, and actions... [and feel] like being no person at all—at least no person that matters (330). However, with the encouragement of Alberta, "an idealized other" (Brown, *Toward* 128), Deedee becomes aware of her own competence. After Alberta sees the truth of Deedee's marriage life, she tries to persuade Deedee in the following words:

> You should go home before you forget how mad you are. You don't have to put up with what he's doing. You can if you want to, if you think you can't make it without him, but you don't have to... your own face in the mirror is better company than a man who would eat a whole fried egg in one bite. (*Collected Works* 83)

Alberta's words stresses Deedee's own subjectivity and encourages her to have her own choice out of her own will.

Alberta knows that it is not easy for Deedee to leave Joe and have a life of her own because of her poverty and lack of economic options. However, life with a man who does not care a bit about her is worse than being by oneself. Facing the truth of her life courageously, Deedee learns the possibility of the change of her life with a renewed self-knowledge which Alberta has bestowed on her. As the stage lights go down, it dawns on Deedee that she can embrace her aloneness in a new way and enjoy the "peace and quiet" (*Collected Works* 84) which she has always felt being a torment before.

Different from Deedee who is very much dislocated, Alberta seems to be self-assured despite her unfamiliarity with the corner laundromat far from her own better-off neighborhood where she deliberately chooses to go in the small hours of the morning. Unlike Deedee who comes to the laundromat to avoid the torment of waiting for a late coming husband, Alberta has planned the washing in advance for a long time. Not responding to Deedee's words initially, she gradually makes conversation with Deedee in an evasive way. Although she "really wanted to be alone tonight" at the beginning of the play, she is grateful to Deedee that "you talked me out of it" (*Collected Works* 84) when her washing is over and she leaves the laundromat with a new sense of life. As Alberta facilitates in helping Deedee realize the truth of her life, Deedee, as "a surprisingly attentive and compassionate listener" (Kane 263), "assuages Alberta's loneliness ... [and] brings Alberta out of her shell by curbing her chattiness and becoming an active listener to Alberta's pain" (L. Brown, *Toward* 135) .

The self-absorption and introversion of the bereaved Alberta can be understood through Freud's terms of mourning and melancholia ("Mourning" 20 – 21). According to Freud, the first term refers to profound mourning which is the normal reaction to the loss of the beloved. In mourning, the mourner has some typical mental features—the feeling of pain, loss of interest in the outside world and turning from active effort that is not related with thoughts of the lost beloved. Through remembering and repeating the memories of everything connected with the lost object, the mourner works through the trauma of loss. After a lapse of time, the work of mourning can be completed and overcome and the ego can turn to new attachments. However, melancholia is a state in which melancholic people are possessed by the past and compulsively and narcissistically indentified with a lost object of love. As a pathological mourning, melancholia involves the inhibition and circumscription of the ego similar to that in normal mourning. Not being able to leave the past behind, the melancholic seems to be stuck with no sense of direction for the future. The melancholic always reacts with withdrawal and grief and even tries to retain forever in fantasy what has long since been lost in reality. As a result, the loss of a loved person or object becomes transformed into the loss of the ego itself.

Because of the death of her husband Herb, Alberta rejects the outside reality, totally absorbed in a state of mourning. Despite Herb's death, he continues to occupy a palpable emotional space which causes intense grief and emotional stress for Alberta. She is unable to comprehend the reality of separateness and the existence of the lost object is psychically prolonged. Alberta still retains her husband's clothes including the stained shirt her husband wore when he died. Having kept the clothes since her husband's death, she has not made her mind to wash them because she is still in the throes of mourning the irrevocable loss of her husband.

The clothes of her dead husband are paradoxically used to signify his presence despite his irrevocable absence. Alberta is startled and stops Deedee with a loud "No!" when Deedee tries to help her put the stained shirt into one of the washers. Taking the shirt from Deedee, she seems to be tongue-tied because of the nervousness caused by Deedee's intrusive behavior. Although Deedee is desperate to talk to any one who she may meet oblivious to whatever condition the person may be in, she is sensitive enough to feel the peculiarity of Alberta's treatment of the shirt. Feeling insulted by Alberta's reluctance to talk with her and unwillingness to let her touch Herb's shirt, Deedee explodes with the following words:

> You not only don't want to talk to me, you didn't even want me to touch that shirt. Herb's shirt is too nice for me to even touch. Well, I may be a slob, but I'm clean. ... That ain't it at all. Herb is so wonderful. You love him so much. You wash his clothes just the right way. I could

never drop his shirt in the washer the way you do it. The stain might not come out and he might say what did you do to my shirt and you might fight and that would mess up your little dream world where everything is always sweet and nobody ever gets mad and you just go around gardening and giving each other little pecky kisses all the time. Well, you're either kidding yourself or lying to me. Nobody is so wonderful that somebody else can't touch their shirt. You act like he's a saint. Like he's dead and now you worship the shirts he wore. (80 – 81)

Living in a lower-class neighborhood, Deedee has never seen a man like Herb whose clothes deserve to be treated with such care. Deedee's utterances indicate her jealousy of the life of the upper class which is utterly different from her own. Alberta's sanctification of her husband causes her to be irritated over the image of such a perfect man while she is living with an imperfect one. However, when she is informed of the death of Alberta's husband, she is aware of Alberta's feeling of great loss. With Herb's death, Alberta experiences no less loneliness than her. The following dialogue toward the end of the first act reveals both women's loneliness.

> DEEDEE: I'm really lonely.
> ALBERTA: I know.
> DEEDEE: How can you stand it?
> ALBERTA: I can't. (*Pauses.*) But I have to, just the same. (*Collected Works* 84)

The laconic dialogue between the two women shows Norman's adeptness of language in revealing the characters' debilitating sense of loneliness.

As she has kept her husband's clothes, she also retains the gardening tools—rake, hoe, spade and trowel, which were intended to send to Herb as her gift for his birthday. His sudden death before his birthday made Albert unable to give them to him.

Although Esther Harriot argues that Alberta's concealment of her husband's death is only a "dramatic device to produce suspense and then a moment of revelation" (136), the secret in fact reveals Alberta's unwillingness to accept her husband's death. She finally tells Deedee about his death: "I've been avoiding it for a long time" (*Collected Works* 81). Like her aunt Dora who suppressed her grief after the death of her pet rabbit Puffer, Alberta has also contained her grief for her husband's death. However, from what Alberta observes about what happened to her aunt afterwards, we can see that her inner conflict concerning the shirt reveals her struggle with Herb's death. Coming to wash Herb's clothes is the first step for facing the truth of his death which is necessary for her future life. Her effort for getting out of the pain of loss is also reflected from the selling notice she has posted on the bulletin board before Deedee's arrival. Trying to sell the gardening tools indicates her desire to walk out of the shadow of her husband's death.

That Alberta still cannot wash the stained shirt which Herb wore when he died is because she feels guilty for his death. Unlike Herb who likes to let her watch him turning over the soil with a rototiller in his garden, Alberta cannot stand Herb's watch when she does kitchen work despite their long-term marriage. However, she had never told him not to watch her in a direct way. Instead, Alberta always sent her husband to the store during her preparation for Thanksgiving to avoid his watching in the past ten years. Also because of her uneasiness being watched, she asked her husband to take out the garbage when she was making his birthday cake. Unfortunately, Herb had a heart attack and died unexpectedly, covering himself with the garbage.

As Deedee's remembering of her giving present to Joe shows his abusive attitude toward her, Alberta's recalling of the scenario that Alberta sent Herb a fishing pole rather than a hat (which he really wanted) as a present after seeing Herb's picture of a man standing in water fishing, reveals to us that they, like Deedee and Joe, also do not express directly their true needs to each other. Alberta says that she still does not have a clue why "men wanting you to watch them do whatever it is..." (*Collected Works* 69) when she hears Deedee's words that Joe also likes her watching him working on his race car. While men, disregarding class or age, feel that women's presence in their work can offer them a sense of accomplishment and an affirmation of masculinity, women regard male attention rarely empowering. Both Alberta and Deedee rather prefer solitude at some point in the play because "People just can't always be where we want them to be, when we want them to be there…. You don't have to like it. You just have to know it" (*Collected Works* 72). Considered it as "a key statement" of the play, Harriott observes that "Facing the truth, always a high value in a Norman play, is the first step for each of these women in "getting out" of their respective traps" (137) .

Accepting the death of her husband and walking out of the confines of mourning and memories related to him is crucial for her future life. In her past life before Herb's death, Alberta had experienced the suffering resulting from her mother's and aunt's deaths. She even quit teaching because she had to take care of her sick mother. Their deaths seem to her that she had been cut from her past life. However, the loss of her husband is like the death of her present life to which she has been accustomed. Even the beachball in their basement has been regarded as containing his breath. As she tells Deedee, without facing her because she does not want Deedee to notice her sad facial expression, she "can't let the air out of it. It's his breath in there" (*Collected Works* 82). With this remark which had given rise to a collective sigh in the audience (Kane 264) , Alberta expresses her deep sense of loss. What's more, even after almost a year, the death scene of her husband is fixated deeply on her mind. She remembers clearly the gray suit, the red tie with a silver stripe through it and white shirt which Herb wore and even the stuff that the garbage bag contained. However, it is surprising even to Alberta herself that under Deedee's interrogation, she does not know what kind of shoes Herb wore when he died and whether he had shoes on in his coffin. The contrast of Alberta's accurate memory and amnesia makes more than a modicum of sense. Garrett A. Sullivan writes about the salutary nature of forgetting in the following manner: "Forgetting entails not merely the loss of memory traces, it also clears a space for and initiates a fresh act of judgment; it is the precondition for something new being done" (47) . In fact, what Norman suggests by Alberta's loss of the memory trace is that what matters most currently to Alberta is not the memory of the dead husband but the continuation of her own life with meaning despite the loss.

As it is not easy for Deedee to leave Joe, it is also hard for Alberta to walk out of the memory of her dead husband. The closure (or lack of closure thereof) of the first act is that Alberta still retains the shirt with the stained cabbage soup and takes the selling notice of her husband's gardening tools off the billboard. This accounts for why Spencer considers that nothing happened because the "fleeting contact ... changes neither woman's life" ("She-Tragedies" 148). However, as Bigsby argues, both women "have significantly changed" (*Contemporary* 223). As Deedee is not in a hurry to go back to her apartment to meet her returned husband and tries for the first time to enjoy the feeling of being a-lone, Alberta may walk out of her delayed mourning of her husband by giving his clothes away to those who need them, "to close the book on the past and move on" (*Contemporary* 223). Before the night's encounter, both women "have filled the spaces in their lives with stories, consoled themselves with fantasies, constructing myths which they separately inhabit" (*Contemporary* 222). The midnight experience makes it possible for them to realize that their nostalgia is not facilitating but debilitating to their survival. Through confronting the past and the truth of their lives, they not only gain some sort of redemption, but also a sense of self and personal wholeness which they have never been able to feel before.

Just as the death of Alberta's husband haunts the memory of Alberta, the death of Shooter, the master pool player, haunts both his friend Willie and his son Gary Wayne, who calls himself Shooter to Deedee and Alberta. However, if it is arguable that Alberta has not prepared well enough to get out of the grief caused by her husband's death, Willie and Gary Wayne accept the death of Shooter. Their midnight conversation is the first-time heart-to-heart talk which reveals their longing for the dead Shooter. Walking out of the nostalgia for the past helps them to remove the estrangement and misunderstanding between each other.

Most of the dialogue reveals much of Willie's reminiscence of his tight friendship with Shooter and George. Shooter, George and Willie were formerly called three-blind mice by Shooter's wife for their being inseparable friends.

However, since one must always die before the other is the law of friendship, "their friendship … have been structured from the very beginning by the possibility that one of the two [or three] would see the other die, and so surviving, would be left to bury, to commemorate, and to mourn" (Brault and Naas 1). Unfortunately, Shooter committed suicide by jumping off a bridge for his losing a pool game. The sudden death of Shooter and the imminent death of George make Willie a survivor to endure the pain of losing the beloved. Having already lost one best friend, he decides to sell the pool hall to pay for the medical treatment of George who has only six months to live. Like the laundromat which is symbolic of the loneliness of Alberta and Deedee, the pool hall has also an evocative meaning. Despite its seediness and smallness, it bears much weight of Willie's memory because it "was once the centre from which evolved the weal and woe of three old friends" (K. Morrow). It signifies "the specific history and aspirations of Shooter, and in the evocation of a powerful sense of decline and isolation by implicit comparison with its more vivacious past" (Grantley 150). It is very hard for Willie to make a decision to sell the place because it has got "Shooter's tracks all over the floor" (*Collected Works* 88); it is the only place "George got to go every night" (*Collected Works* 88) and it is the only thing he got to show for his whole life. As Deedee claims that it is " [h] ard to tell what year it is in here" (*Collected Works* 101) when she comes to the pool hall to bring G. W.'s clothes, Willie's mind seems to stay in the past when the three of the friends shared each other's joys and commiserated with each other's misfortune.

Indifferent to and unconcerned about his present life, Willie is a mnemophiliac because he is addicted in reminiscing whatever happened to the three. The very first words between Willie and G. W. confirm this. Their conversation goes like this:

> SHOOTER: How's it goin'?
> WILLIE: Gets any busier I'll have to stand up.
> SHOOTER: Or at least *look* up. (*Collected Works* 85)

G. W.'s emphasis on the word "look" reflects Willie's nonchalant attitude toward his business and his present life. Jeffrey Blustein, regarding "reminding", "reminiscing" and "recognizing" as the three forms of the content of our memories of the dear departed, comments on reminiscing as follows: "when we reminisce about the departed, we not only recall facts about the person's life or character or deeds. We insinuate ourselves back into that person's life in a way that brings the person him or herself back to life" (250). Put otherwise, reminiscing implies the desire to relive the past wistfully. Likewise, Willie's memories of Shooter and George contain the tiny details of the forever – flown past.

In presenting the nostalgia of Willie for Shooter, Norman makes Shooter's and George's absence present through Willie's quoting or repeating the words of them. Examples abound in the play. Sometimes he imitates the voice of George's "dumb cow voice" (*Collected Works* 86), and at other times, he describes and relives the anecdotes in his past life with Shooter and the past scenes between Shooter and other pool players in a vivid way. From Jennifer Ann Workman's point of view, "This allowing of the 'ghost' character to 'speak for themselves' through other characters' imitation of them is almost a cross between description and actual presence as a character" (80). Put otherwise, although Norman does not represent the absent characters on stage, she adopts a mixture of showing and telling for presenting such characters. Nevertheless, what Workman misses in her analysis of Norman's peculiar dramaturgy is Willie's psychological activity through incessant repeating. In the context of his analysis of the theatre of absence of German playwright Thomas Bernhard, William Gruber says that " [t] o defer repeatedly to the words of someone else can represent an abandoning of selfhood or political autonomy" (174). This is illuminating for the illustration of the situation of Willie. As a matter of fact, Willie's obsession in imitating, to a great extent, represents not only his nostalgic desire for the past life with the old friends but also an abandoning of selfhood. In the meantime, Willie's unconscious imitation of the speech or gestures of his friends also suggests a perpetual reenactment of the past which constitutes a pattern of insistent mourning.

With G. W. 's reinforcing his sentient reanimation of the past, Willie feels a sense of fulfillment because he can relive the past momentarily. Having grown up with the three fatherly figures, G. W. has been familiar with the anecdotes happened to them. When Willie recalls the night when the three of them were imprisoned for fighting with one another, G. W. is quick to narrate the anecdote mocking his mother's voice because "I don't know anything like I know that story" (*Collected Works* 94). Willie still is proud that G. W. and Sondra's wedding ceremony was held in the pool hall. As G. W. recollects, "Got a great picture of Dad and George holdin' their cues lookin' down real serious at this what was always their table, but what is now a high-rise fudge cake, you pourin' champagne on their heads" (*Collected Works* 95). As Susan Sontag argues that "[e]ach still photograph is a privileged moment, turned into a slim object that one can keep and look at again" (13), the picture indicates clearly the happy moment which the three old friends had spent together. The description of such a happy moment causes the audience to fill in their own experience of happiness and festivity in marital ceremonies. But at the same time, the audience also feels the sharp pain because of the irrevocable pastness.

Like Alberta who still cannot accept her husband's death, Willie has the haunted longing for Shooter Stevens. Willie's nostalgia for the dead Shooter and reminiscence of the good old days indicates the devotedness of a friend. Since Shooter's death, he has never played pool with anyone, especially G. W. because "Shooter was the only game I had in this town. So he's gone, so why bother?" (*Collected Works* 93). Willie seems to believe that if he does not immerse himself in the past Shooter will not be remembered. Manifestly, Willie has a frustrating kind of desiring for the dead Shooter, a desiring for the impossible. However, as Blustein has keenly pointed out that "love is a way of *valuing* a person" (256; italics original), his love for the now dead Shooter is love of him as he was in their lives together. In his mind, Shooter is unmatchable either in his devotion to or his exquisite skill in playing the pool game. He cannot allow G. W. to appropriate his father's name and play his game. In *Memoires for Paul de Man*, Jacques Derrida gives an analysis of the essence of the proper name represented by Paul de Man as follows,

At the moment of death the proper name remains; through it we can name, call, invoke, designate, but we know, we can think that Paul de Man himself, the bearer of the name and the unique pole of all these acts, these references, will never again answer to it, never himself answer, never again except through what we mysteriously call our memory. (48)

To Willie, the memory of Shooter and what they had done together in the past are closely related to the name of Shooter. Therefore, allowing G. W. to use his father's name is to obliterate the memory of Shooter.

Shooter's death makes Willie more conscious of his responsibility for G. W. Willie expresses his sense of responsibility to G. W. explicitly: "You're my business. You want somethin' I can get for you, I'll get it. Till then, I'm keepin' you from makin' the mistake of your life" (*Collected Works* 90). From the day G. W. was born, Willie has taken care of him like a father. Despite his emphasis that he paid for G. W. to be born, what he cares most is his friendship with Shooter rather than money. In effect, when G. W. tries to offer him money for what his father had cost him, Willie refuses him because in his eyes friendship cannot be measured in monetary terms. He even blames G. W. for his ignorance of friendship asserting that "Shooter was my friend. And I don't see that you got any friends, so you don't know nothin' about friends, so you shut up" (*Collected Works* 104).

As a matter of fact, just like Willie who cannot forget Shooter, G. W. also harbors nostalgia for his father and the past life. While Willie's nostalgia is demonstrated through his self-effacing imitation and repetition, G. W. attempts to identify with his father through naming himself with his father's name and learning to play his father's shots. Although he explains to Deedee that because he does not like his real name Gary Wayne he addresses himself Shooter, G. W. really wants to carry on his father's legacy of playing pool. The presence of the cue case is a confirmation of the fact. The cue case, as a prop, is a reminder of the dead Shooter. What is more important, G. W.'s insistence to play pool with the cue against Willie's reluctance provides a psychological tension between them concerning the memory of the dead Shooter. Paradoxically, while addressing himself Shooter and playing pool represents his nostalgia for his father, G.

W. realizes the passing away of the wistful past and his insistence also causes Willie to accept the reality.

G. W. 's nostalgia for the past is also manifested in his dissatisfaction with the present marriage life with Sondra, the daughter of George. Sondra's immoderate consumption and unwillingness to have a baby makes G. W. feel his life empty and he is careless about what he does to make a living. He wants to have his own baby who can carry on the tradition of playing pool of the Three Blind Mice.

Just like Willie who still cannot walk out of the woe because of Shooter's death and always immerses himself in reminiscing their time together, G. W. cherishes his father's pictures above all other things in the world. Willie's criticism of G. W. confirms this point. When Willie blames him for wanting to leave Sondra, he says that "You lose her and you're gonna lose it all. Then all you'll have left is some lousy grams of cocaine and pictures of your daddy" (*Collected Works* 90). Susan Sontag argues in her book *On Photography* that

> photographs actively promote nostalgia…. All photographs are *memento mori*. To take a photograph is to participate in another person's (or thing's) mortality, vulnerability, mutability. Precisely by slicing out this moment and freezing it, all photographs testify to time's relentless melt. (11)

The pictures of his father signify "both a pseudo-presence and a token absence" (Sontag 12). Holding onto the pictures which Edward Casey regards one type of "reminiscentia" (111), G. W. treasures the particular past moment which his father had spent. However, the absent reality registered by the photographs is no longer present and is in fact irrecuperable.

G. W. 's job as a DJ does not accord him any sense of accomplishment because the names of the singers or bands are of no significance to his life. Although the meeting with Deedee who recognizes that he is the "Number One Night Owl" (*Collected Works* 61) gives him a sense of masculinity, he feels that he is just like a "record player" to many lonely audiences rather than a man who has his own delicate sentiments and tender feelings. The job enables him to make considerable money but can not make him happy. When Willie recommends him to try something else which makes him happy, he retorts him angrily, "How am I supposed to know what makes me happy? And what difference does it make? You don't work to be happy. You work to make money" (*Collected Works* 96). Like Deedee who is never happy, G. W. makes joke of his identity of being black and thinks himself to be "a certified, wholly owned, shipped-to-the-plantation slave boy, property of ...Mastercharge" (*Collected Works* 97). G. W. 's self-mocking tone underscores his lament of the absence of happiness, love and passion with which the pool hall was replete in the former times.

Having heard that Willie is going to sell the pool hall without knowing the real reason, G. W. has a special aim coming to the pool hall on this very night. Being always aware of the fact that the pool hall is of special significance to both his dead father and the sick George who has now been reduced to a wheelchair, he cannot imagine what may happen to George without the pool hall any more. Before learning the truth of what causes Willie's sale, G. W. expresses his anger toward Willie for his selfishness in an agitated way:

> All my life I watched Dad and George depend on you. And maybe you got a rest coming, but you can't do it yet. If you leave now, while he is sick, then all that friends talk was just talk, and all those friends stories must be made up, and all that you-be-good-to-Sondra-because-she's-my-friend-George's-little-girl lecture is nothing but lies, because if you leave him all alone, you are not his friend and you never were. (*Collected Works* 105)

It is worth noting that the foregoing passage has a special function in the play. It immediately changes Willie's view of G. W. as one who did not have any sense of responsibility. Furthermore, it paves the way for them to walk out of the nostalgia for the past and to confront the reality. Willie is unable to forgive Gary Wayne who was at Miami Beach when Shooter Stevens died. However, G. W. 's censure of his selfishness makes Willie change his attitude toward him. Contrary to his opinion that G. W. does not care about his father, G. W. regrets about not being able to be present when his father died. Till this night, he still cannot imagine that his father committed suicide just because of "a lousy run" (*Collected Works* 92) in playing pool. Willie's explanation that Shooter did not want to "give himself the slightest chance of pullin' outta that dive a-live" (*Collected Works* 93) clears up his doubt about why his father jumped off the bridge to the side of the salvage yard instead of the river.

It is also the foregoing passage that causes Willie to tell G. W. George's imminent death. The sense of unattainability of the dead and the wistful past and the imminent death of George make G. W. and especially Willie recognize their own mortality. The imminent death of George strengthens Willie's apprehension of loneliness still further. His request of G. W. making a special funeral for him after his death reveals Willie's solitary confusion in a seedy and backward pool hall and the underlying terror by the prospect of the ineffable loneliness being laid in a frozen tomb. He envisions his being in his coffin hearing the people play pool on a table immediately beside it:

> I want a table, set right next to my casket, so right after "Don't he look nice," I'll hear "Little nine-ball?" I mean, if I gootta lay there dy-in' for a beer, least I can have a game to watch. Boys cussin' and carry-in' on, balls flyin' off the table, crushin' carnations in my wreath I'm wearin' says "Bartender" . (*Collected Works* 107)

Willie's description of such a scene is morbid. But in the meantime it e-vokes a strong sense of melancholy underlying.

In fact, as his objection to G. W.'s appropriation of name shows his un-willingness to accept the death of Shooter, there is also the anxiety of being for-gotten and erased deep in his mind because of the awareness of his own mortali-ty. Deedee, who comes to the pool hall to bring G. W.'s clothes but is driven out by Willie, speaks much truth about the interdependent relationship among the three old friends in her words about the three-headed mouse which she saw on her trip, "They said it had, I mean, they, the heads… only had one heart. That's what killed them, it, the mouse" (*Collected Works* 102). Willie's sense of loss makes it hard for him to live a life without his friends. However, if he is to survive, it is of crucial importance for Willie to walk out of the web of the past and committed to the present life.

The night talk between Willie and G. W. makes them aware of each other's inner suffering under the façade of assuredness. Toward the end of the play, after G. W. accepts Willie's suggestion that he should not leave Sondra, Willie, accordingly agrees to play a game of pool with G. W. and both speak out Shooter's favorite words "Give me a break" (*Collected Works* 108). We agree with Bigsby in claiming that "[t] he game which ends the play, therefore, marks a crucial moment of reconciliation, not only between Willie and Shooter but between Willie and his memories, between Willie and himself" (*Contemporary* 225 – 226) .

Both acts of *Third and Oak* deal with the nostalgia for the wistful past which has become an impossibility and the necessity of facing the truth of the present. Regardless of gender, class and ethnicity, Norman gives a naturalistic portrayal of the characters' emotional depth undergoing their respective losses. The night 's experience is important for them and also for the audience to reflect on their unproductive nostalgia for the past and treat their present life constructively. Norman makes her point clear that to work through the losses properly and to avoid the corrosive effect of the memories on their capacity to move on with their lives, they should not persist in clinging to their memories which hold sway over them with a potency that is relentless and enfeebling. Rather, developing an individual identity apart from their former relationships with spouses or friends is of crucial importance for their survival in the future.

2. Mourning the Western Outlaw Era in *The Holdup*

The Holdup, [1] Norman's fourth play, is set around a cookshack in New Mexico in the fall of 1914. The play consists of two acts. The first act begins

---

[1] It was first developed in a 1980 Actors Theatre of Louisville workshop directed by Norman herself. After being featured by Circle Repertory Company in 1982, it was produced as a full production at American Conservatory Theater in San Francisco in 1983.

with the prayer of Archie Tucker, a seventeen-year-old boy who comes back from a town travel at midnight. Followed by a coyote which may at any time attack him, he prays to God to save him. He safely arrives at the cookshack where Henry, his thirty something elder brother, is punished to look after for the wheat – threshing crew because of his cheating in the card game and his breach of the prohibition on the use of a gun. The Outlaw, whose real name is Tom McCarty, breaks into the cookshack and threatens the two brothers with a gun. Lily, a hotel manager who was formerly a dance-hall favorite in the frontier, arrives in a car for a rendezvous with the Outlaw who has disappeared for yeas to avoid the lawmen's pursuit. Henry, a voracious outlaw story reader, is excited to find a real outlaw in front of him and provokes the Outlaw into a showdown scene. The act ends with Henry's being gunned down and Archie commands the Outlaw to dig a grave for Henry.

The second act begins with the funeral for Henry. After the three of them say the prayers, the Outlaw is remorseful for killing Henry and tries to commit suicide by swallowing a large dose of morphine. Due to the great efforts of Archie and Lily, the Outlaw is saved. After the Outlaw awakens in the morning, he agrees to leave with Lily in her car to begin a new farm life with a new name. Archie, after sexually initiated by Lily, prepares himself to enter the upcoming World War I. The act ends with the sound of a train whistle and the strains of some World War I song.

Set at the transitional period of American history in 1914, the play continues Norman's concern with the entrapment of the wistful past as in *Third and Oak*. Despite Norman's claim that the protagonist is Archie, who is largely based on her grandfather from whose stories the play draws, this study argues that the play is about the Outlaw who undergoes a transitional adaptation from nostalgia for the western outlaw era to the new era. Although Bigsby maintains that this play is "about characters who are trapped by history" (*Contemporary* 228), Norman's comic ending indicates her celebration of human beings' adaptability and flexibility in times of change.

In the play, nostalgia for the western outlaw era is represented through the Outlaw and Henry. However, what they yearn for is a past which is "violence-ridden, macho, and sterile" (Blatanis 23). With the death of Henry and the suicide attempt of the Outlaw, Norman pronounces her opinion that irrational nostalgia for the past should not be advocated.

Springing from the western frontier, a setting which is always associated with violence and daring, the western outlaws represent both an era and a region. Frank Richard Prassel describes the American outlaw figure in a vivid way:

> He gallops toward us on a magnificent black horse, alone. His face is obscure, for his head is turned to look behind for pursuers. He holds a smoking revolver in one hand, and his saddlebags appear to be bulging with loot. This ominous rider may pose a grave danger; he threatens our security and safety. However, the outlaw also represents resistance to oppressive authority; he defies odious burdens imposed by corrupt society. The horseman should pass by and disappear into the darkness, but he will certainly leave behind a feeling of excitement and a confused memory. (xi)

From the foregoing depiction, it is worth noting that the black horse is a signatory feature of the outlaw, while a white horse is reserved for the hero figure. Moreover, the description also shows the contradictory aspects of the figure, representing "crime, violence, and fear" on the one hand, "fearlessness, independence, and dedication" (Prassel xi) on the other.

However, the appearance of the Outlaw in Norman's play does not seem to fit in the description of the typical western outlaw figure. It is no denying that the Outlaw's threatening gun intimidates the Tucker brothers, which immediately causes the audience to feel the intensity of the action. Nevertheless, the backstage gunshot before his appearance on the stage indicates that the outlaw's trademark horse has been shot to death by himself for its senility, leaving him only the saddle and the satchel. An outlaw without his horse loses the signifying virility related to the figure. Indeed, the dead horse, which is to be substituted by the car, the modern transportation, indicates the passing away of the western outlaw era in a symbolic way.

In fact, Norman creates the Outlaw based on the legendary Tom McCarty who was famous for his many criminal activities, such as train raids, cattle thieving and bank robberies, especially his last bank heist with his brother Billy and his cousin Fred, in which unfortunately the other two died and he disappeared because of the pursuing lawmen. Unlike those earlier outlaw tales which, in many cases with exaggeration, detail the activities of the outlaws in their prime years, Norman's play begins from years after the disappearance of Tom McCarty during which tales about him and his fellow gangsters have been voraciously read by those who are nostalgic about the outlaw era. The Outlaw, with his generic name, according to Norman's description, "a wily survivor of the Hole-in-the-Wall era" (*Collected Works* 164), is "a sort of 'Platonic Outlaw'" (Cooperman 100) because of its synecdochic function to represent all the western outlaws. His reappearance after twenty years at the crossroads means life or death for him and the western outlaw era, metaphorically.

The Outlaw's nostalgia for the past is expressed through his dislike of the technological progress made in the modern era. Under the influence of the technological progress from the east, the old west where the outlaws experienced in their prime years has changed into one almost beyond recognition. The old way of wheat threshing has been replaced by the new separator which spends less time doing more work. Automobiles are increasingly used as a transportation tool. Human flight is no longer a dream. Information transmission is accelerated with the installation of telephones.

The Outlaw's distress about the technological advancements is in sharp contrast with Archie's excitement. This is shown immediately after Lilly comes on stage. Lily's wearing a Barney Oldfield-type duster causes his deep dislike because his first words on seeing it are "What the hell?" (174). On the contrary, when Archie learns that Lily really drives a Buick to the place, he wants to run out to see it for sure. Having killed his beloved horse, the Oultlaw is disappointed that Lily drives a car instead of riding a horse to meet him. As he tells Lily explicitly, "the girl I knew... [w] oulda brought me a horse" (*Collected Works* 180). Actually, Lily still remembers the image of the Outlaw in the old days, as she tells Archie: "He'd blow in like the breath of God, horse sleek and black, and all you'd see was his flyin' coat and this big hat, and he'd make everybody else I'd ever met look real tired" (*Collected Works* 208). Nevertheless, when she comes to meet the Outlaw in their former rendezvous she forgets to bring a horse for him: "I just... didn't think about it. I forgot" (*Collected Works* 208). Lily's forgetting is indicative of her adaptability to the new era with the newest advancements. This point is further confirmed through the contrasting photos of the two. While Lily has taken a new birthday photo " Beside my Buick. In front of my hotel. Wearing my duster and goggles. Looks like I cut it out of a magazine" (*Collected Works* 178) , the Outlaw's wanted poster has been age-old. Having been out of the reach of the police for about two decades, Tom has actually lagged behind the pace of economic development and the changes in the society under the influences from the east.

What's more, even people's way of doing things has been utterly different. As he tells Lily, "these new people... there's nothing to 'em. All talk" (195). He is disappointed at finding that people have changed their way of doing things when Henry tied up his own brother Archie to win his favor. Although he does not show this when Henry is willing to tie up Archie, he directly asks Henry to tell him the reason later:

> Tell me why you tied up your brother. Nobody I know ever *tied* up his brother. Why'd you do that? I mean, we got rules out here for this sort of thing, or used to. Is this how people do now? 'Cause if it is, I don't want any part of it. I'm goin' right back where I been and I'm stayin' put this time. (*Collected Works* 186)

A remnant from a discarded world, the Outlaw still wants to do things according the rules in the past era. However, as Lily tells him, people no longer play fighting games except in school's recess time and celebration of the Frontier Day. The context of the celebration of the Frontier Day and the performative nature of the fighting games, insist on the inherent past-ness of the western outlaw era.

Despite his claim that he wants to return to where he had been, it is impossible for the Outlaw to go back. Spending the past twenty years dodging the pursuit of the lawmen, he eventually outlives the outlaw era. Without the circumstances like the Hole-in-the-wall era, the outlaws are all dead or have escaped to foreign countries. However, he is more distressed by his current status which does not provide any reason for him to go on living. Cherishing the image of Lily as a woman whose former life depended on the men around her, the Outlaw is surprised and feels lost seeing that Lily has changed to a tough woman who has made herself adapted and prospered in modern society. Lily's hotel is a symbol "representing the civilized domesticity that the Outlaw has always rejected" (Wattenberg 510). His own helplessness is in sharp contrast to Lily's independence. Although it seems that he is really sorry for killing Henry because he swallows an overdose of the never – touched morphine which a doctor had once prescribed for him to kill pain for his broken leg, he actually relinquishes his hope for life, a sequestered life without the encroachment of modern civilization which he has visualized for him and Lily together in Bolivia. The morphine, in a way, is symbolic of his nostalgia for the outlaw era. Too much will have fatal consequences.

In fact, responding to Henry's request of his name with "Kilpatrick", "Sundance", "Billy the Kid" and "Jesse James" (*Collected Works* 186), Tom is just a representative of the outlaws who have entered another era. Society has entered a phase wherein the outlaw figure has become more mythic than real. As Konstantinos Blatanis observes in his book *Popular Culture Icons in Contemporary American Drama*, Tom himself cares more about his own image in the mind of the people giving his latest photograph to Lily to update the wanted poster (165). The outlaw image for those who are nostalgic for the outlaw era stands for the masculine qualities of physical strength, competitiveness and ambitiousness.

Frustrated by his circumscribed state of working as part of a wheat-threshing crew, Henry is among the contemporary cowboys who are intoxicated by the outlaw imagery which has been made popular by the media. Around the end of the nineteenth century and beginning of the twentieth century, for the potential profit of the outlaw stories, writers of popular literature and producers of popular films and music draw from the materials of the outlaws for the consumption of the masses. Dime novels were printed and sold in great numbers and attracted a sizeable readership. Based on real or fictive outlaw figures, the Hollywood movie industry created the Western film genre which evolved into an inimitable international product. Despite their lawlessness and violence, they stand for the frontier ideal of masculinity. The use of firearms with swiftness and accuracy and horseback riding with adeptness as well as virile physicality are prominent characteristics of the outlaws. The popularity of the outlaw stories as a result of the rapidly growing media transforms the western outlaw from a criminal to a myth.

Entrapped by such a myth, Henry cherishes a nostalgic feeling for the past era. He spends most of his spare time obsessed in reading stories of the outlaws, which explains why he possesses a remarkably detailed knowledge about the outlaws' lives. Immersing himself in the stories, Henry harbors a belief in the individuality and machismo of the outlaws and nostalgically regards "the outlaw territory as the ideal and desirable state of being" (Blatanis 165) .

However, Henry is frustrated by Archie who is considered an encumbrance for him to get away from home and realize his dream of being an outlaw. Venting his anger toward Archie, he shouts at Archie angrily:

> My whole life I spent so you could go to school, so you could dream about airplanes, so you could go to church. I'm out here feedin' half-starved cattle and raisin' scrub crops, still working for Dad when I oughta belong gone all because you can't do nuthin' and never could. The most help you can ever be is just get out of my way, Archie... (*Collected Works* 183)

Henry's dissatisfaction with Archie is also manifested in his trying every way to humiliate the latter. He taunts Archie with degrading and emasculating names like "runt coward", "Diddly" (*Collected Works* 168), "priss" (*Collected Works* 172) to which the latter opposes indignantly. Using those words connoting weakness and feebleness, Henry puts Archie in a status of emasculation. Moreover, he also chides at Archie's ignorance for hoping to be a pilot in the air force to enter the First World War. As in many of Arthur Miller's and Sam

Shepard's plays, the conflict between brothers in Norman's play reflects one of the topoi in western culture and literature. Similarly, these two brothers are the living embodiment of two contrasting attitudes toward the past and the future. Although both of them want to escape from their present life, the destination of their routes are different, one to the past and one to the future. In the book *The Escape Motif in American Novel*, Sam Bluefarb begins with the sentence that "The presence of escape or flight in the modern American novel has long reflected a dominant mood in American life" (3). It is also the case in many plays. Norman herself is one of the many playwrights who deal with the theme of escape. In one of her interviews, after elaborating her grandfather's influence upon her work life, Norman states that "Granddaddy's stories were always about escape, and I, to a certain extent, write about escape today" (Norman, "An Interview" 12).

However, Henry's route to the past is a dead-end. For Konstantinos Blatanis, what Henry is in quest for is in fact a definitive image of the western outlaw (167). Henry wishes himself to be a real outlaw. Like the outlaws who always resort to unlawful activities, he also cheats at playing whether childhood games like egg hunts with his brothers or poker games with his colleagues. Making an analogy between the childhood games and the machismo deeds of the outlaws, Norman impels the audience to reevaluate the playfulness of both. With the real outlaw in front of him, Henry's romantic reading and dreaming about the outlaw era break out into the real world that he inhabits. However, Henry's eagerness to become an outlaw actually accelerates his death. Forcing the Outlaw to a duel, he imagines himself to be a real outlaw who is adept and accurate at gunfighting. Visualizing the death of the Outlaw after the fight, he says "my *picture* with you propped up dead on the ground beside me. Change my whole life" (*Collected Works* 190; italics original). But it is ironic that it is he himself who turns out to be the one who will be dead. Using Jean Baudrillard's theory of simulation and simulacrum, Konstantinos Blatanis, however, justifies Henry's death in the following manner:

In order to realize his image as an outlaw, Henry knows that he has to

> kill himself. He is in effect shooting at himself when aiming at the Outlaw.
> The moment he shoots he falls dead. The space of simulation interferes de-
> cisively with the real when the Outlaw serves as merely a third agent who
> helps Henry, the simulacrum of an outlaw, shoot at Henry, the frustrated
> cowboy. (167)

Despite Blatanis's justification that Henry has to kill himself in order to realize his dream of becoming an outlaw, Norman intends for the audience to respond critically to the absurdity of Henry's life and death. The Outlaw is right
commenting on Henry's life in Henry's funeral at the beginning of the second
act, "he just has a short time on this earth, but he spent it, well, to tell the
truth, he pretty much wasted it…Lie, cheat, steal" (*Collected Works* 196).
Spending most of his time intoxicated by the stories of the outlaws, Henry has no
sense of self. Consequently, he is totally confused about what to say when the
Outlaw asks him "who are you?" (*Collected Works* 183). Appropriating stories
that he has read in *Police Gazette*, he lies to the Outlaw about his life, most of
which he in fact spends "breaking horses" and "threshing soybeans with a
stick" (*Collected Works* 185) as is revealed by Archie.

In effect, the era of the outlaws loses its intrinsic worth and becomes a
mere function of market operations with the stories of the cowboys prepackaged
and commoditized. As authors of the popular dime novels probably meant to provide entertainment for weary train travelers and other idle people, the editors of
the *Police Gazette*, recognizing and creating a public demand for the stories,
"adhered closely to reported dates, names, and places while making up episodes and anecdotes to complete interesting tales" (Prassel 165). However,
"[s]ince the stories carried the superficial appearance of being both current
and accurate, all the contents tended to become accepted as facts" (Prassel
165). The barber shops in which Henry read the *Police Gazette* provided the stories of the outlaws for customers to kill time while waiting to be served or getting
their hair cut.

Henry's excitement in recounting the details of what happened to the Outlaw
after the latter specified the place where he buried Tom McCarty alive speaks

much of his intoxication in the stories. Having met many a lot young cowboys who are just like Henry, the Outlaw has pointed out perceptively to Henry that "All you got in your life is my story to tell" (*Collected Works* 189) .

Henry's death, to a great extent, shows that abnormal yearning after the vanished past is doomed to failure. Darryll Grantley accuses Norman of not giving much space for Henry whom he considers as a character with potential interest and disposing him even before the end of the first act (152). Actually, the reason that he makes such an accusation is just because he misconstrues the point of Norman's intention in writing the play. As a matter of fact, Henry's violent death signifies the inevitability of the passing of the outlaw era.

In addition to that, the death of Henry also facilitates the transformation of the Outlaw. With the last believer in the outlaw myth dead, the Outlaw sees no reason for his own existence. His suicide attempt is a declaration of his despair over the passing of the outlaw era. However, Norman's play does not end here.

Designating Lily and Archie to save the Outlaw and displaying the Outlaw's flexibility to adapt to the new era, Norman expresses her humanist view which privileges life over violence, insisting on the need to survive over nostalgia for the past era. Rather than holding up the western outlaw era as heroic, this play performs an elegy for the passing era and suggests that while the past is a stage of our life, we must also progress beyond it.

With a "life-affirming" horizon, Norman invites the audience to witness the rebirth of the outlaw to show the adaptability of human beings. His unrealistic nostalgia for an impossible outlaw era changes his resistant attitude to be forgotten. The Outlaw's giving up his name and adopting Archie's nickname Doc signifies his willingness to continue his life with the new identity. The Outlaw's anxiety of eraser is transformed into an embracing of the new era.

The death of Henry causes the Outlaw to reflect on his nostalgia for the past and the actuality of his present condition. The funeral on stage for Henry at the beginning of the second act has a ritualistic function. It is a mourning ritual not only for the one whose death is brought about because of his nostalgia for the western outlaw era, but also for the passing of the western outlaw era. The inevitability of the passing of the outlaw era contributes an elegiac mood to the play.

Northrop Frye explains the elegiac when he talks about the tragic mode: "the elegiac is often accompanied by a diffused, resigned, melancholy sense of the passing of time, of the old order changing and yielding to a new one" (36–37).

Henry's grave on stage for the whole second act is a constant reminder for the Outlaw of the fact of the ending of the past era. Robert Cooperman is right in pointing out that Henry's death is significant in that "it creates a feeling of remorse in the Outlaw" (101). Responding to Lily's reprimand that he shows no sorrow for Henry in earnest, he says, "I am sorry. (*Louder.*) I'm sorry, Henry. (*Genuine.*) I really am sorry... (*Getting Crazed.*) I'm sorry..." (198). Speaking out several "sorrys" consecutively to the dead Henry reveals the Outlaw's genuine apology for killing him. In fact, his remorse is not only directed toward Henry but also self-directed. To a great extent, Henry's funeral also mourns the obsolescence of the outlaw in the modern world. Having killed the one who shares a similar nostalgic feeling for the past era, he feels at a loss about what to do and what to say in the modern era. Always cherishing nostalgia for the past, he does not have a sense of belonging. His going back to the Hole-in-the-Wall aggravates the sense of rootlessness because he cannot find anybody that he knows. While Henry's death is "a suicide brought about by the existential angst that accompanies a shattering of belief" (Cooperman 101), the Outlaw's suicide attempt to show his sorrow for Henry is out of his disillusionment with the wistful past which has become an impossibility. Lamenting that "Nobody knows how to shoot anymore either!" (198), he admits the reality of the present era.

Designating Archie and Lily, the two characters who share a hopeful view about the future, with the role in saving the Outlaw reflects Norman's acclaim of the life-affirming attitude of the two. Unlike Henry and the Outlaw who idealize the past, Archie and Lily embrace the future with their optimism. Although the Outlaw has killed Archie's brother and Lily is not sure whether the Outlaw will still behave violently and indifferently as he did in the past, they determine to save him. The lengthened process of saving the Outlaw is equivalent to a "battle between the past and the present" (Cooperman 102). However, the past which is evoked is a past of violence, rather than a comforting vision. This is confirmed by the Outlaw's fragmented memory of the past violent events in the state of delirium. Both Lily and Archie try their utmost to recall names of the western outlaws to activate the Outlaw in order for him not to fall into a coma. However, the Outlaw does not have any response to a name such as Daniel Boone[1] because he does not belong to the Outlaw's time. Archie and Lily's failure in recalling names belonging to the Outlaw's era not only signifies the fact of the pastness of the era but also indicates their repudiation of violence.

Archie and Lily not only bring about the rebirth of the Outlaw, but also change his attitude toward the past and his identity. The Outlaw's attempt to imbue Archie with the rules made by Jesse James[2] for the outlaws that "you have to kill 'em while you got the chance, or else you'll just have to fight 'em again some other day" because "This is how things are... here" (*Collected Works* 215) meets with Archie's doubt about the formula's applicability for the present in changing the Outlaw's words from the present tense into the past tense. Although the Outlaw persists in using the present tense in a stronger voice, Archie's words "Not anymore" defeat him and cause him to admit the reality.

Through burning the Outlaw's wanted poster, newspaper articles and all the evidence of the Outlaw's exploits, Archie removes the Outlaw of his former identity. The Outlaw has insisted on the preservation of those things as a way of maintaining a link with the past. In allowing Archie to burn them, the Outlaw rescues himself from the nostalgia for the past. The ritual of burning is key to the Outlaw's transformation as he accepts the need to destroy his past identity in order to move forward into the future.

Claiming "All the outlaws are dead. McCarty was an outlaw. McCarty must be dead" (*Collected Works* 216), Archie suggests that the Outlaw forget what happened to him in the past and start anew. The Outlaw's voluntarily identifying

---

① Daniel Boone (1734 – 1820) is the American frontiersman and legendary hero who blazed a wilderness road to Kentucky and built a major settlement in early Kentucky—Fort Boonesborough. Norman's *Loving Daniel Boone*, which will be discussed in the next section, is drawn from the Boone myth.

② Jesse James (1847 – 1882) is one of the most famous outlaws of the American West. A guerrilla fighter for the Confederates during the Civil War, he later became a bank and train robber whose trail of robberies and murders led through most of the central states.

himself with Archie's nickname Doc at the suggestion of Lily signifies his willingness to accept Archie's proposition. If letting Archie burn the papers which
are evidence of his past life is the first step to being assimilated to the new era,
renaming himself is the second step because it indicates his will to a new identity
and a different self-image. Addressing himself Doc in a cheerful and light-heart-
ed manner, the Outlaw sloughs off the identity that would yoke him to the western outlaw era. However, to some extent, the Outlaw's renaming himself is a
way of transformation instead of negation. As he asks questions Archie when he
suggests him to forget the past and begin a new life with Lily: "If I forget everything that's happened, then what do have I have she would want, boy?" (*Collected Works* 216). His renaming in fact is a way to address the external instead
of the internal. As he says to Lily who advises him to use some other name to
call himself: "It won't work. Roy Luther will know it's me" (*Collected Works*
218). But Lily's words that he will call him whatever he wants to relieve him.
In this sense, the Outlaw's self-refashioning is a way to formulate a new identity
which is used to avoid the past instead of to forget the past. Through the Outlaw
's refashioning, Norman expresses her view that identity is a process rather than
a fixed and rooted essence. The change of times does not permit us to continue
to live in the past, but we can still retain the knowledge of the past.

Lily's nurturing spirit has done much in helping the Outlaw's adaptation to
the new era. The first time in many years not having to threaten people to prepare some food for him, the Outlaw feels the warmth of a family after he awakens
from his drug-induced coma. The scene with the two generations on stage preparing for breakfast seems like any common family of three, added with their
talk of favorite food. In fact, Norman has her special purpose in specifying eggs
as the Outlaw's favorite food. As eggs are used to symbolize creation, rebirth
and spring, the Outlaw's request of eggs cooked by Henry is an obvious indica-
tor of his love of life. Even though he tried to kill himself as repentance for killing Henry, it is because he shot his "last real admirer" (*Collected Works* 215)
as Archie said. When he really feels the approach of death, he appeals to Archie and Lily for saving his life, crying out "I don't want to die. Don't let me
die…" Taking his last chance to ask his former lover to go to another country,

he is unreconciled to live a life hiding from place to place any more. However, the reality does not accord with what he had expected. After his narrow escape from death, he is refreshed with eggs prepared by Lily. Despite Lily's toughness as a businesswoman, the Outlaw is ultimately convinced by her kindness and love for him. Endowing Lily with the traditionally feminine qualities of nurturing and caring, Norman is at the risk of being criticized of essentialism. However, the feminine qualities are not necessarily negative, just as the masculine qualities are not certainly positive. Setting the play at the inception of the First World War, Norman maps the epochal and cultural shifts in American society in which women have played a crucial role. With a receptivity to accept the changes of the society, women show the energy of their life instincts against men's death instincts or destructive energy with their unwillingness to face the reality.

It is worth noting that it is of significance that Norman sets Henry's death scene and the long and strenuous process of saving the Outlaw's life during the night and the rebirth and leaving scene in the morning. Making an analogy between violence and darkness, rebirth and light, Norman makes it succinct that the turbulent violence has passed and they can look to the future with hope. With the peaceful scene in the morning, Lily dispels her misgivings about the Outlaw's resorting to his violent ways which paves the way for their reunion.

Echoing the gunshot at the beginning of the play, which suggests the death of the Outlaw's old horse, with the slam of the car doors at the end of the play, Norman expresses her favor of the advances of a progressing civilization. The Outlaw's leaving with Lily in her car evinces that he is ready to adapt to the new era with its technological developments. Through the union of Lily and the changed Outlaw, Norman presents her version of the new west which is a combination of the transformed old west and east civilization and technological advancement.

Norman's anti-nostalgic vision toward the past frames the western outlaw era as inherently violent and life-negating. Presenting a transformed relationship with the past, Norman demonstrates a futuristic outlook which idealizes the present and the future. The present, or more accurately, the future, with the promise of progress and prosperity, are considered to be more productive than the past.

3. Deromanticizing the Frontier Hero
in *Loving Daniel Boone*

Loving Daniel Boone,[1] a play "about heroes, dead and alive" (*Collected Works* 332), continues Norman's reevaluation of nostalgic feelings toward the past. The play begins with two buckskin-clad men equipped with rifles, Daniel Boone and Russell in the forest indicating the frontier life in the 18th century. But the scene can only be seen by Florence, the cleaning woman of a Kentucky history museum which features Daniel Boone, the legendary frontier hero. It is stated clearly in the stage direction that "there will be no barriers to Flo's movements between the worlds" (*Collected Works* 333). Florence is addressed as Flo by others except Hilly, who, for vandalizing a Boone statue, comes to perform community service and replace her position. She is attracted to Mr. Wilson, the curator of the museum. However, because of Mr. Wilson's homosexual orientation, she develops a love affair with Rick, a married mechanic who conceals his marriage from Flo and has no intention to divorce his wife. Frustrated by the present bleak prospects to have a fruitful love, Florence falls into love with Daniel Boone, which, according to Bigsby, is "a relationship doomed by more than the two-century difference" (*Contemporary* 246). She finds that she can go back to Boone's time through stepping into a teepee, which also becomes a conduit for the other time travelers and fights along with Boone against the Indians. [2] Living in the past in Boone's time with herself as the center, she decides not to come back to the present in which she always meets with frustration. She resigns from her job which will be taken over by Hilly who is keen enough to find out Flo's frustration and secret love for Boone. After Flo's disappearance,

---

① Initially entitled *D. Boone*, it was commissioned especially for Kentucky's bicentennial and premiered at Actors Theatre of Louisville at the 16th Humana Festival of New American Plays, March 1992, under the direction of Gloria Muzio.

② Here and in the following analysis of the play, the Indians refer to Native American warriors.

Hilly leads the other two male characters to the past through the teepee. After defending the fort at Boonesboro against the Indians, they finally persuade Flo back to the present through their heroic deeds.

The juxtaposition of the two times makes the play a fantasy piece which enables Norman to probe into the relationship between the past and the present. Through erasing the boundary between the past and present, Norman shows that history and memory are alive in the present, informing and shaping the choices that Flo makes. Neither a fanatic believer nor a banisher, Norman takes a detached view concerning the myth of Boone. Through her portrayal of the heroine's nostalgia for and disillusionment with Daniel Boone, Norman reevaluates the Daniel Boone myth. The heroine's realization of the mythical nature of Boone enables her to come back to the present with a renewed view of hero and herself.

Several scholars assert that nostalgia does not mean that the nostalgic wants to return to the past. Naughton and Vlasic writes: "We may look back through rose colored glasses but few want to live in the past for the sake of authenticity" (qtd. in Wilson 26). Similar to them, David Lowenthal, in his book *The Past is a Foreign Country* maintains that "few admirers of the past would actually choose to return to it" (28). However, in this play Norman's heroine does return to the yearned era as a result of the intensity of her nostalgia. Thus doing, Norman presents a female time traveler. With a female as the protagonist which is atypical in backward time traveling stories, the play follows the structures initiated by J. S. Barrie:

> The first structure is a frame story set in the present that anchors the temporal fantasy that is central to the time-travel drama. The second repeated structure is the main action of the play itself: a romantic/sexual triangle that forces the time traveler to choose between remaining in the fictive past or returning and confronting a difficult present. (Dee 12)

It points out two characteristics of time-travel plays. One is the coexistence of two time frames and the other is the romantic element. In Norman's play, the alternating between or juxtaposition of the present and the past invite the audience to see Flo's stasis with her job in the museum and her mobility of with Boone in the past.

Just like the articles displayed in the museum which have no organic role in the society, Flo is spiritually estranged from the society as she considers that there is no one to communicate with her. She gloomily expresses her sense of alienation to Hilly: "Everybody I see here is dead. Dead people walkin' the streets. Dead people askin' me how I am. If I have to spend my life with dead people, I'd rather be back there, where the dead people did things" (*Collected Works* 342). Edward Martin Dee, in his doctoral dissertation titled *Time travel to the past in twentieth-century Anglo-American drama*, states that "the wish fulfillment element is at the heart of time-travel stories involving journeys into the past" (10). Similar to other time travelers such as Stephen Minch in Maxwell Anderson's *The Star-Wagon* or Peter Standish in John L. Balderston's *Berkeley Square* who are unhappy or feel confined, Flo is so frustrated in the present that she feels "like there was nobody in the whole world I wanted to see. Nobody I wanted to call. And nobody I wanted to call me" (*Collected Works* 384).

Flo's present desolateness sharpens her feelings of nostalgia for the past. Commenting on Miller and Williams' characters who retrogress to the time of innocence, Julie Adam says that "[t]he escape into the past represents a flight from unbearable actuality into possibility because in a world without future, all hope and potential lies in recreating the past to suit one's needs" (100). This is also the case for Flo. But the destination of her escape is not a time in her personal history, but one that has been recorded in history books and invented through her, or Norman's, imagination. In the book *Race to the Frontier: 'White Flight' and Westward Expansion*, John V. H. Dippel illustrates the frontier as refuge as well as a romantic allure:

> For most, the Western frontier was the nation's backdoor, the unlocked exit through which one could slip quietly and undetected, leaving all one's woes behind...the frontier served as a kind of safety valve, siphoning off those who faced failure, or the fear of failure, and needed to escape. It

was their sanctuary. (2)

Actually, what Dippel describes is the state of mind of many Americans during the late 18th and 19th centuries. To Flo, the twentieth-century woman, the frontier has been long past. But the alluring frontier, especially Daniel Boone as the paragon of hero, beckons to her across time. By walking into the teepee in the museum "quietly and undetected", Flo achieves her wish to return to Boone's time and the frontier. Juxtaposing the two time frames and dividing the stage into two parts, Norman makes uses of the pliability of stage space to make it possible for Flo to return to the frontier era through the obsessively unrealistic time travel.

To escape her upsetting life, she is in search of a life of meaning going back to Boone's time which she deems as a romantic refuge. To Flo, Boone's era offers a fresh start, a new beginning for her. Traveling back to Boone's time, she is able to enjoy the kind of freedom and cherished visibility unavailable to her in the present life. Despite her role as an expert on Boone's handwriting for Mr. Wilson, she never achieves the kind of importance as she does to Boone. A cipher in her present life, she is both unknown and unnoticed. Having never socialized with other people, her last night working at the museum is spent as quietly as any other night without anyone saying goodbye to her.

Lowenthal maintains that " [d] isenchantment with today impels us to try to recover yesterday" (33). Among the many forms (including a devotion to relics, the treasuring of antiques and souvenirs, a tendency to value what is old simply because it is old, the rejection of change and etc.) which the discontent may take, time travel tops the most obsessive one. Flo's job makes it possible for her to obsess herself with the displayed exhibits whenever she is distressed. Her obsession displays her intense nostalgia for the Daniel Boone period which she fantasizes a romantic possibility to ameliorate her present desolation. Her total despair about the present and the irresistible allure of a romanticized past makes her resort to the most extreme way.

An important reason causing Flo's desperation at the present is that she cannot have the love that she desires. In the present, Flo is frustrated because there is no prospect of her marrying a man she wants. She is attracted by Mr. Wilson but is only objectified by him. To him, Flo is just any woman with whom he can form a marital relationship without caring about whether they have their own emotions or not. When his homophobic doctor suggested to him to marry a woman as a therapeutic strategy instead of continuing to live with his partner, Mr. Wilson considers Flo available, thinking that Flo likes him and they have common interests. As he tells Flo, "I don't know what women want. I have a good income. And I'm a decent, responsible man. I just want to know if that will be enough" (*Collected Works* 354). When Mr. Wilson offers her a ride home, she feels profoundly insulted because " [m] y same car I've parked in the same spot beside your car every day for the last two years" (*Collected Works* 355). But she falls into a habitual process to inhibit her anger from bursting out in front of Mr. Wilson. Only after he walks out of hearing does she express her anger because she still attempts to keep herself as an ideal image in Mr. Wilson 's mind. In addition to Mr. Wilson's indifferent treatment to her, Rick does not take their relationship seriously. Despite that Flo has formed a love relationship with Rick for a long time, it is futureless because it seems very bleak that Rick will divorce his wife for his habitual delay. Because of not being loved efficiently and not being able to produce change in the love object, Flo feels painful and angry.

Despite the existence of anger, she does not display her anger externally. As one who has received the conventional opinion that any sensible woman should not be carried away by anger, Flo's anger is internalized, repressed and self-destroying, and ultimately emotionally disabling as if she has frozen herself in a state of lifelessness. Habitually passive, she has not learned appropriate social skills which enable her to interact with others. When Hilly comes to replace her as the cleaner of the museum, she does not know how to talk with him and is so restrained as not trying to express any emotion toward him.

Additionally, in a society in which women are often unseen and unheard, women's expressions of anger often take forms less recognized as displays of anger than men's. Despite the fact that both Flo and Hilly have their objections to their immediate circumstances, they show great contrast in venting their discontents. Hilly's anger is outwardly turned. As a display of his anger toward Boone as the ideal hero image to which he always feels belittled, he vandalized the Boone statue in Cherokee park. Like Agnes in '*night, Mother* who always burns her house to attain a sense of accomplishment, Hilly seems to gain a sense of contentment through his iconomachic behavior. On the contrary, much aware of the personal and social constraints on her life, Flo's anger is turned inward. She does not admit to the men around her about her depression. Superficially, she appears to have nothing wrong with her, as Mr. Wilson tells Hilly that "[s] he seemed happy enough" (*Collected Works* 364). Without proper ways to express her anger, she fantastically finds a way to the past from where she has no intention to come back if it were not for Hilly's quest for her without any reservation.

In fact, Flo's resignation from the present world is a result of being deprived of proper help which may enable her to channel her anger in positive ways. As Lois P. Frankel argues, "[t] he stereotypes we have for gender appropriate behavior have ironically deprived both men and women of the kind of help they need" (3). Since women are not supposed to express their anger directly, Flo has never shown her anger despite felt pain underneath. Flo's attempt to seek help from both Mr. Wilson and Rick who are the most probable to provide assistance shows that she is no longer able to endure the lifeless life. Nevertheless, neither of them takes her words seriously. Flo submits her resignation to Mr. Wilson with the reason for ceasing employment because of her intention to go to Boonesborough. Noticing her behaving strangely recently, but with his own problems with his partner, he even does not take the trouble to ask whether there is something wrong with her. Likewise, Rick, with his skeptic mind, does not believe that Flo has fallen in love with Daniel Boone, not to say that she will go to Boonesborough. Flo, after seeing Rick follows Hilly and Mr. Wilson to the fort, pours out her grievance toward Rick, "You didn't even think I was crazy for saying it. You didn't even say I should go see a doctor. You have no idea how hard it was for me to tell you those things. And all you did was laugh" (*Collected Works* 371). Flo's words demonstrate her frustration at Rick's not taking her serious and indifference toward her.

Women's anger, as "a highly politicized subject" (Harris 264), involves a politics of recognition. As Cynthia L. Wimmer argues, recognizing women's anger indicates respect while "denying the existence of anger expressed by women denies their authority and their power" (96). As a keen observer, Hilly finds out that Flo is able to disappear and come back as she wills. In his reprimand of Mr. Wilson who is deemed by Flo as her last hope, Hilly rightly points out Flo's plight and desperation before deciding to go to Boonesborough, "Damn right you should have [asked]. She was counting on you, and him, whatever his name is, Rick, to hear what she was saying and stop her. Catch on. That's what she was hoping for, for somebody, somewhere, to catch on. But nobody did" (*Collected Works* 364).

The frustrations in the present life cause Flo to retreat into her nostalgia for a past which she deems as a romantic golden world. Imbued with the Daniel Boone myth, Flo, like many Boone fans, equals Boone to the archetypical hero with whom she can form a romantic relationship. However, the time traveling experience to Boone's time deromanticizes Boone.

Setting the play in a historical museum actually provides Norman a suitable place for a more critical engagement with the past and its links with, or contingency on, the present. To Edward Martin Dee, the museum in the play provides a locus in space which "gives the audience a firm grounding that allows the dramatist to explore the temporal dimension" (94). In the last decades of the 20th century, there has been an international boom of history museums and places of remembrance as people are increasingly concerned with history and the past. The fictional history museum which features Boone is such an institution which attracts customers who are interested in his life and his times.

However, as many fake displays in the American landscape which are used to reinforce a national myth and commemorate a patriotic past, nothing, except a cast of Boone's skull whose impression is believed to be taken after his death, among the displayed artifacts in the museum, such as the rifles, the hunting shirt as well as the centerpiece of the museum—the tree stump, really belongs to Boone. To get to know the past, relics and documents are extremely significant. However, without authentic relics, the visual experience of fake artifacts can also provide museum visitors with a vivid awareness of the tangible past with similar effects. Umberto Eco, in his collection of essays on the USA called *Travels in Hyper Reality*, contends that in the United States "the past must be preserved and celebrated in full-scale authentic copy," and "where the American imagination demands the real thing, and, to attain it, must fabricate the absolute fake" (6). The museum, through creating a managed community of memory, presents kind of authoritative knowledge of the history. Many people hold on to the symbol as authentic since it conveys the story of a heroic pioneer who has helped establish a state. Not only that, as Mr. Wilson maintains, " [E] ven false views of historical personages are nevertheless, interesting to historians" (*Collected Works* 350). James B. Gardner specifies that in order to shorten the gap between historians and the public in understanding the role of the museums and of history, the historians and curators have the responsibility to help the public to

understand how museums have shifted from preoccupation with the authenticity of artifacts to issues of significance and meaning; that the selection of artifacts for exhibition is itself a subjective act, a way of shaping perspective, establishing point of view; and that artifacts never stand as objective evidence. (15)

In the official history, Daniel Boone, as a cultural icon, "who combined the occupations of hunter, trader, cattle-raiser, farmer and surveyor" (Turner 18), was generally considered the founder of the State of Kentucky. His name was involuntarily popularized by John Filson in a real-estate brochure entitled *The Discovery, Settlement and Present State of Kentucke* in 1784. This initiated a myth which was passed down to later generations. Idolized as the most heroic of explorers of the American West, his name was inscribed among the noblest of the United States in the Hall of Fame.

However, despite the many circumstances which are united to promote the unity of opinion, some historians have punctured the myth of Daniel Boone at the risk of being accused of ungraciousness and irreverence. Clarence Walworth Alvord, based on substantial evidence, claims that contrary to the popular assumption, it was not Boone who discovered the Kentucky wilderness which until

Boone's time was already known and explored by many explorers. As a matter of fact, "The forces which brought about the settlement of Kentucky were of too complex a nature to be simplified into the naive symbolism of the Daniel Boone myth" (Alvord 29).

Despite the efforts of social historians who helped debunk the falsehoods about Boone, particular versions of the Daniel Boone myth have persisted. In his study of collective memory, Gary Alan Fine has demonstrated that history, to a great extent, is a biographical one which focuses on the great man who serves as a synecdoche for a historical period or set of events (7). Only until the recent past decades, new historians shifted their focus to examine the historical events from the perspective of the average citizen, from the bottom up. For the new historians, those patriotic and celebratory tales are just part of the drama of American past. The reason a community or a nation celebrates and commemorates historical figures is because they represent their ideals. In his study on Columbus and the national origin myth, Timothy Kubal, from the constructionist point of view, maintains that "collective memories are partisan interpretations of the past that have become widely shared across historical time and institutional spaces" (XIV). As liable as any other groups to be subject to external forces, such as political currents, social trends, cultural conflicts and intellectual upheaval, professional historians have produced historical memory in aggrandized and distorted form. Peter Pericles Trifonas, in his analysis on Barthes's idea of history, maintains that "The texts and images of history, like those of myth, are thoroughly penetrated by ideology and the rhetorical techniques of the historian" (24).

Nevertheless, despite the centrality of the history of behaviors of elites, the American past is not fraught with dissension and conflict. The contestedness and constructedness of collective memory makes the belief that history as a series of unproblematic and objective facts profoundly shaken, if not shattered. With a poststructuralist sense of history, Norman takes up the cudgel of revisionism with a portrayal of Daniel Boone which challenges the official version as well as the belief in one, objective and authentic history. The official history is dialogized by alternative versions.

Through the exploration of the cultural themes of history and memory, Norman's play causes the audience to reformulate some of their assumptions about the historical figures, the background of their appearance and representation of them in mainstream culture. In her play, Norman pens the mythopoetic wildman as a romantic wanderer whose adventures are a strategy to free himself from family obligations and the civilization that he helps to expand. Believed by Flo as one who can handle everything to his will, Daniel Boone in fact "have never known where I was going" (*Collected Works* 348). Bigsby has pointed out that Boone's "heroism is another word for disinterest and detachment, even from his own life" (*Contemporary* 246). Translating Boone's experiences and adventures into more personal and psychological terms, Norman demystifies Boone.

Disparate from what he recorded in his autobiography, Boone's wanderings are results of his cowardice rather than of his ambitious goal to explore. From Boone's daughter Jemima's mouth, Flo gets an opinion of Boone which goes against the hero image in her mind: "He's afraid of Mother. He's afraid of Colonel Calloway. He's afraid of the British. He's afraid of the whole state of North Carolina. And most of all, he's afraid of honest work" (*Collected Works* 369). Departing markedly from generally idealized representations of the frontier hero, Norman's portrayal of Boone reminds us of the henpecked Rip Van Winkle.

Boone is not an omnipotent hero but a pragmatist. Rather than "the bravest man that ever lived in this country" (*Collected Works* 369), Boone is a "guileful pragmatist, playing diplomacy" (Gussow, "About Death" C22). Marya Bednerik maintains that in Norman's play, Boone is created out of the tradition of the trickster figure because he "manipulates situations, misleading the participants and disarming his audiences" (149). Escaping from the Indians' camp, he goes back to his own fort which has only a few people left without enough food and water to sustain, let alone powders to defend the Indians' attack. However, faced with the various shortages, Boone resorts to the tactics of beguilement. To make an illusion of a normally running fort to the Indians, he asks the soldiers including the just arrived Mr. Wilson to walk around the palisade all day to give the Indians an impression of a large number of soldiers. To prove to the Indians that they have enough food rather than starve, Boone asks a party including Rick who does not even have an idea of what is a buffalo to go out and kill one which they just spot. Taking Hilly to the front gate where the Indian soldiers can see them, Boone asks him to "spill as much as you can while you're drinkin' it. I want Blackfish's boys to get really thirsty just watching you" (*Collected Works* 372). They are in effect also in shortage of water for they have poured all the water on their roofs to prevent them from burning if the Indians set fire on them.

Despite the vividness of the past life which sets Flo's stagnant life in the present in sharp relief, Flo's retreat into the past does not change her status as a woman to a significant degree. As a woman, her status in the past is no better than that in her own time. Because Boone never takes the trouble to tell his family his whereabouts, Flo shows sympathy toward Rebecca, the absent wife of Boone who spends lots of sleepless nights worrying about her husband and has six children to raise. As wife and mother, Rebecca, as many others, is the one who is left and returned to, a fixed position in a male universe. Despite their role in facilitating explorations and adventures, they are always invisible in patriarchal legends.

When Boone tells her that he has lost the fight to Hilly and she and Hilly will be married at the Indian's Camp, Flo is angered because she is also objectified by Boone who ironically regards Flo's reaction as being scared. Like Mr. Wilson who never considers the feelings of Flo, Boone takes it for granted that Flo is willing to marry Hilly because Hilly has stated clearly that he comes to get Flo back. He not only persuades the Indian Chief Blackfish to give Flo as a present to Hilly and perform the marriage in the Indian camp, but lies to Flo that Hilly has won the fight. Actually, as Hilly tells Flo honestly, Boone just wants to use her as a delaying tactic and win time for the fort to prepare for the Indians' attack.

Boone's treatment to his daughter Jemima also intensifies Flo's disillusion of Boone's heroic image. Believing that Boone would protect his own daughter at any cost, she urges Jemima against the latter's will to go to the Indians because "your father wouldn't ask you to come out there if it was dangerous" (*Collected Works* 369) when the Indians ask Boone to have a look at Jemima. However, when Hilly asks Blackfish to spare Flo for him, Boone says that Flo belongs to him and Hilly can have Jemima if he wants to. The words show that he evinces a casual lack of concern for his own daughter's security. Living at the time that war dominated, women's fates were determined by men and they were in no place to have their own way. Since women were figured as prizes to be possessed and exchanged by men, Flo and Jemima, the only two women in the fort met with the kind of treatment.

Rather than finding a consolation with her ideal lover, she is in a state of confusion not knowing where to go. Comparing Flo with Jessie in 'night, Mother who steps into another world by killing herself, Bigsby maintains that Flo's imagination creates for herself another possibility which saves her from death (*Contemporary* 247). In his view, Flo's time traveling not only provides her a new way of life but also urges her to look at the present life from a new perspective which gives impetus to return to her life in the present.

However, despite her freedom and importance in the past, this kind of life is still a result of non-involvement and escape. As her ideal love object, Boone stands for the best traits which she desires her lover to have. Commenting on Norman's choice of the "tall, broad-shouldered" Gladen Schrock to act as Boone who in actuality was short and small, Marya Bednerick maintains that Norman "follows the pattern in her heroine's choice of man" (148). Wearing a fringed, suede jacket, the figure of Boone as the metaphoric frontiersman for whom Flo has given up the present, the dream pathfinder assumes the audience's acquaintance with the ethos of cinema westerns. However, only when she lives with Boone intimately does she realize that so-called heroes have their own shortcomings. The heroic image of Boone is cumulatively punctured and he is only a normal specimen of imperfect humanity. What's more, although she forms a romantic relationship temporarily with Boone, she faces the danger of losing her life with Boone and those people at the fort which is to be attacked by the Indians. Even though they can survive the attack, Flo cannot go with Boone back to his family in North Carolina, because as Jemima tells her, "Mother is there" (*Collected Works* 380). While time-traveling to the past rescues Flo from the confined and despairing present life, it is also potentially fatal and similarly restricting.

In fact, as science fiction writer Alfred Bester has concluded in *Hobson's Choice*, "Through the vistas of the years every age but our own seems glamorous and golden. We yearn for the yesterdays and tomorrows, never realizing that we are faced with Hobson's choice... that today, bitter or sweet, anxious or calm, is the only day for us" (126). Learning that the past is only a mirage which reflects only her idealized imagination and she has "look [ed] for love in all the wrong places" (Mason 12), Flo is ready to come back to the present to accept Hilly's affection for her. Since escaping to the past cannot ensure her survival with dignity, it is worth a try to come back with a person who "is willing to pay for it" (*Collected Works* 390).

As the present counterpart to Boone, Hilly does not possess the traits which Boone is supposed to have. However, Norman thwarts the audience's proclivity to valorize Boone and depreciate Hilly. Hilly's earnestness in trying to talk with her and listen to what she says and his determination to fetch Flo from the past reconfigure Flo's view of him, her idea of the romantic and the hero. In fact, what Flo really wants is not a hero but one who can listens to what she says and respects her self. She realizes that Hilly, the man who does not have many masculine traits, rather than Boone, the universally acknowledged frontier hero, is "the first man I ever knew who actually just... heard what I said" (391).

The first person who really listens to what Flo says to him, Hilly is also a man who has self-determination and courage. Thinking that Flo is able to travel back and forth between the past and the present, he is sure that he can also come back to the present if he is able to travel to the past like Flo. Despite Mr. Wilson's discouraging words that Flo will not come back to the present, Hilly's reply "this time...isn't over yet" proves his confidence that he has some influence upon Flo. Unlike Hilly whose goal is to bring Flo back to present, Mr. Wilson only wants to "pick up some stuff for the museum" (*Collected Works* 370), as Hilly tells Flo when she catches the first sight of Mr. Wilson in the fort. Before they decide to go to the past to fetch Flo, Mr. Wilson is hesitant because he is afraid of not being able to come back. Angry at Mr. Wilson's unconcerned attitude about the disappearance of Flo, Hilly states his opinion that "〔w〕e have to go get her" (*Collected Works* 361) .

Creating a man who does not accord with the standard of conventional masculinity, Norman disrupts the stereotypical categories of men and women and posits the harmonious relationship between them without either being pigeonholed. With a formulaic happy ending like that of a fairy tale, Norman prophesizes a union of Flo and Hilly which helps Flo out of her dwelling on the past.

Assumed to be a commemorative play, *Loving Daniel Boone*, in fact, as Bigsby rightly points out, shows Norman's "ambiguous gesture toward the State of Kentucky" (*Contemporary* 247). The carnivalesque occasion of the Louisville festival provides an opportunity for Norman to question and challenge the myth of Boone. In the book *The Politics of Performance: Radical Theatre as Cultural Intervention*, Baz Kershaw explains in detail the relationship between community and efficacy of performance. Classifying communities into those of location and interest which are always intersecting, he maintains that the ideological integrity of a community is crucial to the efficacy of a performance. He gives further explanation as follows,

〔T〕he ideological transaction of performance must deal with the fundamental constitution of the audience's community identity in order to approach efficacy. In so doing it may reinforce or modify that ideological identity, but in either case efficacy depends on the identity being challenged. (33)

The demystification of the myth of Boone is sure to discomfort the audience in the community. Challenging the ideological assumptions of the community, Norman triggers the audience to reconsider their collective memory to prevent it from being hegemonic and exclusive.

Chapter Three

AVOIDANCE TO CONFRONTATION: MAKING SENSE OF THE FICTIONAL PAST

While the protagonists with a traumatic past in the first chapter try to evade the painful events, and nostalgic characters in the second chapter harbor a longing for the wistful past, the protagonists in 'night, Mother and Trudy Blue have a purpose in remembering the fictional past and want to make sense of the past. Their retrospective focus implies that, rather than simply waiting passively, they move forward with a searching eye to meet the past which has been lived through without interacting with truth and reality.

The term "fictional" is used with its two meanings: one is unreal and the other imaginary. The first meaning is related to Norman's metaphorical allusion to Plato's allegory of the cave. Having mentioned that her playwriting is influenced by Plato's allegory, Norman uses it as a central principle, especially in 'night, Mother ("Conversation with Brustein" 189). As the prisoners in the cave have only access to the shadow of the reality, in 'night, Mother, the heroine has undergone a past which is masked and misrepresented by her mother. The second meaning is used to refer to its fantastical nature. In Trudy Blue, the heroine's fantasies shield her from her family and the real world. Superficially alleviating themselves from the unpleasantness of the actual world, the fictionality of the past renders them inactive and injuriously deprives them of their true selves. To end the conditions of avoidance and inauthenticity in their lives, they sense an imperative to conduct an existential quest to find the ultimate meaning of life. Consequently, they confront their past through exposing its lies and cutting ties to the past. Through the confrontation with the past, even through death, the heroines display their self-determination and power in controlling their own lives.

1. Unearthing a Past with No Self-Control in *'night, Mother*

Up to now, *'night, Mother*[1] has been Norman's most famous play, and is garlanded with the 1983 Pulitzer Prize for Drama. Always referred to as a realistic play because of its naturalistic treatment of characters and setting, Norman transcends a superficial realism by the incorporation of symbolic, temporal, psychological and philosophical elements in the play.

In the Time = Time play[2] of ninety minutes, Norman presents the last night of Jessie Gates, an epileptic who lately resumes control of herself and but determines to commit suicide after preparing her mother as well as herself for her suicide. Giving equal force to both sides of the fighting partners, Norman gives both Thelma Gates, the mother and Jessie, the daughter their respective voice to state their reasons whether or not to continue to live. Norman shows her acute powers of observation with respect to individual psychology in circumscribed circumstances. Living a seemingly peaceful life with her mother, Jessie has undergone a turbulent interior conflict concerning "to be or not to be" since the Christmas before. To Jessie, her last conversation with her mother aims to dis-

---

[1] It was first produced at the ART with Robert Brustein as the artistic director and Tom Moore as the director in Cambridge, Massachusetts in December 1982. After receiving critical and popular applause, it opened on Broadway March 31, 1983, at the Golden Theater and played over 380 performances. It has been played in almost every language around the world except Latin, which Norman wishes it to happen in the future so that she can be completely fulfilled (*Collected Works* 404). It was adapted to a movie in 1986, not to Norman's satisfaction because it loses the intensity of the suspense potential which usually sustains the audience's attention in a theatre. Mainly a piece primarily of the domain of college students during the years after its Broadway debut, it was successfully revived on Broadway in 2004.

[2] Jeffrey Hatcher calls plays which cover the exact amount of time it takes to watch the play Time = Time plays. In addition to *'night, Mother*, his examples include Lanford Wilson's two-character love story *Talley's Folly*, and German writer Franz Xavier Kroetz's wordless one-character play *Request Concert. The Art & Craft of Playwriting*. 9.

claim her mother as liable for her suicide. However, this "only" night of no-holds-barred conversation between mother and daughter unearths the past of lies and truths which both parties of the emotional tug-of-war excruciatingly confess to each other. Their present life is sedimentation of the past which is revealed gradually in their "debate of great emotional suspense, the ancient Greek agon in slippers and sweaters, the ultimate domestic conversation" (Kroll, "End Game" 41).

The dramatic impact of the play derives from the overwhelming sense of loss and frustration felt by Jessie through unearthing the past lies and truths about her and her mother's lives. Her confrontation with death is her own way of self-assertion through ending a past without any self-control. Dramatizing a heroine who determines to confront a life through death to end the passivity to the existential condition, Norman prompts the audience to reflect on the philosophical question of the significance and meaning of life.

In describing her impetus to write the play, Norman remarks that her purpose is trying to understand the psychology of the person who determines to commit suicide and the one who wants to obstruct the action. She talks about her creative intention with L. Elisabeth Beattie as follows:

> At that time there were five or six people that I knew well whose children had killed themselves. It was kind of epidemic, I felt. I was stricken by it. I wanted to know why they did it, and whether there was anything I could have done. And I wanted to know if I were ever to be in that situation, whether there was any way that I could be saved. ("Marsha Norman" in *Conversations* 294)

Putting the mother and daughter in circumscribed circumstances in which they are entrapped, Norman makes it possible for both parties to express their opinions of life.

Not satisfied with another play—*Whose Life is It, Anyway?*, [1] which is purported to deal with the suicide topic but in fact has not put the issue at the center, Norman makes the play "like heavyweight bout" ("Marsha Norman" in *Conversations* 294) which results in the form of *'night, Mother*. Although the contained form has been used in her earlier plays, *Third and Oak* and *The Holdup*, she makes maximum use of it in this one. Several minutes after the beginning of the play, Jessie declares to her mother, "I'm going to kill myself, Mama" (*'night, Mother* 13), intending to do so that very night. The audience-unsettling announcement throws the mother into a desperate battle to win her daughter's life, trying every means which she can resort to. The gunshot before the curtain falls realizes Jessie's goal of ending her life of insignificance and gaining self-control by claiming her body to herself. Intermissionless, the play evolves into a debate between mother and daughter which elicits a retrospection of their incredibly boring existence in the past which is based on Mama's concoction and misrepresentation.

Having mentioned that Plato's allegory of the cave has to a great extent influenced her writing ("Conversation with Brustein" 190), Norman imbues the Platonic sense of As in other plays where setting is adeptly deployed to symbolize the past, Norman in this one uses the extrascenic space of the attic to achieve this aim. The attic which contains items of antiquity towering above the mother and the daughter can only be accessed through a pull-down ladder: "A pull cord in the hall ceiling releases a ladder which leads to the attic" (*'night, Mother* 3). The attic with the various items like rusted wagon wheel, the churn, the old milk can and her father's shoeboxes is symbolic of the non-nurturing past life of stagnation and secrets. Jessie's searching through the shoeboxes for the father's gun signifies her determination to find out the truth of her past life. As only her mother knows in which shoebox the father's gun lies, she is also the one who has concealed the secrets of their past life.

Thelma's withholding the truth of Jessie's being an epileptic since her

---

[1] *Whose Life is it, Anyway?* (1978) is a play by British playwright Brian Clark. Set in a hospital, the play revolves around the protagonist Ken Harrison, a sculptor by profession, who was paralyzed from the neck down in a car accident and has no further desire to live.

childhood deprives of her daughter the right to have a full knowledge of life and even learn how to live a life. An epileptic like her father, Jessie was closely controlled by her mother since she was five years old. However, the fact of her inborn illness has not been disclosed to her until this very night. It is undeniable that Thelma has undergone a lot of difficulties in bringing up an epileptic daughter. But her keeping the truth of Jessie's illness a secret speaks much of her feeling disgraced for having such a daughter. Like Amanda who refuses to acknowledge her daughter's disability as a cripple in *The Glass Menagerie*, Thelma insists that Jessie's coming on of epilepsy as fits instead of seizures. She has kept it a secret from the people and especially Jessie herself. "I didn't want anybody know. Least of all you" (*'night, Mother* 70). Holding the tenet that "Things don't have to be true to talk about 'em" (*Collected Works* 41), she has weaved a web of lies in her past life. Her dishonesty with Jessie, to a great extent, reflects her feeling of guilt, which many parents experience when their children do not abide by conventional norms. As Arlene's mother who searches from herself the reason which leads to her children's deviation, Thelma blames herself for Jessie's illness:

> Maybe I fed you the wrong thing. Maybe you had a fever sometime and I didn't know it soon enough. Maybe it's a punishment... Because of how I felt about your father. Because I didn't want any more children. Because I smoked too much or didn't eat right when I was carrying you. It has to be something I did. (*Collected Works* 71)

Mama's unwillingness to tell the truth of the history of Jessie's epilepsy and the fact of her husband as an epileptic, as Craig argues, "exposes Mama's motives as truly being more protective of herself than of her daughter" (*Family Ties* 336). Mama's overprotection intends to prevent Jessie from the unpleasantness and misery of life, but is of no avail.

Although she "has gained control of her mind and body" (*Collected Works* 4) in the past year without having a fit, Jessie has harbored a sense of lack of self-control because of epilepsy for many years. Reading her epilepsy in symbolic terms, Bigsby argues that "her fits, involuntary actions, are a symbol of her lack of control, her inability, to date, to affect her life or determine her fate" (233). Gerald Weales concurs in reading the illness along this line, "The restrictions implicit in her epilepsy, in the response to it rather than the disease itself, reflect a society of limited possibilities, mandatory roles .... [It] is another example of the way in which these women are...caught in a social and psychological web that gives very little room to maneuver" (370). The past experiences of losing control of her body are traumatic for Jessie. Talking about symptoms of her fit with her mother calmly this very night, she shows her sense of humiliation by her ugliness and unconsciousness. Because of her repeated bouts of unconsciousness during her epileptic seizures, Jessie's has a "paranoic sensitivity about her privacy" (Elliott 138). Recollecting about the consequences of her epilepsy, Jessie is frustrated at her incapability of holding any job, whether it is the telephone sales job, or the one at the hospital gift shop where her smile makes the customers rather uncomfortable. And also because of her unpredictable epileptic seizures, she even cannot do an adequate job as a bookkeeper for her father.

It is Mama who rendered it possible for Jessie's marriage with Cecil by enticing him to build an unnecessary porch for the house. Mama's assuming responsibility for Jessie's life and deprivation of Jessie's opportunity to make decisions about her life are manifestly illustrated in Jessie's marriage with Cecil. In fact, Like Laura's mother in *The Glass Menagerie* who tries every way in order to have her daughter married, Mama is also "an 'agent' of patriarchy" (Paige, "Off" 99) because she accepts the patriarchal order and its values: "I wanted you to have a husband" (*'night, Mother* 117). Bending to the socially sanctioned norm which regards marriage as a must for a girl, she thinks that her daughter should be taken care of by a husband without considering Jessie's true feelings.

Although she is successful in marrying her daughter to the man whom she chooses for her, their married life is not happy as assumed. Out of her love for her husband Jessie is always trying very hard to satisfy him, but to no avail: "I tried to get more exercise and I tried to stay awake. I tried to learn to ride a horse. And I tried to stay outside with him, but he always knew I was trying, so it didn't work" (*Collected Works* 59). Because of her seizure, her efforts to learn riding resulted in her falling down from the horse. Her husband's leaving her to the voyeuristic scrutiny of others is extremely traumatic for her. Although her husband has constructed their house so strong that it "will be still standing at the end of the world" (*Collected Works* 57), he lacks the commitment to stick to their marriage.

Although Thelma knows that Cecil leaves Jessie because he has an extra-marital affair with her friend Agnes's girl, she has not told Jessie the truth until this last night of Jessie's life. Mama's concealing the truth has resulted in Jessie's feeling powerlessness toward her marriage. Her sense of powerlessness and loss of dignity gets across to the audience through her recounting of her futile attempt to keep Cecil from leaving her: "But I did beg him to take me with him. I did tell him. I would leave Ricky and you and everything I loved out here if only he would take me with him, but he couldn't and I understood that" (*Collected Works* 61). With her husband walking out of the marriage, Jessie felt herself deserted like garbage and wrote Cecil's goodbye letter herself out of shame. However, like Alberta in *Third and Oak* who never feels at ease when her husband watches her doing kitchen work, Jessie admits that "it was ... a relief in a way.... I never was what he wanted to see, so it was better when he wasn't looking at me all the time" (*Collected Works* 61). To a great extent, during her marriage life with Cecil, she has never lived her own life because she has directed her energies to trying to please Cecil and has no chance to develop a sense of her own self.

Although Jessie performs the maternal role for her mother after she divorced and moved back to her mother's house, it is in fact that Thelma has been affecting incapacity and manipulating the situation. Isolated from all the other relationships, Jessie has performed the role of "symbiotic servitude" for her mother, "a benevolent despot" (Harriott 138). Jessie has been a dutiful daughter to her mother despite her epilepsy and her loss of memory as the side effects of the drugs. Comparing Jessie and Thelma's inverted daughter-mother relationship to that of May and her bed-ridden mother in Samuel Beckett's *Footfalls*, John

Kundert-Gibbs argues that Jessie is "a daughter who is essentially mother to her mother" (51). Zhang Jinliang also maintains that Jessie lived her mother's life (137). Jessie takes up the task of doing household chores and has demonstrated her capacity with the help of listing to overcome her poor memory. Everything is in good order. Even during the last night talk with her mother, she is still busy filling the candy jars, cleaning out the refrigerator, putting the slipcover back on the sofa, and preparing the grocery lists. In addition, the ritual Saturday night manicure is one occasion which shows Jessie's scrupulous care for her mother. To use Kundert-Gibbs' words, they "live a life of private repetition, going through the same motions day after day in a cycle of habit that crushes the women, yet is sought after for its familiar safeness" (58).

Living under the same roof with her mother, Jessie has been closely watched by Mama. It is no wonder that Thelma is surprised that Jessie has prepared for her suicide in advance without her knowledge. Thelma always asks Jessie "where was I while this was going on?" ('night, Mother 15) or "When did you do all this? During my naps, I guess" (Collected Works 85). Minutes into the play, she commands Jessie to fetch her knitting basket and her eyeglasses and then to cut the six inches of yarn she needs. Like a child she has a sweet tooth and litters snowball wrappers casually for Jessie to clean up. In addition to these details, Jessie's other household chores also speak much of her caretaking role. Without any sense of herself, Jessie is totally at the mercy of her mother's experiences. Her last request for her mother to make a caramel apple shows that Jessie have never had her own say in making decisions. Lynda Hart suggests that " [w] hat will be eaten and how it will be prepared are questions that often form the basis for mother/daughter struggles" (76). According to her mother, she cannot have a caramel apple without having supper. Despite Jessie's explicit request that she does not want marshmallows added to the hot chocolate, Thelma insists that "You have to have marshmallows" (Collected Works 39). Through the preparation details, Norman makes her point clear about Mama's assertion of her power and her habitual denial of Jessie's initiative.

Mama's never telling her about the details of her epileptic fits and her brother Dawson's being in the know make Jessie feel a strong sense of invasion. Jessie expresses her infuriation at their knowing more about her than herself in the following words: "They know things about you, and they learned it before you had a chance to say whether you wanted them to know it or not. They were there when it happened and it don't (*sic*) belong to them, it belongs to you, only they got it" (*Collected Works* 23). She is furious at her brother Dawson and sister-in-law Loretta because without her permission, they opened her mail containing her bra with rosebuds which is mailed to their address by mistake. She is angry at Dawson "calling me Jess like he knows who he's talking to" (*'night, Mother* 23). To Jessie, in so doing, he behaves like an "all-seeing patriarch" (Burke 118). Furthermore, the slippers he bought as Christmas presents for Jessie are not fit for Jessie's feet at all. In Jessie's mind, Dawson's attitude toward her represents the indifference of others who has no real care for her at all but tries to define her in their own ways.

To some extent, Norman contrasts the potency of Dawson, whose place is out of sight, with the comparative powerlessness of Jessie and Thelma who are on stage. Dawson's offstage presence is played off against events in the lives of both mother and daughter who are materially present on stage and who speak and act. Like the other male characters in the play, Dawson is never present on stage. But Dawson's name appears from the very first lines of Mama who is suspicious of his having stolen her treats. In fact, he has deprived both women of something more crucial than the non-nurturing sweets—autonomy. When Jessie tried to go up the attic, Mama says that "I thought Dawson told you not to go up those stairs" (*'night, Mother* 9). His discursive power also manifests in that it is his name on their charge accounts at the grocery store. Furthermore, the details concerning how Dawson helped Jessie obtain the new bullets for her father's gun reveal Dawson's condescending attitude. As Jessie tells Mama, "He took it as a compliment. He thought I might be taking an interest in things. He got through telling me all about the bullets and then he said we ought to talk like this more often" (*Collected Works* 15).

Thelma's lies about her friend Agnes make it impossible for Jessie to have a true knowledge about Agnes' life and Agnes' attitude toward herself. Jessie accuses Thelma of lying about Agnes: "You lied about setting fire to all those houses and about how many birds she has and how much okra she eats and why she won't come over here" (*Collected Works* 44). Because Jessie is reclusive, Thelma always provides details about things and people around. Nevertheless, the details concerning Agnes are in the aggregate puzzling to Jessie. What troubles her most is why Agnes never comes to the house. Just like she feels a sense of invasion by Dawson, she is afraid of being disliked by the surrounding people. When Thelma tells her that Agnes is in fact scared of her rather than dislikes her, Jessie is greatly relieved. As a matter of fact, Agnes's fear of Jessie shows her fear of mental and physical degeneration which she deems to be contagious. Since Jessie's epilepsy is only intermittently visible, Agnes's fear also signifies the social fear of the invisible Other, who is perceived to be enormously different. This explains why Thelma misrepresents Agnes and withholds the reason that she does not come to their house.

Through the retrospective telling of both mother and daughter, it is revealed that Jessie has had a life without any sense of control because of her mother's intentional misrepresentation. Commenting on Jessie's seemingly throw-away line with China, Demastes observes that it is indeed an indication of Jessie's awareness of her lack of control in all things in her personal life, not to say international affairs (*Beyond* 151). Unwilling to continue this kind of life to which Jessie thinks that she can do nothing, she determines to stop her life of insignificance. Rejecting "the formal 'Beckettian' approach of waiting" (*Beyond* 149) which has been handed down to her by her fatalistic mother, Jessie plans to act to enact change in her own way.

With regard to the death end of Jessie, critics have disparate readings of the suicide, both negative and positive. To Sarah Reuning, Jessie's state of mind and her ultimate action is due to her depression, the undiagnosed disability. Considering depression as "a debilitating disease", Reuning argues that Jessie's suicide is "a relinquishing, rather that a regaining, of control" (55). Similarly, Jenny S. Spencer, updating the eighteenth-century form of *she-tragedy* to apply to Norman's three women-centered plays *Getting Out*, *The Laundromat* and *'night, Mother*, implies that Jessie's suicide cannot be regarded as a final triumph ("She-Tragedies" 156).

Contrary to the negative readings, Norman and many other critics show their positive interpretation. Despite the death of Jessie, Norman considers the play as one "of nearly total triumph" rather than one with "a despairing act" (Marsha Norma *Interviews* 339). Anne Marie Drew considers that Jessie "embraces suicide as her way of triumphing over time" and her death "must not be viewed as a negation but rather as a triumph (87 – 88). Raynette Halvorsen Smith, holds that Jessie's suicide as one form of violence, is an agent that brings "freedom, autonomy, and individualism" (279). Linda Ginter Brown also shares a similar view that despite her death, "Jessie triumphs because she, alone, decides what constitutes her proper nourishment" ("A Place" 84). Liu Yan, in her book *A Study of Motherhood in Modern Western Drama*, also holds the view that "Jessie's suicide should be interpreted from a positive perspective, because the play's significance derives from her suicide" (294). Reading Jessie's suicide in light of Theodor Adorno's negative dialectics, Demastes argues that "her death has not, ultimately, been a defeat" because "Jessie has served the future by presenting a cognitive process that will itself serve the future" ("Jessie" 117). The study maintains that Jessie's resort to suicide is to control her own body, disengage herself from the control of others and claim a self by ending the self which has been constructed and defined by others in the misrepresented past.

Jessie's self-annihilation is firstly a means to control her own epileptic body. Unlike her carpenter husband Cecil whose prowess as a craftsman invites her jealousy and anger because he is sure of the things he built, Jessie never knows when her next seizure comes. Like Mama's friend Agnes who always burnt down her own houses for "a feeling of accomplishment" (*'night, Mother* 39), Jessie destroys her body, a metaphorical house, for self-control. Thus doing, she will no longer suffer the sense of invasion as a result of her unconsciousness during her seizures. To Linda Rohrer Paige, the self destruction signals Jessie's rebellion against "patriarchy's claim to her body" ("Off" 396). What needs to be pointed out is that despite Mama's efforts to discourage Jessie from carrying out her self-annihilating plan, Mama's comments on Agnes' pyromania unwittingly explains Jessie's logic. As she explicates her understanding of Agnes pyromaniac activities, "The houses they lived in, you knew they were going to fall down anyway, so why wait for it, is all I could ever make out about it" ('night, Mother 39). In justifying Agnes' burning, Mama's words show unintentionally to Jessie that her "house" should also be destroyed.

Jessie's suicide is to exert control over her life, which has been lived with her mother's assuming responsibility for everything. Even if she reiterates that her killing herself has nothing to do with her mother, Jessie has unconsciously showed her anger toward her mother for making her an extension of and appendage to her. Responding to Mama's "You are my child" (Collected Works 76), Jessie speaks out her sense of loss of a self and incapability to have her own self in the state of mere existence:

> I am what became of your child. I found an old picture of me. And it was somebody else, not me. ... That's who I started out and this is who is left. (There is no self-pity here.) That's what this is about. It's somebody I lost, all right, it's my own self. Who I never was. Or who I tried to be and never got there. Somebody I waited for who never came. And never will. (Collected Works 50)

The baby photo offers a powerful metaphor of innocent beginnings. But the process of her development from child to adult is just one that leads to her increasing consciousness of suffering and meaninglessness of her existence.

Refusing to continue to live in this world represents Jessie's determination to cease to live a boring and meaningless life which her mother has colluded with her. Both mother and daughter live their life without much interest, not to say passion. To Jessie, Mama's life is what she does not want to have. Thelma has enjoyed herself watching TV, crocheting, solving puzzles, gossiping with the neighbor and has been addicted to eating sweets like sugary snowballs, peanut brittle and Hershey bars. For Mario Jacoby, an excessive love of sweets "reflects a longing to 'make life sweeter', especially in those cases where the individual cannot find anything worthwhile in him or herself, when everything tastes dry and hollow and there is no-one whose caring can give the individual a sense of self-esteem" (65). Laura Morrow also argues that sweets are for her "a happy substitute for genuine human interaction", and provide for her "the sensual gratification and the sense of fullness which she failed to obtain from her marriage" (24).

Like the Tyrones in O'Neill's *Long Day's Journey into Night* who "tolerate life rather than live it, [and] ... endure rather than survive" (Adam 127), Thelma blindly accepts the arbitrariness of life and her lack of control over it, and lives a life of apathy and shallowness. She thinks that "Family is just accident" (*'night, Mother* 23), and does not have a kind of commitment to things because to her "There's just not that much *to* things that I could ever see" (*Collected Works* 44; italics original). It never occurs to her to reflect on her own life wholly: "I don't know what I'm here for, but then I don't think about it" (*Collected Works* 49); "I don't like things to think about. I like things to go on" (*Collected Works* 52). Life to her, like doing laundry, is a mainly kind of waiting, "Things happen. You do what you can about them and you see what happens next" (*Collected Works* 58). Although she has done a lot of things in her past life, she "didn't know enough to do half the things I did in my life" (*Collected Works* 58). Envisioning no other ways to live, she blindly accepts life as one "composed of contingency and serendipity" (Bigsby, *Contemporary* 233) and is fearful for her own death. Weales comments that admitting her intense fear of death, Mama "has mastered the limitations of her life by embracing the small activities and inactivities that fill a day with busy work which has no meaning beyond itself. That is not enough for Jessie" ("Really" 371).

Feeling aloof toward her own life, Mama has taken her daughter's life for granted. Having thought that her daughter belongs to her, she did not regard her as one with her own subjectivity. Despite their physical closeness, she has never launched any endeavor to probe into her daughter's inner world. The following dialogue speaks much of the fact:

> JESSIE: You have no earthly idea how I feel.
> MAMA: Well, how could I? You're real far back there, Jessie.
> (*'night, Mother* 55)

Initially regarding Jessie's wanting to kill herself as joking, Thelma launches every available "communication strategy" (Breding 78) ranging from aggressive verbal assault to pep talks to sustain her daughter's life when she sees Jessie's resolution. However, whatever she offers for suicide intervention is ineffectual because nothing can change Jessie's mind at all. Linda Rohrer Paige argues that Mama's failure at stopping Jessie's suicide is because she does not really know her daughter and what she provided as options only strengthens Jessie's resolve to kill herself (*The "Other"* 115).

Unlike her mother who is willing to continue her life of desperation, Jessie opts out of a life of insignificance. Although it is set in the kitchen, the play gives us a sense of confinement, but also coziness. The refrigerator, like the one in Sam Shepard's *Curse of the Starving Class*, contains little nourishing food. Having never really liked rice pudding or cornflakes for breakfast, Jessie has lost her "appetite" for life. She cannot stand the stasis of this kind of life in which nothing has happened and nothing will happen, as she assumes. In the past ten years, she deliberated to make change to her life, but never carried out. She vainly hoped change externally. But even her birthday presents are predictable because everybody around her is indifferent to her. As she told her mother, "I'm tired. I'm hurt. I'm sad. I feel used" (*'night, Mother* 28). She is tired of "[i]t all" (*Collected Works* 28), "[t]he way things are" (*Collected Works* 30). No longer can she postpone the alternative to her life, she changes her deliberation to action.

Her clear headedness and sightedness as a result of the improvement of her illness and memory enables her to reflect on her life and make the violent decision. Commenting on her characters in general, Norman remarks:

[I]t's people who need ultimately and finally to find out what the truth is, and who are willing to know it, whatever it cost them. They are not interested in suffering, they are not interested in pretending and they want to know how things are. They want the real story. ("Interview with Marsha Norma" in *American Volces* 152 – 53)

The foregoing passage reveals her characters' courage and determination to know the truth of their life. Jessie's action to make sense of her life even at the expense of her life further confirms Norman's point.

Indeed, as she tells her mother, "Once I started remembering, I could see what it all added up to" (*Collected Works* 68). The "what" is "the fact that she is living in a life without true meaning or purpose and has the power to end such a pointless existence, thereby paying herself the respect of believing that she is at least the author of her own fate" (Bigsby, *Contemporary* 232). Seeing no possibility of improvement of her life, she chooses to stop the mere existence. Proclaiming her determination to control her own life, she compares life to riding a bus: "Well, I can get off right now if I want to, because even if I ride fifty more years and get off then, it's the same place when I step down to it. Whenever I feel like it, I can get off. As soon as I've had enough, it's my stop. I've had enough" (*'night, Mother* 33). Realizing the existential reality of her life is a life of despair, she opts to deliver herself from the condition of living death through suicide.

Her decision to kill herself instead of staying alive makes her mother realize that Jessie has always been under her control. With all the alternatives that she provides for Jessie failing to dissuade Jessie from carrying out her plan, she says, "Look, maybe I can't think of what you should do, but that doesn't mean there isn't something that would help. *You* find it. *You* think of it. ... I'll pay more attention to you. Tell the truth when you ask me. Let you have your say" (*Collected Works* 75; italics original). For the first time Mama allows Jessie to make a decision by herself. Nevertheless, what Jessie finds that can help her is to say no to her life. Refuting Mama's opinion of her action as resignation, Jessie gives an explanation of her choice in the following manner:

> I'm not giving up! This is the other thing I'm trying. And I'm sure there are some things that might work, but might work isn't good enough any more. I need something that will work. This will work. That's why I picked it. ... This is how I have my say. This is how I say what I thought about it all and I say no. (*Collected Works* 75)

Having never been able to control what happens to her in the past, Jessie makes it sure about the certainty of her action. Demastes states Jessie's self-murder in the following: "Limited as Jessie is in her choices, she chooses to act in a way that authoritatively says 'no' to her world and that finally does put her in control of her life. She refuses to wait and has no other means to take control that literally to take her life" (*Beyond* 151). Roudané also argues that Jessie's death is her redefinition of survival. He says: "if her survival paradoxically relates to her death, her survival is equally the product of a new-found self-reliance, based on personal choice, that, for Norman, at least, defines her heroism" (*American Drama* 131). Put otherwise, through making a decision to kill herself, she is capable of creating significance. Elizabeth Stone claims that the point of the play is not that Jessie "chooses to *die*" but that "she *chooses* to die" (58; italics original). To Kate Stout, Jessie's death is "more than an act of desperation, it is an accomplishment" (33) because her decision is her means to take control of her life and reclaim her dignity. Challenged that suicide is not survival, Norman replies that "by Jessie's definition of survival, it is. ... Jessie has taken an action on her own behalf that for her is the final test of all that she has been" (*Interviews* 339). Through an extreme way, Jessie endows her life with significance.

Jessie's suicide not only enables her to claim autonomy and self-assertion, but also makes it possible for her to exert her control over Mama and Dawson. Analyzing the play as a power struggle between mother and daughter, John Kundert-Gibbs considers that Jessie's suicide alters the status quo because she has mapped out her mother's actions for the future after her final exit from the world. Although her past life is a collaborated one by others, through her death, Jessie "has shaken herself loose from her mother's control by 'revolving' their plot forward—taking authority over the future 'script' of the pair" (Kundert-Gibbs 58). Even though from the opening of the play Jessie has shown her resistance to and neglect of Mama's order as a sign of her control, by stipulating what Mama should do after she dies Jessie changes the balance of control. Returning Dawson's presents for her and providing a list of presents for Mama for Christmases and birthdays in the years to come in her letter for Dawson,

Jessie expresses her anger and avenges herself by controlling Dawson through her nonexistence. As she says in response to Mama's doubt whether Dawson will o- bey, "I think he'll feel like a real jerk if he doesn't. Me telling him to, this and all" (*'night, Mother* 84).

Jessie's watch as a present to Ricky is imbued with significance. Linda Ginter Brown argues that Jessie wants to nurture Ricky by leaving her watch to him because he can sell it to buy a good meal or some good dope ("A Place" 80). Nevertheless, the study maintains that since the watch is an instrument to tell the passing of time, it suggests indirectly Jessie's message to Ricky to live a life of significance during the finite time of one's life.

To some extent, the watch corresponds to Norman's deployment of clocks on stage running the same time with the audience time. In addition to the func- tion of arousing the audience's sense of urgency, the clocks also suggest that Jessie's past life under the control of others has been nothing compared to the last ninety minutes which culminates in her self-sacrificing action of self-asser- tion and self-control.

2. Piercing the Net of the Imaginary Past
in *Trudy Blue*

Unlike *'night, Mother* which is Norman's most naturalistic play, *Trudy Blue*[1] is the most expressionistic one since it delineates the innermost activities of Ginger Andrews, composed of memories and fantasies, when she struggles with her imaginary self whether to tell her husband and her daughter about her fatal illness and how she will live the rest of her life.

The play begins with Ginger Andrews, a novelist holding her thirteen-year-

---

[1] The play was first written in 1994, and the next year it premiered at the 19th Annual Humana Festival of New American Plays at Actors Theater of Louisville where several of her plays made their first appearance. Norman had rewritten the play in the subsequent five years and it was restaged at MCC Theatre in New York in 1999. The present study discusses the final version which is published by Samuel French, Inc. in 2002.

old daughter Beth in her lap before bedtime. Despite the warm scene, both have their own anxieties. Beth worries that she may fail her Science class because she has dumped her mice in the trash which were supposed to be used in her science project. What is on Ginger's mind is graver for it involves the matter of life and death. Contrary to an earlier diagnosis that she is free of cancer, Ginger has been told by her pulmonogist that she may have only two months to live. Although she feels that her life is not as good as she expected, Ginger was completely caught off guard by this diagnosis. The fear of the imminent death throws her into deeper perplexity. In fact, most of the thirteen scenes of the play transpire in Ginger's mind during the moment which she searches in her mind a- bout the thing she has to do before she tells her husband the bad news from her doctor. The searching process of what she has forgotten composes much of the play. Through her looking back at what happened during the last twenty-four hours in which her destiny changed greatly because of the doctor's initial misdi- agnosis, the audience is able to have access to her whole life in retrospect.

Being a novelist, she has led a double life with one in the real world and the other in the imaginary world. The title of the play, "Trudy Blue", is multi- referential. It refers to Ginger's alter ego, an imaginary companion for Ginger's private needs. Moreover, it is also the heroine of her novel-in-progress, *Trudy Blue: A Girl in Love*. Over the course of the play, Trudy Blue, her alter ego, has become a source of internal conflict and provides a great obstacle to Ginger' s action in the imminent future. Toward the end of the play, after an admixture of memories and fantasies, Ginger finds out that Trudy Blue and the imaginary world are the reasons that she has not lived a committed life and makes a deci- sion to walk out of her imaginary world peopled by invisible figures. Her reaching out to her daughter and her husband at her life's end embodies not only her search for a new self but also her endeavor to find the true meaning of life.

As any play which may receive both criticisms and accolades, critics and actors have expressed different views on the play. Those critics who express neg- ative comments on the play focus on the episodic structure which, in their opin- ions, causes much confusion for the audience. Reviewing on the performance of the play at MCC Theatre, Charles Isherwood criticizes it as "unfocused" because it is hard for the audience to discriminate Ginger's nonstop fantasizing and the real world among the repetitious series of incidents, and the play is "an hour of wheel-spinning replays that simply aren't written with enough wit or revealing insight" (51). Likewise, Les Gutman thinks that the play "seems to lack a cogent target" and "Norman also seems eager to make her story theatrically hip, shredding up her time line, rewinding and replaying shards of her 'moment' and juxtaposing the tangible and intangible" . [1] The critics' attack on the play's lack of focus fails to do justice to Norman's efforts in meticulously establishing the connections between the episodes. Those episode are Ginger's purposeful retrospect of the last twenty-four hours of her life to find out the thing she has to do before telling her husband about her cancer. The theatricality of the play which is added by the double-and-triple casting in which one actor plays several characters in effect creates a notable Brechtian V-effect which alerts the audience to analyze the meaning of Ginger's interior searching rather than take it as an odd slice of mental life.

Regarding the play as being anti-naturalistic, John Simon does not think it innovative at all, speaking sarcastically that " [t]his would have been daringly innovative until 1921, when a certain Luigi Pirandello came out with *Six Characters in Search of an Author*". [2] However, unlike Pirandello's characters who are compelled to demand for enhanced status for their distrust of the author to do them justice, the imaginary characters in Ginger's mind are apparently under the authorial control of Ginger.

Contrary to the above critics' negative views, others speak highly of the play's emotional power. Anita Gates from The *New York Times* regards *Trudy Blue* as "a vivid and stirring reminder of just what a fine observer of the interior life she [Norman] is" and a morality play from which can be drawn the lesson that "alter egos are addictive and no match for the warm-blooded comfort of real human beings, no matter how flawed" (3). Regarding the play as technically complex and emotionally demanding, Nelson Pressley acclaims Jane Beard who

---

① Les Gutman. "A CurtainUp Review: *Trudy Blue*."
② John Simon. Marsha Norman's "Trudy Blue."

played Ginger in The Studio Theatre production for creating "a sympathetic Ev-
erywoman with acting that is direct and unembellished but hardly unemotional"
(C1) and displaying nuances of Ginger's thought and feeling with a full understanding. Making an analogy of Ginger's flowing thoughts to the balls in a pinball
machine, Jean Beard says that the play is not merely about cancer and imminent death but about "being present to your life, about being awake to what's
going on" (qtd. in Horwitz C05).

Actually, by presenting Ginger's mindscape on stage, Norman puts her
notion of the closeness of the visible and the invisible into practice through having "fantasy figures walking around in between conversations that are actually
happening" ("Marsha Norman" 191), like her adoption of time travel and
multiple story frames respectively in *Loving Daniel Boone* and *Sarah and Abra-
ham.* She explains her notion in detail as follows:

> What I like best to play is the notion that the visible and the invisible
> are quite close and in fact they are both sensible and active realms in which
> we play. That the invisible is woven around and through the visible in our
> daily lives. By the invisible I mean there are people from the past, people
> who are dead, people who never existed, people we dreamed of, ideas
> that we had, dreams, hopes, fears, those things all might as well be
> characters that are walking around on a stage. ("Marsha Norman" 191)

Ginger's world is composed of the visible and the invisible—her real life
with her family and the society and her inner world with the imaginary people. Although her past life has been addicted to the invisible, the fact of her imminent death compels her to make up her mind to live in the visible. Presenting
Ginger's invisible world on the stage, Norman makes the play a process of Ginger's
reflection of her past life which has been lived in a fictional world. Ginger's self-
knowledge gained at the end of the play comes through a process of inner conflict
rather than *peripetia* of a more tangible kind. By overcoming her alter, and thus,
herself, Ginger comes out of her isolated past to connection with her family. Through Ginger's final decision, Norman conveys to the audience that the

kind of human existence lacking genuine connection is fundamentally absurd and life with meaningful human contact instead of life in isolation is the essence of the meaning of life.

The play is about Ginger's deliberate self-searching through a relatively controlled mental re-enactment of the past. In this sense, it belongs to the category of memory play which is used by Tennessee Williams and some British playwrights like Peter Shaffer and Brian Friel, whose influence upon Norman is credited on several occasions ("Marsha Norman" in *A Search* 245, 247; "Marsha Norman " in *In Their* 181; "Conversation with Brustein" 191). According to Kramer, a memory play is

> a play in which all the stage action, or a large part of it, represents events as putatively recalled by one of the characters. In the course of dramatization, the remembered experience is altered, distorted, perhaps even invented, typically revealing the state of the narrator's psyche. The presentation of events usually seems purposeful and well rehearsed, but sometimes memories assert themselves despite the attempts of their owners to suppress them. That characters' earlier self…is also an active characters in the scenes recalled by the older self, the memorist/narrator. (14)

From Kramer's definition, we can see several characteristics of such a memory play. Firstly, the play takes place in the mind of the protagonist. Then, because of the subjectivity of the mind, the events may be distorted by the protagonist. Thirdly, there is an imperative for the protagonist to recall the events which are remembered in an orderly way. Fourthly, there are two selves of the protagonist, the narrator as the older one and the earlier self as the participant of the events in the memory. But Norman exploits the form with some alterations. Without violating the decorum of the "fourth wall" tradition of the theatre, Norman does not allow Ginger to talk directly to the audience. Hence, she is not exactly a narrator but performs a similar function. As those plays dramatize events belonging to a much earlier time, the earlier selves of the narrators are of a quite different disposition from the present one. However, because what Ginger recalls is the immediate past, the two Gingers are not disparate from each other. Although the recalling is similarly purposeful, it cannot be well rehearsed because it is mind searching for a forgotten thing. Nevertheless, just like Tom in *The Glass Menagerie* who "constructs himself as the one who remembers in order to organize his past, make sense of it, and to forget" (Favorini 142), Ginger's memory performs a similar aim in making sense of and prompting her to confront the past.

To accommodate the memories of Ginger, Norman employs the episodic structure. Consisting of several episodes which are an admixture of Ginger's memories and fantasies, the play belongs to what Jeffery Hatcher classifies as one of three types of plays whose plots are not in a forward-moving fashion— plays in a non-linear fashion. According to his opinion, in such plays, " [e] vents in a character's life may be *remembered*, *fantasized* and *depicted* onstage in a nonlinear fashion" (10 – 11; italics original). At the beginning of the play, Ginger is accompanying her daughter Beth to go to bed. Only after three lines of talk with Beth, Ginger resorts to the imaginary Trudy Blue for advice whether she should tell her husband about the doctor's bad news of her illness. Trudy's habitual prevention of Ginger to have intimate talks with her husband makes Ginger hesitate. However, her words "But there was something I had to do before I told him" (*Trudy Blue* 9) put the audience in a suspense about what she wants to do. From Scene 2 to Scene 12 is Ginger's searching for the thing which encompasses Ginger's memory of what happened during the last twenty-four hours. It is superficially chronological since the scenes are from the night before through to this evening. However, the events and conversations, specified in the author's note to the play, "are drawn from many days, both past and future, and many states of consciousness, waking and non, fictional and non" (*Trudy Blue* 6). Unlike her earlier plays in which Norman's deployment of stage space is meticulously detailed, the play has a minimalist stage because "Rooms, furniture and props mentioned in the script need not exist on the stage" (*Trudy Blue* 6). Space here is elastic which accommodates the fluidity of the memories and fantasies of Ginger. From the audience's point of view, Norman's bare setting provides an imaginative space for a theatrical journey into the depths of Ginger's mind.

Although the play takes place in one moment, it has the weight of an entire life's revelation. Ginger seems driven to burrow inside the memory of the past twenty-four hours which is, in the meantime, a process of trying to fathom her past life which she mixes fact and fiction, confusing her real life with the imaginary one. Over the course of the drama in which memories and fantasies overlap, it is revealed that Ginger's past life is a process of sinking deeper into a solipsistic shell which she formed around herself since childhood. Her imaginary self Trudy Blue, created out of her isolated childhood, accompanied her throughout her imaginary past. Her writing career is a continuation of her fantastical life which is rendered in a fictional form. And her imaginary lover James is her strategy to deal with her unsatisfactory marriage life with Don.

Notwithstanding the veridicality of Ginger's memory can be challenged since the play is filtered through Ginger's mind, the sporadic memories of her dead mother reflect Ginger's emotional traumas as a result of childhood isolation and her mother's restrictive demands in her upbringing. Just like Norman's fundamentalist mother who never allowed her to play with the neighborhood children, Ginger's mother thinks that being inside the house and having her own world all to herself can be the best way for her daughter to be happy. The mother 's monologue in the second scene in the first version of the play shows this most tellingly:

Ginger was a happy child. So happy. Happy all the time. Singing and dancing and playing by herself. I kept telling her how nice it was outside, but I have to admit it was sweet that she wanted to stay down in the basement with me. None of the other neighborhood children were well … good enough to play with her, really, so I would iron and she would play school, making little books, writing things. Even before she knew how, she was writing, scribbling on the paper and then hiding her little messages behind the runner on the stairs. She didn't know I knew, but I did. But I didn't read them. (*A moment.*) If she had wanted me to know what she thought, she would've just told me. ①

The monologue has been deleted in the final version of the play. But it is quoted at length to show Norman's struggle with her material as she struggles with herself concerning her mother's mixed influence over her. Moreover, Ginger's mother's tendency to be overcritical and fault-finding had planted a strong negativism in her who did not want to communicate but withdrew into herself mentally. In her memory, her mother is never a considerate one with whom she can share joys or pains but one who is difficult, cold, unfriendly and judgmental (*Trudy Blue* 30). The mother-daughter discord is shown clearly through the imaginary dialogue between Ginger and her dead mother in Scene 8.

> GINGER's MOTHER. Ginny. It's O. K. Ginny.
>
> GINGER. Come around to gloat, did you, Mother?
>
> GINGER's MOTHER. That's not necessary.
>
> GINGER. What is necessary, Mother? Maybe if you have another daughter someday, you could try passing that along. Not what isn't necessary. What is.
>
> GINGER's MOTHER. You don't have to be this way.
>
> GINGER. I don't have to be dying?
>
> TRUDY. I think it would be best if you were quiet right now.
>
> GINGER's MOTHER. I am here to comfort her.
>
> GINGER. Since fucking when!
>
> GINGER's MOTHER. Fine. (*Trudy Blue* 49)

Despite her desperate need for comfort which is unintentionally revealed by a tear on her face specified in the stage direction, Ginger can not imagine herself accepting consolation from her mother.

As a matter of fact, Norman creates a schizophrenic character modeled on herself as a result of the restrictions imposed on her. Norman, through Ginger,

---

① Marsha Norman. *Trudy Blue. Twentieth Century North American Drama.*

constructs her own subjectivity in the face of her personal self-divided-ness. Although Frieda Fromm-Reichmann's concept of a ' schizophrenogenic' mother (qtd. in Shorter 177) , ① which means that a mother's behavior and faulty mode of communication cause her child to be schizophrenic, had been aban-doned in the nineteen seventies, it seems that Norman still holds the concept true. Although she later reflects that her isolated childhood is conducive to her career of writing which coincides with D. W. Winnicott's statement that solitude is conducive to creativity, ② she regards her mother's way of bringing her up as problematic because she just "fill [s] somebody up, separate [s] them from all of their friends, do [es] nt let them play with anybody else, and fill [s] them all full of these ancient stories of conflict over moral issues" ("Marsha Norman" in *Conversations* 284). Growing up "in a world of silence, a world of enforced good cheer," Norman remarks that " [t] here wasn't place for all the things I felt to go, except into some kind of internal dialogue" (Norman, "An Interview" 11). With such a narcissistic mother, to use Alice Miller's term, a person has to accommodate to her needs which leads to the "as-if personality"③ and there is no way for others to guess what is behind the mask (12). However, for Norman, the silence "does not breed quiet minds; it breeds inner dialogue, inner talk, inner voices. And then the hothouse effect takes place. These things grow and change and morph and take on their own lives rather than the real voices" ("Marsha Norman" 42). In other words, under the seemingly serene facade, there are intense inner activities which are not easily detected by the

---

① Frieda Fromm-Reichmann states: "The schizophrenic is painfully distrustful and resentful of other people due to the severe early warp and rejection he encountered in important people of his infancy and childhood, as a rule, mainly in a schizophrenogenic mother" (qtd. in *A History of Psychiatry: From the Era of the Asylum to the Age of Prozac*) .

② According to Winnicott, creativity is linked to the true self and compliance is related to the false self. States of solitude is a way to live in a subjective world that protects the true self from the external world which dilutes and thwarts creativity by exacting social compliance. (*Playing and Reality*, 53 – 85) .

③ According to Miller, accommodation to parental needs often leads to the "ass-if personality", which is similar to Winnicott's term "false self" . Such a person "develops in such a way that he reveals only what is expected of him and fuses so completely with what he reveals of him, and fuses so completely with what he reveals that—until he comes to analysis—one could scarcely have guessed how much more there is to him" (12).

surrounding people.

Just like Norman, who in her childhood invented Bettering as an imaginary playing pal as a countermeasure to her mother's restrictions of forbidding her to play with neighborhood children, Ginger succumbs to her imaginary world. The creation of an imaginary self Trudy Blue is a reaction to the formulating forces of familial and societal pressure and tradition which Ginger, as Norman's surrogate, views as prisons to be struggled against. As a result, what ensues is that Ginger is deliberately insulated against other people because "I'm afraid of them. I'm afraid of my family and afraid of my friends. I'm afraid I won't measure up and they won't want me" (*Trudy Blue* 71). Like the divided self in R. D. Laing's existential study of schizophrenia, she seeks to achieve a relationship with herself that is "scrupulously sincere, honest, frank" despite her relationship with others abounds in "pretence, equivocation, hypocrisy" (83). This is confirmed by Beth's accusation of Ginger that "You lie for a living, Mom" (*Trudy Blue* 13).

Consequently, Ginger has locked herself into a relationship with Trudy Blue which has precluded herself from having a direct relationship with real things and real people. To use Laing's schema, Ginger is in the situation of a vicious circle, self-(body/other), rather than a benign circle, (self/body) – other (82). Considering her relationship with her own body as equivalent to that with the true object world of the other with which she may have a relationship, Ginger is precluded from "a full experience of realness and aliveness" and there is no "mutual enrichment of the self and the other" (82) at all. Admitting her feeling of not-presentness to Sue, her oldest friend and book agent, she says that "I feel like I'm here, and my life is over there somewhere" (*Trudy Blue* 20).

Ginger's career as a novelist is a continuation of her childhood fantasies which helped her get through her childhood isolation. Bigsby maintains that "[h]er (Ginger's) career as a novelist seems to be an extension of the fantasies she had as a child, her desire to live what she calls 'her other life'" (*Contemporary* 251). Norman herself also says that what she has portrayed in her work, is "a sense of what you would like to say, of the conversations you would like to hear, of how it goes when people *do* say those things" ("Conversation with Brustein" 184). Categorizing child's play, daydreaming or fantasy and art in one group for their difference from reality, Freud, in "Creative Writers and Day-Dreaming" (1908), maintains that "The creative writer does the same as the child at play. He creates a world of phantasy which he takes very seriously-that is, which he invests with large amounts of emotion while separating it sharply from reality" (144). Ginger's profession as a novelist affords her to continue to retain the pleasures associated with play and childhood and live a life according to the pleasure principle instead of the reality principle. As Norman's surrogate, Ginger enjoys the fantastical world which seems to offer her omnipotence and freedom which she cannot gain in her relationship with the people in the real world. Anita Gates remarks in her review of *Trudy Blue* with the following words: "Successful novelists are the luckiest people. When something really bad happens to them, when they need to hash out the meaning of their lives, they have alter egos to talk to: always available and never bored, if not always sympathetic" (3). Laing interprets the sense of freedom of an imaginary self as follows,

> Since the self, (*sic*) in maintaining its isolation and detachment does not commit itself to a creative relationship with the other and is preoccupied with the figures of phantasies, thought, memories, etc. (imagos), which cannot be directly observable by or directly expressed to others, anything (in a sense) is possible ... In phantasy, the self can be anyone, anywhere, do anything, have everything. (84)

Likening *Trudy Blue* to *Getting Out* in its use of split selves, Bigsby argues that in the play "there are, in effect, multiple selves, some a product of social or familial roles (friend, wife, mother), others a product of an imagination which peoples the world with projections of private need" (*Contemporary* 251). While the real world has limited Ginger in the traditional roles, the fantastical world affords her the freedom to impersonate several people, dead or imaginary. Freud also argues that because fantasy is the fulfillment of a wish, only unhappy person fantasizes. People escape into fantasy just because it seems to cure the dissatisfaction that they cannot otherwise escape. He explains in the following manner: "We may lay it down that a happy person never phantasies, only an unsatisfied one. The motive forces of phantasies are unsatisfied wishes, and every single phantasy is the fulfillment of a wish, a correction of unsatisfying reality" (144). Through the fantastical life Ginger has experienced vicarious satisfaction which up to the moment seems to have successfully contributed a therapeutic function for the real life in which she always feels unhappy and angry.

Unlike other popular writers who write romances which can be optioned as a movie, Ginger makes use of the fictional form mainly to convey her unhappiness and rage. Replying to her imaginary lover James' question about what she has done with all her rage, Ginger says that she " [s]old it. Made something out of hurt and loss, like a book or something and sold it. And the rage nobody wanted to buy, well, I buried it" (*Trudy Blue* 36). She has published in the past several Trudy Blue novels in postmodern fashion. Through writing novels, Ginger projects her fantastical world into the fictive form which registers her feelings indirectly. In addition to that, she has written journals which contain "the precious little secret stuff I couldn't tell anybody" (*Trudy Blue* 74).

Ginger's habitual resort to her imaginary world causes disharmony in her married life. Ginger's self-directed isolation makes her inscrutable to Don. Even though they have married for years, Don has never been able to gain a complete understanding of Ginger. Apparently, Ginger is frustrated with her marriage with Don because she thinks that he lacks in "perception, understanding and compassion" (Bigsby *Contemporary* 249). Consequently, there is much distrust, misunderstanding and lack of communication between Don and Ginger which has set them far apart from each other. Don has a bias against her being a novelist because he does not consider writing as work. In Scene 3, when Ginger asks Don who he would become if he could, Ginger is astonished by Don's answer "Of course you. Isn't everybody's dream to make a living by not going to work? (*Trudy Blue* 19)" In Don's eyes, what Ginger does is just talking on the phone and having lunch with friends. What is more infuriating for Don is that instead of communicating with him, Ginger has put all her feelings in her writing. Don's accidental reading of a piece of paper containing the heroine's meeting another man in Ginger's novel-in-progress makes him interrogate her whether she is having an affair. This scenario triggers Don's words about his desperation to know his wife's inner world,

> I just want you to know that if anything ever happens to you, if you die... the first thing I'm going to do, after I stop crying, is go into your study and read everything you've written. Not just your short stories and books, but your notes, your journals, your letters... everything you've ever written. (*Trudy Blue* 27)

Instead of having intimate conversations with Don, Ginger has always resorted to paper as an outlet for her feelings and thoughts.

Ginger's immersion in her own thoughts has caused much trouble for her to hear others' words. In her memory of trying to communicate her confused mind to Sue, Ginger says "For years now, I have real conversations with imaginary people, and imaginary conversations with real people" (*Trudy Blue* 33). Drawing from her own experience, Norman explains the feeling, "When people talked to me I wasn't listening to what they were really saying. I would hear what I *thought* they said or what they *probably* meant. I was listening on so many *under* levels" ("Marsha Norman" 40; italics original). Visualizing Don's response after she tells Don about her being sick, Ginger over-interprets Don's question "What do you mean sick? (*Trudy Blue* 49)" In one breath, she pours out her dissatisfaction with Don and her marriage:

> Sick. I'm sick of you thinking everything is either a nuisance or a joke. I'm sick of sleeping with someone who'd rather be on the sofa. I'm sick of wishing I had it all to do over. I'm sick of memories and call waiting and bank accounts and bargaining with you for the things I need. I want someone to talk to me in a clear, plain way and say what he means. I want to tell the truth without deciding to first. (*Trudy Blue* 49)

The frequent occurrence of her not being able to hear what other people say causes her husband to think that she has hearing problems. However, after seeing seventeen doctors in the past month, Ginger's hearing has not improved much not only because the doctors have identified different causes, but also because it is really her being in the two worlds at the same time that have brought about her conflicting mental state which sometimes causes her auditory senses to psychosomatically shut to the outside world.

As a figment of her imagination, Ginger's ideal lover signifies her dissatisfaction with her present marital life. Having always lived two disparate lives in fantasy and in reality, Ginger is accustomed to resort to the imagined rather than the real people. To use Laing's words, " [t]he [divided] self can relate itself with immediacy to an object which is an object of its own imagination or memory but not to a real person. This is not always apparent, of course, even to the individual himself, still less to anyone else" (86). To Bigsby, because the whole play is a dramatization of Ginger's mindscape, what we see must have a level of distortion (*Contemporary* 249). To Ginger, who has felt that passion has drained from her life, her marriage cannot meet her emotional needs. Consequently, she says to Don that "I don't feel like you love me" (*Trudy Blue* 42). Norman comments on Ginger's feeling of not being loved by Don in the following words: "the idea of marriage ends here where two people obviously feel some kind of love for each other but cannot communicate that consistently enough to make the other person believe it. So it becomes empty" (L. Brown, "More" 209). Unlike Don who cannot even make Ginger feel his love for her, James, on the contrary, speaks a lot of sugar-coated words which lead to Ginger's longing for him. In contrast to her husband, James is the perfect man who would agree with whatever she says and knows how to love her. Consequently, Ginger wishes to stay with James: "I want time to stop. It doesn't have to be for long. I just want one week with you where I don't have to work or worry or plan anything or remember anything or call anybody, or anything" (*Trudy Blue* 59). Because of her feeling of unhappiness and sense of frustration, Ginger wants to escape from the real world where she has to shoulder the responsibilities of being a wife and a mother.

Ginger's memory shows that in her past life she has lived both in the material world and the fantastical world. Although the imaginary world has allowed her to escape from the dilemmas in the real world and contributed to her writing career greatly, the imminent death propels her to reconsider the meaning of her existence. In effect, what Ginger really needs is the feeling being cared for and loved by other people. She also wants people to realize her love for them. She expects to have a sense of belonging, which is a relational and reciprocal condition that encompasses connection and community. Her getting out of the imaginary world toward the end of her life enables her to embrace the essence of life.

Although her imaginary world to which she has devoted her past time more than anything else has proved its value to her life, till the end of her life, Ginger realizes that contact with the real people is more important. Through her determination to break away from her imaginary lover James, get rid of Trudy Blue and cease to resort to her memory of her dead mother, Ginger finally walks out of the imaginary world which has for the past years "propose [d] a coherence, a pattern, a shape to experience not always observable in the seeming contingencies of daily life" (Bigsby, *Contemporary* 251).

Uncommitted to the real world, Ginger has enjoyed herself in the seemingly unconditioned freedom, power and creativity her fantastical world has provided her. As to Trudy Blue's question "What makes you think Don is going to get nicer?" (*Trudy Blue* 68), Ginger expresses the omnipotence of her fantasy: "If I want to imagine people getting nicer, then I can. It's the funeral fantasy. I can have anything I want. I can have white light and a guardian angel bringing me lemon meringue pie if I want" (*Trudy Blue* 69). However, as Laing argues, the self's

> freedom and its omnipotence are exercised in a vacuum and its creativity is only the capacity to produce phantoms. The inner honesty, freedom, omnipotence, and creativity, which the "inner" self cherishes as its ideals, are cancelled, therefore, by a coexisting tortured sense of self-duplicity, of the lack of any real freedom, of utter impotence and sterility.
> (89)

As a matter of fact, Ginger's freedom in fantasizing is at the expense of the real people in the material world to which she has not committed. As she says to Sue who stays beside her bed but has not been seen by her in her imagination of a scene of her deathbed in hospital, "All my life I've seen people who weren't there. Now I'm not seeing people who *are* there" (*Trudy Blue* 69; italics original). Ginger's final decision to stop living in her mind with the imaginary people toward the end of her life enables her to see her family in a new way.

Ginger's farewell to her imaginary lover James signifies the beginning of her walking out of the imaginary world. Scene 11 "Dinner with a friend" is Ginger's last conversation with James. From this scene we can see that the invention of James is Ginger's way to drive away her loneliness and she is unaware of the unreal nature of her fantasy. However, the sense of the unrealness of her fantasy creeps more and more into her consciousness:

> Please don't let this be true, you're not real. You're in my mind. ... And then you said something I had been praying somebody would say to me somebody, and suddenly, you were the one. The perfect man. You know what I needed. You knew how to love me. And before I knew it I was dreaming about you all night, and talking to you all day. But it wasn't you. I wasn't talking to you. I was talking to my idea of you, my idea of what would make me happy. (*Trudy Blue* 60)

Although James says that "the things in your mind are as real as everything else (*Trudy Blue* 60)", she "want [s] to feel like I'm actually talking to somebody. In contact with somebody" (*Trudy Blue* 33). It finally dawns on her that she has to stop living in her mind because "I have two months to live! I can't spend it with somebody I made up... I have to say goodbye to the people I really had... not the people I wish I had" (*Trudy Blue* 61). The sense of approaching death makes her summon up her courage to confront her husband in the real world and face the fact of death. In fact, Ginger's waking up to the fact that James is her wish instead of a real person has been brought about with the temporary absence of Trudy Blue. Ginger realizes this point and responds to Trudy's regret for her exorcizing of James with the following words: "Oh, and with you not there, I could see who he really was, is that it?" (*Trudy Blue* 61). Ginger's rupture with Trudy furthers her move away from the imaginary world.

To a great extent, the whole play is Ginger's making decision to get out of the imaginary world in which Trudy Blue reigns. At the beginning of the play, because of her chaotic mind as a result of her unpreparedness for her cancer diagnosis, Ginger suffers from temporary memory loss. She wants to tell her husband the bad news about her illness, " [b]ut there was something I had to do before I told him. I thought of it as I was coming home and then ... maybe it was about you, Trudy. I don't remember" (*Trudy Blue* 9). Toward the end of the play, after she realizes that Trudy Blue was the reason that she felt estranged from her family, she remembers "that was what I forgot to do today, Trudy, get rid of you" (*Trudy Blue* 71).

In Freudian psychological structure, Trudy Blue is the id, the instinctive component of personality that operates according to the pleasure principle, which is considered by Michael Vannoy Adams as a "fantasy principle" (5). Trudy Blue has always tried to prevent Ginger from any real contact with the surrounding people, especially her husband and her daughter. Even at the critical moment of Ginger's crisis, she still urges Ginger to go to Peru instead of telling Don and Beth about her illness. The last line of Scene Four also shows this point clearly, "Ginger? Let's just stay out all day, what do you think? Don't check you messages. Don't call home" (*Trudy Blue* 28). In addition to that, Trudy Blue always deliberately seeks to sow discord between Ginger and Don. After learning the devastating news, Trudy spurs Ginger to blame Don for her illness because "If you'd been happier in your marriage, you wouldn't have gotten sick" (*Trudy Blue* 48). Pointing out that Don and Ginger want different things from their life in saying that "He wants things to stay the way they are ... You want things to be better" (*Trudy Blue* 20) , Trudy tries every way to dissuade Ginger from telling Don about her illness. The imminent death makes Ginger realize the real nature of Trudy Blue. Ginger is finally angry at Trudy and criticizes her that she was " [a]lways telling me I was out of control. Giving me your little thoughts on everything, pointing out how badly they were treating me" (*Trudy*

Blue 70).

Having only the next two months of life, Ginger decides to get rid of her i-maginary self Trudy Blue. Always feeling that Trudy Blue is the only one who understood her, Ginger has finally waken up to the fact that "you, Trudy Blue, are nothing but my fear of these people that I love, and maybe they love me too, but I won't know that til I get out of this net, this web you've [weaved] ..." (*Trudy Blue* 71). In fact, Trudy Blue is not a separate individual with her own personality. As one side of an internal mental conversation, she is more the con-soling company which Ginger finds lacking in the real life. Commenting on Gin-ger's isolation from the other people in her life, Norman utters her opinion as follows:

> The boundaries are purely arbitrary and are there between people out of fear. Trudy says, "You're not like other people," and Ginger says, "That's not true. You keep telling me that but that's not true. I'm not dif-ferent from them. I'm afraid of them. " Ginger understands that she is vir-tually the same as her husband, her daughter, her mother, her friends— all the voices, they're all her. We go to great lengths to avoid knowing a-bout this commonness, and yet when we actually run into it we are faced with the degree to which we are exactly the other. We are not just like other people; we actually are them. And it's such a relief. ("Marsha Norman" 41 – 42)

Deciding at last to get off Trudy Blue— "the wrapping or the cellophane" which has separated her from the other people, Ginger tries to get into real con-tact with the real people: "I'm going to deal with them skin to skin now, and if it's only for a couple of months, well, that's better than nothing" (*Trudy Blue* 71). Just like Sam in *Traveler in the Dark* who finally establishes connection with his family, Ginger also determines to do so.

In fact, the co-existence of the two selves on American stage can be traced back to Eugene O'Neill's *Days without End*. In the play, John Loving is a nov-elist who is in the process of writing an autobiographical novel. In *Trudy Blue*,

Ginger is also a writer who is struggling with autobiographical material. To a great extent, both works give us a sense of mirrors reflecting mirrors. The struggles with their material during the protagonists' writing process reflect the authors' difficult groping which is not only an artistic one, but also an existential one. The battle between John Loving's two selves, John and the masked Loving, symbolically good and evil, is like that in a morality play which ends with good conquering evil and the soul of the Everyman character being saved by returning to the once-forsaken religious faith. Without the religious part, Ginger also subdues the not so Mephistophelean Trudy Blue. Ginger's crying out and collapsing to the ground shows that the loss of Trudy has caused great pain for her because "Trudy was the one thing Ginger had always had, and had always thought she couldn't do without. And now she is gone. The loss is unimaginable" (*Trudy Blue* 72). However, the memory of her dead mother after Trudy's disappearance immediately rejuvenates her: "It is like a kind of life coming back into her" (*Trudy Blue* 72).

Ginger's decision to stop talking to the memory of her dead mother demonstrates her complete retreat from her imaginary world. Unlike James and Trudy Blue who are invented to satisfy her needs and desire, Ginger's mother always performs the role of superego which postulates the powerful critical force. Norman expresses her creation of the mother figure in the play: "clearly this is mother as projection. This is mother as introjection. Here she is—she's dead, and she doesn't go away. She's there still judging and holding her standards" (L. Brown, "More" 205). In Ginger's memory, her mother never stops urging her to improve her failings. She is always upbraided by her mother in a harsh manner because she broke the multifarious rules which she set in a rigid way. To Ginger who has almost been in the grip of death, her mother comes to gloat over her because what she did in the past in rebellion against her mother—talked to strangers, did not get enough sleep and did not drink enough water (*Trudy Blue* 54). However, the last imaginary conversation with her mother in her future projection after her death not only reveals Ginger's forgiveness toward her mother but also prompts her to really communicate with her daughter and husband in a way that she has never done before. Having already gotten rid of Trudy Blue,

Ginger resorts to asking her mother about what it is like after death,

> GINGER. Will I be able to talk to them? Touch them? Can I communicate with them in any way?
>
> GINGER's MOTHER. No, Ginger. That's what your life is for.
>
> GINGER. But I still have things to say. I need to talk to Beth. (*Trudy Blue* 73)

Her mother's words point to her the fact that only during life can a person establish connections with one's intimate family. However, since she has always lived in her own imaginary world, she has never been able to really care for her daughter.

A writer who mostly works at home, Ginger has not provided enough care for Beth because she has been too attentive to her work. As a result, in her daughter's eyes, she is a serious mother who "wouldn't know fun if it bit her on the ass" (*Trudy Blue* 56), and does not love her at all. Ginger's mother's last words that she has only two months to live and should not speak with her bring Ginger back to the real world. Ginger's realization that her contribution as a novelist does not matter much in comparison to her love for Beth motivates her to express her love and concern for her. Norman conveys the feeling of the transformed Ginger through her stage direction: "Ginger becomes aware of Beth in a new way. Without Trudy there, she can actually see her very clearly. Ginger is present, simply and clearly present, perhaps for the first time" (*Trudy Blue* 75). The ending dialogue between Ginger and Beth, in which Ginger tries to talks with Beth about how to recover from a failed science project, further confirms Ginger's desire to become a good mother who is willing to share her daughters' worries and try to help solve her problems.

Only after she comes out of the imaginary world can Ginger shed her fear of her family, express herself distinctly and feel their love for her in a genuine way. No longer being afraid of her husband's cold and indifferent reaction to her illness which has been predicted by Trudy, who has always maintained a distorted view of Don, Ginger courageously tells Don the bad news. The long pause after Ginger's desperate words reminds us of Samuel Beckett or Harold Pinter who in their plays display silence as an effective tool for communication. Despite Ginger's claim that she cannot feel Don's love for her, the emotionally-charged silent scene which ends the play convinces Ginger and the audience Don's love for her. As Norman's stage direction shows, "He comes over to sit beside her on the bed. There is a long moment. In slow steps, he takes her hand. She rests her head on his shoulder. Finally he puts his arm around her. His eyes water" (*Trudy Blue* 77).

As Bigsby argues, the play is similar to Arthur Miller's play *Mr. Peters' Connections* which also takes place entirely inside the mind of the eponymous main character (*Contemporary* 251). As an old man toward the end of his life, Mr. Peters "is free to roam from real memories to conjectures, from trivialities to tragic insights, from terror of death to glorifying in one's being alive" (A. Miller Vii). As Mr. Peters finally finds out that connections are of great importance to his existence, Ginger, likewise, till the very end of the play, reaches out to her family members for the first time in her life. Like Jessie who decides to commit suicide to control herself, Ginger also takes charge of her life, in a totally different way, however, by finally casting off the imaginary world and deciding to take up her responsibilities toward the people around. If Jessie shows her courage in killing herself to resist the absurdity of life, Ginger shows hers in trying to understand the meaning of life through putting herself in the web of human relationships. Through consoling her daughter and telling her husband about her fatal illness, she begins her first step of having real contact with them which is also what Norman really wants for her parents between whom she never considers there is any real contact at all (L. Brown, "More" 219).

Breaking out of the cocoon of solitariness to establish connection with her husband and her daughter, Ginger "is forced to stop living in her mind and face terrifying realities about herself and her relationships to her mother, husband, daughter" (Craig, *Women* 173). Ginger "reach [es] the moment of sureness ... a moment of great peace and arrival" and experiences "a moment of profound personal redemption where the world suddenly opens up. The doors of her life are blown open and she's in the world" ("Marsha Norman" in *BOMB* 40). The last two months of Ginger's life are relatively short, but they may be the most valuable because only until the end does she see deeply the true meaning of life.

Like many of her other plays which have much autobiographical detail, the play is also based on Norman's own experience of misdiagnosis of lung cancer which was a blessing in disguise because it triggered her to reevaluate and reflect on her life as a whole. Unlike its creator who was released from the death sentence of the fatal disease, Ginger is put in the grip of death. Adopting the theatrical form, Norman imbues a fabricated persona with the psychological circumstances of herself—the sense of approaching death which caused "this frozen panic of fear and horror" ("Marsha Norman" in *BOMB* 38) and led to a sudden realization that "I am not attached enough to my life, [*sic*] I am not living in a way I have respect for" ("Marsha Norman" in *BOMB* 38). Bringing the silent inner movements of the protagonist onto the stage to show "the effects of trying to make a decision" (L. Brown, "More" 205), Norman succeeds in projecting her most intimate concerns on stage which makes it possible for the audience to experience the quandaries of many women who face similar problems. More importantly, through ending the play with Ginger's facing her family courageously, Norman attempts to stimulate the members of the audience to observe their lives critically.

CONCLUSION

Throughout her oeuvre, Marsha Norman has displayed her concern with the past and memory and their lingering effects on the present. This study has probed into Norman's dramatization of the past and memory in seven of her original plays. In Norman's plays, there are three different pasts, namely, the traumatic, the wistful and the fictional. In representing different pasts of the characters, Norman makes an adept use of multifarious dramatic resources. It is demonstrated that Norman's vivid dramatization of the past and memory grants her characters psychological complexity and subtlety. Showing her characters in the historical nexus between past, present and future, Norman reveals that the characters are able to come out of their entrapment in the past through connection with the surrounding environment and the community and take actions and make decisions confronting their existential crises accordingly.

In Norman's plays, traumatic experiences are devastating to the protagonists. In *Getting Out*, Arlene suffers overwhelming sense of powerlessness and pain as a result of childhood sexual abuse, sexual exploitation and prison violence. In *Traveler in the Dark*, Sam has a developmental disruption with the loss of his mother which results in his insulation from the other people and the inhibition of his capacities for mature love. Yet, Norman tries to show that an empathic relationship can be collaborative and empowering in healing the protagonists from trauma. The traumatic past in Norman's plays has made the protagonists emotionally and psychologically scarred. The life-shattering quality of the trauma has caused the protagonists to repress them. However, the repression, rather than helping them forget the traumas, incites severe crises in their lives. The research herein shows that Norman underscores the necessity of reintegrating the

traumatic past into the present life of the protagonists. The recovery of the protagonists from the traumatic memories is facilitated with the empathic community
as listeners to the victims' recounting of the traumatic events. After reconciling
themselves with the traumatic past with the help of the empathic community,
the protagonists enable themselves to reintegrate their selves and their lives.

Unlike the traumatic past which causes the characters to choose repression
due to its disruptiveness, the wistful past in Norman's plays cause the protagonists to yearn for it. Their nostalgia not only conjures up images of a previous
time when life was supposed to be good, but also provides them a sense of continuity of their life. In *Third and Oak*, the characters reminisce about their lives
before the loss of marriage and in the ripe of their time. In *The Holdup*, the Outlaw indulges in the outlaw era. The heroine in *Loving Daniel Boone* is nostalgic
for the archetypical frontiersman. However, while it seems that they can be temporarily and superficially released from the present miseries, their indulgence in
the past is in fact debilitating and dysfunctional. As a result, the nostalgia causes them to be more isolated and estranged from the surroundings. Nevertheless,
the protagonists' interaction with the community propels them to reflect on their
obsession with the past and the reality of the present.

For the nostalgic who harbor a yearning for the past through rose-colored
lenses, it is the unfavorable circumstances in the present that prompt them to do
so. To the protagonists with a fictional past, the uncongenial reality in the past
caused others and themselves to mask and avoid the reality. In *'night, Mother*,
Jessie's real situation in the past is severely distorted and misrepresented by her
mother. In *Trudy Blue*, Ginger always avoids the real world through immersing
in her own fantasy. Shielded from reality, the protagonists are rendered to inac-
tivity and isolated from things that constitute the essence of life. The existential
crisis acts as a catalyst provoking them to dig into the fictional past. Their confrontation with the fictional past signifies their self-control and self-determination
through cutting ties with it.

Through an exploration of Norman's dramatic representation of the traumatic
past, the wistful past and the fictional past, the study demonstrates Norman's
views on the dynamics between past, memory and present and her philosophical

meditation on human existence. Influenced by Kierkegaard's doctrine of recollection, Norman presents in her plays the backwards understanding of life. Taking their lives as a continuum, her protagonists construct a present transcending the past with openness toward the future. As recollection for Kierkegaard is not simple memory but a transformative vision, the engagement with the past and memory of Norman's protagonists is to get their lives as a whole and grasp the meaning of life. In the process, Norman underscores the importance of connection. The presence of an empathic community proves facilitating for the protagonists to come to terms with the past, returning to reality or confronting the past.

In some senses, dramatizing her characters out of their entrapment in the past may reflect her unconscious rebelliousness toward her own past, from which she wants to escape. As one who has grown up with a sense of isolation as a result of a strict Christian fundamentalist family background, she remarks that writing can express her feelings which cannot be done otherwise. As for the characters in her plays, she says that "Somebody once told me that the people in the plays are all the folks Mother wouldn't let me play with as a kid" ("Interview with Marsha Norman" 158). In fact, what causes her to write about those characters is the uncanny resemblances between them. As she states, she "choose [s] to represent certain people in the world and our reasons for these choices are probably undiscoverable, except that I think we feel there is something of our own selves in that person" (Gross 256). In the introduction to *Getting Out*, Norman says that she "wasn't writing about Arlie, I was writing about myself" (*Collected Works* 3). Talking about her writing in general, Norman says,

> I feel that we are all working toward one goal, which is the documenting of what it has felt like to be alive in our time. And that we all write the parts of it that we see. You can't possibly do the whole thing so you just do your little part and trust that the assortment of you is great enough to pretty much cover it. ("Marsha Norman" 42)

Despite some of the autobiographical elements in her plays, Norman manages to display a universal significance which extends beyond the personal. With her transmogrifying powers of an aesthetic procedure, Norman creates an oeuvre of plays that make us examine our life and our own pasts.

The study includes Norman's seven original plays which are representative of Norman's art at her best and her concern with the past and memory. As a matter of fact, Norman's concern with the past and its impact on the present is not limited to her original plays. Her musical plays and screen plays also display her craft in representing the interaction of the past, memory and the present. For example, in the musical *The Secret Garden* which is adapted from Frances Hodgson Burnett's classic children's novel, Norman changes the plot to have an effect that the play is about "a man exorcising the ghost of his dead wife, rather than on the children who have been damaged by emotional neglect resurrecting themselves and each other through their nurturing of an apparently dead garden" (Tyler 134). Besides that, Norman adds more psychological sense to Mary Lennox through presenting the loss of her parents as traumatic and painful which is a dramatic departure from Burnett's novel. In the screenplay *The Audrey Hepburn Story*, Norman adopts the flashback device for the heroine to relive significant episodes in her past life while she is shooting scenes for the film *Breakfast at Tiffany's*. In the screen play, Norman continues her concern with the past as she says, "The question of how she became Audrey Hepburn was the thing to see" (Weiraub 130). As in her original plays, Norman in these works also engages with the past and memory from whose shackles the protagonists have to free through acceptance and reintegration. Therefore, it is also a viable perspective to conduct research on Norman's musicals and screen plays through her concern with the past and memory.

With a serious infiltration of philosophy and moral values into her plays, Norman believes the enlightening function of the theatre and her endeavors in doing so have prevented her from being labeled merely as a woman playwright. Considering Norman both as a skeptic and a humanist, Kate Stout explains in detail: "From the skeptic grew a commitment to the truth, and from the humanist grew a sense of responsibility to the nameless people who shuffle along the sidewalks of out times, on whose lives society generally turns a blind eye" (33). In some senses, Norman's commitment to truth is displayed in the characters' willingness to have a full comprehension of the past and posit themselves with an appropriate relationship with the past. Of course, in portraying the underdogs of the society and giving voice to those formerly unheard, Norman demonstrates her humanistic concerns. What's more, her humanist concern is also expressed through her persistence in human capacity to reposition themselves for the present and the future by reshaping the memories of the past in human life.

As a major contemporary American playwright, Norman will continue to write for "the least of our Brethren" (Stout 33)[1]. Always meditating on "Why Do Good Men Suffer?"[2], Norman's social conscience and humanistic persistence enable her to continue to write plays about human suffering and how we can emerge from our personal and historical pasts, nightmarish as they sometimes are.

---

[1] Norman will write the inaugural play for Theatre for Humans, an arts and entertainment production company in Northridge, CA. According to Norman, "What I hope to do is to create a play that investigates the ongoing violence toward women and children in the world, and searches for some kind of answer to the question, 'What Can We Do?'" Kenneth Jones. "Marsha Norman Will Craft New Play About Issues Facing Girls and Women. "

[2] It is the title of Norman's high school essay which won the first prize in a writing contest and is regarded by Norman as "the real title of every play I ever wrote" (*Collected Works* 274).

Works Cited

Adam, Julie. *Versions of Heroism in Modern American Drama: Redefinitions by Miller, Williams, O'Neill and Anderson.* London: Macmillan, 1991.

Adams, Michael Vannoy. *The Fantasy Principle: Psychoanalysis of the Imagination.* New York: Brunner-Routledge, 2004.

Alvord, Clarence Walworth. "The Daniel Boone Myth." *Journal of the Illinois State Historical Society* (1908 – 1984) Apr. – July 1926.

Beal, Suzanne Elaine. "*Mama Teach Me That French*": *Mothers and Daughters in Twentieth Century Plays by American Women Playwrights.* Diss. U of Maryland College Park, 1994.

Bednerick, Marya. "Writing the Other." L. Brown, *Marsha Norman* 145 – 158.

Bercovitch, Sacvan. *The Cambridge History of American Literature, V. 7. Prose Writing* 1940 – 1990. New York: Cambridge UP, 1999.

Bergson, Henri. *Laughter: An Essay on the Meaning of the Comic.* Trans. Cloudesley Brereton and Fred Rothwell. London: Macmillan and Co., Limited, 1911.

Bester, Alfred. "Hobson's Choice." *Virtual Unrealities: The Short Fiction of Alfred Bester.* Eds. Robert Silverberg, Byron Preiss, and Keith R. A. DeCandido. New York: Vintage Books, 1997..

Bigsby, Christopher. *Contemporary American Playwrights.* Cambridge: Cambridge UP, 2004.

——. *Modern American Drama*, 1945 – 2000. Cambridge: Cambridge UP, 2000.

Bitonti, Tracy Simmons. "More than Noises off: Marsha Norman's Offstage Characters. " *Shaw and Other Matters*. Ed. Susan Rusinko. Cranbury, NJ: Associated UP, 1998.

Blatanis, Konstantinos. *Popular Culture Icons in Contemporary American Drama*. Cranbury, NJ: Rosemont Publishing & Printing Corp, 2003.

Bluefarb, Sam. *The Escape Motif in American Novel: Mark Twain to Richard Wright*. Columbus: Ohio State UP, 1972.

Blustein, Jeffrey. *The Moral Demands of Memory*. Cambridge: Cambridge UP, 2008.

Bordman, Gerald & Thomas S. Hischak, eds. *The Oxford Companion to American Theatre*, 3rd ed. New York: Oxford UP, 2004.

Boym, Svetlana. *The Future of Nostalgia*. New York: Basic Books, 2002.

Brault, Pascale-Anne and Michael Naas. "Introduction: To Reckon with the Dead: Jacques Derrida's Politics of Mourning. " Jacques Derrida. *The Work of Mourning*. Eds. Pascale-Anne Brault and Michael Naas. Chicago: The U of Chicago P, 2001. 1 – 30.

Breding, Connie J. "Communication and Family Roles: Mother-Daughter Talk in Marsha Norman's *'night, Mother*. " *North Dakota Journal of Speech and Theatre* Vol. 7 1994.

Brown, Janet. *Taking Center Stage: Feminism in Contemporary U. S. Drama*. Metuchen, N. J. : Scarecrow Press, 1991.

Brown, Janet and Catherine Barnes Stevenson. "Fearlessly ' Looking under the Bed' : Marsha Norman's Feminist Aesthetic in *Getting Out* and *'night, Mother*. " *Theatre and Feminist Aesthetics*. Eds. Kathleen Laughlin and Catherine Schuler. Madison: Fairleigh Dickinson UP, 1995.

Brown, Linda Ginter. "A Place at the Table: Hunger as Metaphor in Lillian Hellman's *Days to Come* and Marsha Norman's *'night, Mother*. " L. Brown, *Marsha Norman* 63 – 85.

——. "More with Marsha Norman. " L. Brown, *Marsha Norman* 197 – 220.

——. "Update with Marsha Norman. " L. Brown, *Marsha Norman* 163 – 195.

——. *Toward a More Cohesive Self: Women in Works of Lillian Hellman and Marsha Norman*. Diss. The Ohio State U, 1991.

——, ed. *Marsha Norman: a Casebook*. New York: Garland Publishing, Inc. , 1996.

Brustein, Robert. "Don't Read This Review. " Rev. of *'night, Mother*, by Marsha Norman. L. Brown, *Marsha Norman* 159 – 162.

Burke, Sally. "Precursor and Protege: Lillian Hellman and Marsha Norman. " *Southern Women Playwrights: New Essays in Literary History and Criticism*, Eds. Robert L. McDonald and Linda Rohrer Paige. Tuscaloosa, Alabama: The U of Alabama P, 2002.

Burkman, Katherine H. "The Demeter Myth and Doubling in Marsha Norman's *'night, Mother*. " *Modern American Drama: The Female Canon*. Ed. June Schlueter. Rutherford: Fairleigh Dickinson UP, 1990.

Caruth, Cathy. *Unclaimed Experience: Trauma, Narrative, and History*. Baltimore: The John Hopkins UP, 1996.

Casey, Edward S. *Remembering: A Phenomenological Study*, 2nd ed. Bloomington, IN: Indiana UP, 2000.

Clark, Brian. *Whose Life is it, Anyway?* Oxford: Heinemann Educational Publishers, 1989.

Clark, Robin E. and Judith Freeman Clark, eds. *The Encyclopedia of Child Abuse*, 3rd ed. New York: Facts On File, Inc. , 2007.

Cline, Gretchen Sarah. "The Impossibility of Getting Out: The Psychopolitics of the Family in Marsha Norman's *Getting Out*. " L. Brown, *Marsha Norman* 3 – 25.

——. *The Psychodrama of the Dysfunctional Family Desire, Subjectivity, and Regression in Twentieth Century American Drama*. Diss. The Ohio State U, 1991.

Cooperman, Robert. " 'I don't Know What's Going to Happen in the Morning': Visions of the Past, Present, and Future in *The Holdup*. " L. Brown, *Marsha Norman* 95 – 107.

Craig, C. Casey. *Family Ties and Family Lies: Women's Perceptions of Family, Society, and Self Reflected in the Pulitzer Prize Plays by Women*. Diss. Wayne State U, 1995.

——. *Women Pulitzer Playwrights: Biographical Profiles and Analyses of the Plays.* Jefferson, North Carolina: McFarland & Company, Inc. , Publishes, 2004.

Czander, William M. *The Psychodynamics of Work and Organizations: Theory and Application.* New York: The Guilford P, 1993.

Dee, Edward Martin. *Time Travel to the Past in Twentieth-Century Anglo-American Drama.* Diss. City U of New York, 1997.

Demastes, William W. "Jessie and Thelma Revisited: Marsha Norma's Conceptual Challenge in *'night, Mother.* " *Modern Drama* Mar. 1993.

——. *Beyond Naturalism: a New Realism in American Theatre.* New York: Greenwood P, 1988.

Derrida, Jacques. *Mémoires for Paul de Man.* New York: Columbia UP, 1989.

DeVries, Hilary. "Marsha Norman's 'Traveler' Stumbles into a Pedantic Wilderness. " Rev. of *Traveler in the Dark*, by Marsha Norman. *Christian Science Monitor* 22 Feb. 1984.

Dippel, John V. H. *Race to the Frontier: 'White Flight' and Westward Expansion.* New York: Algora Publishing, 2005.

Dolan, Jill. *The Feminist Spectator as Critic.* Ann Arbor: U of Michigan P, 1991.

Drew, Anne Marie. "And the Time for It Was Gone": Jessie's Triumph in*'night, Mother.* " L. Brown, *Marsha Norman* 87 – 94.

Eco, Umberto. *Travels in Hyper Reality: Essays.* San Diego: Harcourt Brace Jovanovich, 1986.

Eder, Richard. "Stage: 'Getting Out' by Marsha Norman. " Rev. of *Getting Out*, by Marsha Norman. *New York Times* 16 May 1979.

Epstein, Grace. "At the Intersection: Configuring Women's Differences through Narrative in Norman's *Third and Oak: The Laundromat.* " L. Brown, *Marsha Norman* 27 – 46.

Erben, Rudolf. "The Western Holdup Play: The Pilgrimage Continues. " *Western American Literature* Feb. 1989.

Favorini, Attilio. *Memory in Play: From Aeschylus to Sam Shepard.* New York: Palgrave Macmillan, 2008.

Fine, Gary Alan. *Difficult Reputations: Collective Memories of the Evil, Inept, and Controversial*. Chicago: The U of Chicago P, 2001.

Foster, Karen K. *De-Tangling the Web: Mother-Daughter Relationships in the Plays of Marsha Norman, Lillian Hellman, Tina Howe, and Ntozake Shange*. Diss. The U of Nebraska – Lincoln, 1994.

Foucault, Michel. *Discipline and Punish: The Birth of a Prison*. Trans. Alan Sheridan. New York: Vantage Books, 1977.

Frankel, Lois P. *Women, Anger, and Depression: Strategies for Self-Empowerment*. Deerfield Beach, Florida: Health Communications, Inc. , 1992.

Freud, Sigmund. *Beyond the Pleasure Principle*. Trans. and Ed. James Strachery. New York: W. W. Norton & Company, 1961.

——. "Creative Writers and Day-Dreaming. " *The Standard Edition of the Complete Psychological Works of Sigmund Freud*. Eds. James Strachey et al. , 24vols. London: Hogarth P, 1953, vol. 9.

——. "Mourning and Melancholia. " *On Freud's Mourning and Melancholia*. Eds. Leticia Glocer Florini and etc. London: Karnac Books, 2009.

——. "The Aetiology of Hysteria. " *The Standard Edition of the* Complete *Psychological works of Sigmund Freud*. Eds. James Strachey, et al. , 24vols. London: Hogarth P and Institute of Psychoanalysis, 1954 – 1974, vol. 3.

Frye, Northrop. *Anatomy of Criticism: Four Essays*. Princeton: Princeton UP, 1957.

Gardner, James B. "Contested Terrain: History, Museums, and the Public. " *The Public Historian* Autumn, 2004.

Gassner, John and Edward Quinn. Eds. *The Reader's Encyclopedia of World Drama*. Mineola N. Y. : Dover Publications, Inc. , 2002.

Gates, Anita. "Thinking to Live, and Living to Think. " Rev. of *Trudy Blue*, by Marsha Norman. *New York Times* 3 Dec. 1999.

Giddens, Anthony. *The Constitution of Society: Outline of the Theory of Structuration*. Cambridge: Polity P, 1984.

Grantley, Darryll. "Marsha Norman. " *American Drama*. Ed. Clive Bloom. New York: St. Martin's P, Inc. , 1995.

Greiff, Loius K. "Fathers, Daughters, and Spiritual Sisters: Marsha Norman's *'night, Mother* and Tennessee Williams's *The Glass Menagerie.* " *Text and Performance Quarterly* Sept. 1989.

Gross, Amy. "Marsha Norman. " *Vogue* July 1983.

Gruber, William. *Offstage Space, Narrative, and the Theatre of the Imagination.* New York: Palgrave Macmillan, 2010.

Gussow, Mel. "About Death, Bad Dreams And D. Boone Debunked. " Rev. of *Marisol*, by José Rivera, *Bondage*, by David Henry Hwang and *Loving Daniel Boone*, by Marsha Norman. *New York Times* 26 Mar. 1992.

———. "Women Playwrights: New Voices in the Theater. " *New York Times* 1 May 1983.

Gutman, Les. "A *CurtainUp* Review: *Trudy Blue.* " Rev. of *Trudy Blue*, by Marsha Norman. 3 Dec. 1999. Web. 10 Sept. 2010. < http: //www. curtain-up. com/trudyblue. html >.

Hammontree, Patsy. " Family Solitude: Marsha Norman's Modern Gothic. " *Humanities in the South* Spring 2000.

Harriot, Esther. "Marsha Norman: Getting Out. " *American Voices: Five Contemporary Playwrights in Essays and Interviews.* Jefferson, N. C. : McFarland & Co. , 1988.

Harris, William V. *Restraining Rage: The Ideology of Anger Control in Classical Antiquity.* Cambridge, MA: Harvard UP, 2004.

Hart, Lynda. "Doing Time: Hunger for Power in Marsha Norman's Plays. " *Southern Quarterly* Spring 1987.

Hatcher, Jeffrey. *The Art & Craft of Playwriting.* Cincinnati, Ohio: Story P, 2000.

Heney, Jan and Connie M. Kristiansen. "An Analysis of the Impact of Prison on Women Survivors of Childhood Sexual Abuse. " *Breaking the Rules: Women in Prison and Feminist Therapy.* Eds. Judy Harden and Marcia Hill. Binghamton, NY: The Haworth P, Inc. , 1998.

Herman, Judith. *Trauma and Recovery.* New York: Basic Books, 1997.

Hinson, Scott. "The ' Other Funeral' : Narcissism and Symbolic Substitution in Marsha Norman's *Traveler in the Dark.* " L. Brown, *Marsha Norman* .

Honzl, Jind? ich. "Dynamics of the Sign in the Theatre." *Modern Theories of Drama : A Selection of Writings on Drama and Theatre* 1850 – 1990. Ed. George W. Brandt. Oxford : Clarendon P, 1998.

Horwitz, Jane. "In an Emotional Maelstrom : What if You Had 2 Months To Live? Ask 'Trudy Blue'." Rev. of *Trudy Blue*, by Marsha Norman. *Washington Post* 16 Jan. 2001.

Huang, Shih-yi. *Spatial Repression in Marsha Norman's Plays.* MA thesis. Taiwan Chengchi U. 2002.

Isherwood, Charles. "*Trudy Blue.*" Rev. of *Trudy Blue*, by Marsha Norman. *Daily Variety* 8 Dec. 1999.

Jacoby, Mario. *Individuation and Narcissism : The Psychology of Self in Jung and Kohut.* New York : Routledge, 1990.

Janet, Pierre. *Psychological Healing : A Historical and Clinical Study*, vol. 1. Trans. Eden and Cedar Paul. London : Allen & Unwin, 1925.

Jones, Kenneth. "Marsha Norman will Craft New Play about Issues Facing Girls and Women." 11 July 2011. Web. 20 July 2011. < http : // www. playbill. com/news/article/152566 – Marsha – Norman – Will – Craft – New – Play – About – Issues – Facing – Girls – and – Women > .

Jeffreys, Sheila. *The Idea of Prostitution.* North Melbourne, Vic. : Spinifex P, 1997.

Kane, Leslie. "The Way Out, the Way In : Paths to Self in the Plays of Marsha Norman." *Feminine Focus : The New Women Playwrights.* Ed. Enoch Brater. New York : Oxford UP, 1989.

Kershaw, Baz. *The Politics of Performance : Radical Theatre as Cultural Intervention.* New York : Routledge, 1992.

Keyssar, Helen. *Feminist Theatre : An Introduction to Plays of Contemporary British and American Women.* New York : Grove Press, Inc. 1984.

Kierkegaard, Soren. *The Sickness onto Death.* Howard V. Hong and Edna H. Hong, Trans. and Eds. Princeton : Princeton UP, 1980.

Klemesrud, Judy. "She Had Her Own 'Getting Out' to Do." Rev. of *Getting Out*, by Marsha Norman. *New York Times* May 27, 1979.

Kramer, Prapassaree Thaiwutipong. "*The Enclosed, Subjective Universe*" :

Dramatizing the Mind in Modern British Theater. Diss. Purdue U, 1999.

Kroll, Jack. "Before and After Meet in a Girl. " Rev. of *Getting Out*, by Marsha Norman. *Newsweek* 28 May 1979.

——. "End Game. " Rev. of *'night, Mother*, by Marsha Norman. *Newsweek* 3 Jan. 1983.

Kubal, Timothy. *Cultural Movements and Collective Memory: Christopher Columbus and the Rewriting of the National Origin Myth*. New York: Palgrave Macmillan, 2008.

Kundert-Gibbs, John. "Revolving It All: Mother-Daughter Pairs in Marsha Norman's *'night Mother* and Samuel Beckett's *Footfalls*. " L. Brown, *Marsha Norman* 47 – 62.

Laing, R. D. *The Divided Self: An Existential Study in Sanity and Madness*. New York: Penguin Books, 1990.

Lacapra, Dominich. *Writing History, Writing Trauma*. Baltimore: The Johns Hopkins UP, 2001.

Laub, Dori. "Bearing Witness or the Vicissitudes of Listening. " *Testimony: Crises of Witnessing in Literature, Psychoanalysis, and History*. Shoshana Felman and Dori Laub. Eds. New York: Routledge, 1992.

Leach, Robert. *Theatre Studies: The Basics*. London &New York: Routledge, 2008.

Lefebvre, Henri. *The Production of Space*. Trans. Donald Nocholscn-Smith. Cambridge: Basil Blackwell, Inc. , 1991.

Leys, Ruth. *Trauma: A Genealogy*. Chicago: The U of Chicago P, 2000.

Lisker, Donna Eileen. *Realist Feminisms, Feminist Realisms: Six Twentieth-Century American Playwrights*. Diss. The U of Wisconsin-Madison, 1996.

Liu, Haiping and Zhu Xuefeng. *British and American Drama: Plays and Criticisms*. Shanghai: Shanghai Foreign Language Education P, 2004.

Lowenthal, David. *The Past is a Foreign Country*. Cambridge: Cambridge UP, 1985.

Mason, M. S. "Louisville's Window on New Plays. " Rev. of *Loving Daniel Boone*, by Marsha Norman. *Christian Science Monitor* 2 Apr. 1992.

McCann, I. Lisa and Laurie Anne. *Psychological Trauma and the Adult*

Survivor: Theory, Therapy, and Transformation. New York: Brunner-Routledge, 1990.

Miller, Alice. *The Drama of the Gifted Child.* Trans. Ruth Ward. New York: Basic Books, Inc. , 1981.

Miller, Arthur. *Mr. Peters' Connections.* New York: Penguin Books, 1999.

Miller, Jean Baker. "Ties to Others" from *Toward a New Psychology of Women. The Nature of Melancholy: From Aristotle to Kristeva.* Ed. Jennifer Radden. New York: Oxford UP, 2000.

Monaco, Pamela Powell. *The Bond that Ties: The Role of the Family in Contemporary American Drama.* Diss. The Catholic U of America, 1995.

Morrow, Katherine. "Over a Pool Game, the Truth Surfaces. " Rev. of *Third and Oak: The Pool Hall,* by Marsha Norman. *Globe and Mail* (Toronto) 28 Oct. 1989.

Morrow, Laura. "Orality and Identity in *'night, Mother* and *Crimes of the Heart. " Studies in American Drama,* 1945 – Present Mar. 1988.

Murray, Timothy. "Patriarchal Panopticism, or the Seduction of a Bad Joke: "Getting out" in Theory. " *Theatre Journal* Oct. 1983.

Norman, Marsha. "An Interview with Marsha Norman. " By Sherilyn Beard. *Southern California Anthology* Mar. 1985.

———. "Interview with Marsha Norman. " *American Voices: Five Contemporary Playwrights in Essays and Interviews.* Ed. Esther Harriott. Jefferson, NC: McFarland &Company, Inc. , Publishers, 1988.

———. "Marsha Norman. " *A Search for a Postmodern Theatre: Interviews with Contemporary Playwrights.* Ed. John L. DiGaetani. Westport: Greenwood P, 1991.

———. "Marsha Norman in Conversation with Robert Brustein. " *Broadway Song and Story: Playwrights/ Lyricists/ Composers Discuss Their Hits.* Ed. Otis L. Guernsey. New York: Dodd, Mead & Company, 1985.

———. "Marsha Norman. " April Gornik, ed. *BOMB* Spring, 2000.

———. "Marsha Norman. " *Conversations with Kentucky Writers.* Ed. L. Elisabeth Beattie. Lexington: The UP of Kentucky, 1996.

———. "Marsha Norman. " Hatcher, *The Art & Craft* 185 – 94.

——. "Marsha Norman. " *In Their Own Words*: *Contemporary American Playwrights. Ed. David Savran. New York*: *Theatre Communications Group*, *1988.*

——. "Marsha Norman. " *Interviews with Contemporary Women Playwrights.* Eds. Betsko, Kathleen & Rachel Koenig. New York: Beech Tree Books, 1987.

——. *Collected Works.* Vol. I. Lyme, NH: A Smith and Kraus Book, 1998.

——. *'night, Mother.* New York: Hill and Wang, 1983.

——. "Time and Learning How to Fall. " Norman *Collected Works* 398 – 408.

——. *Trudy Blue.* New York: Samuel French, Inc. , 2002.

——. *Trudy Blue. Twentieth Century North American Drama*, electronic edition. Alexandria, VA: Alexander Street Press, L. L. C. , 2005. Web. 10 Mar. 2009. < http: //asp6new. alexanderstreet. com. proxy-um. researchport. umd. edu/atho/atho. result. htmls. aspx? id = PL008672. 4. html >.

Nouryeh, Andrea J. "Flashing back: Dramatizing the Trauma of Incest and Child Sexual Abuse. " *Theatre Symposium*: *Theatre and Violence*. Ed. John W. Frick. Tuscaloosa, Alabama: The U of Alabama P, 1999.

O'Connor, John J. "Mother, Daughter and Hatred. " Rev. of *Getting Out*, by Marsha Norman. *New York Times* 25 Apr. 1994.

Paige, Linda Louise Rohrer. "Off the Porch into the Scene": Southern Women Playwrights Beth Henley, Marsha Norman, Rebecca Gilman, and Jane Martin. " *A Companion to Twentieth-Century American Drama.* Ed. David Krasner. Malden, MA: Blackwell Publishing Ltd. , 2005.

——. *The "Other" Side of the Looking Glass*: *A Feminist Perspective on Female Suicide in Ibsen's "Hedda Gabler"*, *Hellman's "The Children's Hour"*, *and Norman's "'night, Mother"* . Diss. The U of Tennessee, 1989.

Patraka, Vivian M. "Staging Memory: Contemporary Plays by Women. " *Michigan Quarterly Review* Winter 1987.

Perelberg, Rosine Jozef. "Psychoanalytic Understanding of Violence and Suicide: A Review of the Literature and Some New Formulations. " *Psychoanalytic Understanding of Violence and Suicide.* Ed. Rosine Jozef Perelberg. London:

Routledge, 1999.

Porter, Laurin. "Contemporary Playwrights/Traditional Forms." *The Cambridge Companion to American Women Playwrights*. Ed. Brenda Murphy. Cambridge: Cambridge UP, 1999.

Prassel, Frank Richard. *The Great American Outlaw: A Legacy of Fact and Fiction*. Norman: The U of Oklahoma P, 1993.

Pressley, Nelson. "Through a Mind's Eye: 'Trudy Blue' Stares Life in the Face." Rev. of *Trudy Blue*, by Marsha Norman. *The Washington Post* 9 Jan. 2001.

Reuning, Sarah. "Depression—The Undiagnosed Disability in Marsha Norman's *'night, Mother.*" *Peering behind the Curtain: Disability, Illness and the Extraordinary Body*. Eds. Thomas Richard Fahy and Kimball King. New York: Routledge, 2002.

Rich, Adrienne. *Of Woman Born: Motherhood as Experience and Institution*. New York: W. W. Norton & Company, Inc., 1976.

Rich, Frank. "Suicide Talk in 'Night Mother'." Rev. of *'night, Mother*, by Marsha Norman. *The New York Times* 1 Apr. 1983.

Rogers, Karen Kay Keeter. *Responses to Restriction and Confinement in Selected Plays by Women Dramatists of the English-Speaking Theatre: The Susan Smith Blackburn First-Prize-Winning Plays From 1980—1981 Through 1985—1986*. Diss. The U of Texas at Dallas, 1999.

Roudané, Matthew. *American Drama since 1960: A Critical History*. New York: Twayne Publishers, 1996.

——. "Plays and Playwrights since 1970." *The Cambridge History of American Theatre: Post-World War II to the 1990s*, Volume III, Eds. Don B. Wilmeth and C. W. E. Bigsby. Cambridge: Cambridge UP, 2000.

Scaer, Robert C. *The Body Bears the Burden: Trauma, Dissociation, and Disease*. Binghamton, New York: The Haworth Medical P, 2001.

Schroeder, Patricia R. "American Drama, Feminist Discourse, and Dramatic Form: In Defense of Defense of Critical Pluralism." *Journal of Dramatic Theory and Criticism* Spring 1993.

Shorter, Edward. *A History of Psychiatry: From the Era of the Asylum to the Age of Prozac.* New York: John Wiley & Sons, Inc. , 1997.

Simon, John. "Free, Bright, and 31. " Rev. of *Getting Out*, by Marsha Norman. *New York Magazine* 13 Nov. 1978.

——. Marsha Norman's "Trudy Blue. " Rev. of *Trudy Blue*, by Marsha Norman. Web. 4 Sept. 2010. < http: //nymag. com/nymetro/arts/theater/reviews/1685/ >.

——. "Out of the Crucible. " Rev. of *Getting Out*, by Marsha Norman, *La Puce à L'oreille*, by Georges Feydeau and *Tunnel Fever*, by Jonathan Reynolds. *New York Magazine* 5 May. 1979.

——. "Theater Chronicle: Kopit, Norman, and Shepard. " *The Hudson Review* Spring 1979.

Slotkin, Richard. *Gunfighter Nation: The Myth of the Frontier in Twentieth – century America.* New York: Atheneum, 1992.

Smith, Raynette Halvorsen. "'night, Mother and True West: Mirror Images of Violence and Gender. " *Violence in Drama.* Ed. James Redmond. Cambridge: Cambridge UP, 1991.

Solomon, Marion F. "Manifestations of Narcissistic Disorders in Couples Therapy: Identification and Treatment. " *Disorders of Narcissism: Diagnostic, Clinical, and Empirical Implications.* Ed. Elsa Ronningstam. Arlington, VA: American Psychiatric P, Inc. , 1998.

Sontag, Susan. *On Photography.* New York: RosettaBooks LLC, 2005.

Spencer, Jenny S. "Marsha Norman's She-Tragedies. " *Making a Spectacle: Feminist Essays on Contemporary Women's Theatre.* Ed. Lynda Hart. Ann Arbor: Michigan UP, 1989.

——. "Norman's 'night, Mother: Psycho-drama of Female Identity. " *Modern Drama* Sept. 1987.

Stone, Elizabeth. "Playwright Marsha Norman: An Optimist Writes about Suicide, Confinement and Despair. " *MS.* July 1983.

Stout, Kate. Marsha Norman: Writing for the 'Least of Our Brethren. '" *Saturday Review* Sept. – Oct. 1983.

Styan, J. L. *Drama, Stage and Audience.* Cambridge: Cambridge UP, 1975.

Su, Jon J. *Ethics and Nostalgia in the Contemporary Novel.* Cambridge:

Cambridge UP, 2005.

Sullivan, Garrett A. , Jr. *Memory and Forgetting in English Renaissance Drama: Shakespeare, Marlowe, Webster.* Cambridge: Cambridge UP, 2005.

Szondi, Peter. *Theory of the Modern Drama.* Ed. and trans. Michael Hays. Minneapolis: U of Minnesota P, 1987.

Thompson, Elizabeth Rose. *Saving the Southern Sister: Tracing the Survivor Narrative in Southern Women's Modern and Contemporary Novels and Plays.* Diss. U of Memphis, 2010.

Trifonas, Peter Pericles. *Barthes and the Empire of Signs.* Cambridge: Icon Books Ltd. , 2001.

Truitt, Judi. "Marsha Norman: Her Life, Her Literature, Her Legacy." *Kentucky Journal of Communication* Fall 1999.

Turner, Frederick Jackson. *The Frontier in American History.* New York: Henry Holt and Company, 1920.

Tyler, Lisa. " 'This Haunted Girl': Marsha Norman's Adaptation of *The Secret Garden.* " L. Brown, *Marsha Norman* 133 – 44.

Wald, Christina. *Hysteria, Trauma and Melancholia: Performative Maladies in Contemporary Anglophone Drama.* New York: Palgrave Macmillan, 2007.

Wattenberg, Richard. "Feminizing the Frontier Myth: Marsha Norman's *The Holdup.* " *Modern Drama* Dec. 1990.

Weales, Gerald. "A Long Way to Broadway. " Rev. of *Traveler in the Dark*, by Marsha Norman and *Squirrels*, by David Mamet. *Commonweal* 23 Feb. 1990.

——. "Really 'Going On': Marsha Norman's Pulitzer Winner. " Rev. of *'night, Mother*, by Marsha Norman. *Commonweal* 17 June 1983.

Webster's Encyclopedic Unabridged Dictionary of the English Language. Rev. ed. New York, Avenel: Gramercy Books, 1996.

Weiraub, Bernard. "A Teen Queen Follows in Her Idol's Footsteps. " Rev. of *The Audrey Hepburn Story* by Marsha Norman. *The New York Times Television Reviews* 2000. Chicago: Fitzroy Dearborn Publishers, 2001.

Wertheim, Albert. "Eugene O'Neill's *Days Without End* and the Tradition of the Split Character in Modern American and British Drama. " *Eugene O'Neill Newsletter 6 Winter 1982.*

Whitehead, Anne. *Memory.* New York: Routledge, 2009.

Williams, Tennessee. *The Glass Menagerie.* Oxford: Heinemann Educational Publishers, 1996.

Wilson, Janelle L. *Nostalgia: Sanctuary of Meaning.* Cranbury, NJ: Rosemont Publishing & Printing Corp. , 2005.

Wimmer, Cynthia L. *Slicing Silences and Hatchet Words: Operations of Women's Anger in Twentieth Century Plays by American Women.* Diss. U. of Maryland, 2001.

Winnicott, Donald Woods. *Playing and Reality.* London: Routledge, 1991.

Wolf, Naomi. *The Beauty Myth: How Images of Beauty are Used Against Women.* New York: HarperCollins, 2002.

Workman, Jennifer Anne. *Marsha Norman's Ghosts: The Embodiment of the Past on the Stage.* MA Thesis Indiana State U, 1993.

Wren, Celia. "A Bleak Prison Break, 'Getting Out' Explores a Haunted Past. " Rev. of *Getting Out*, by Marsha Norman. *The Washington Post* 12 Sept. 2007: C04.

Wynette, Tammy and Billy Sherill. *Stand by Your Man.* Web. 15 Sept. 2011. < http: //www. stlyrics. com/lyrics/sleeplessinseattle/standbyyourman. htm >.

Zhang, Jinliang. *Language as a Perspective: A Study of Three Contemporary American Dramatists.* Diss. Nanjing U, 2007.

蔡晓燕, 从杰茜的选择看存在的困境—解读玛莎·诺曼的《晚安, 妈妈》. 戏剧文学, 2008 (6): 46 – 49.

岑玮, 女性身份的嬗变—莉莲·海尔曼与马莎·诺曼剧作研究. 山东大学出版社 2009 年版。

陈迈平, 漫谈当前西方现实主义戏剧状况. 中国戏剧, 1984 (10): 29 – 32.

符泉生, 美国公布今年普利策奖获奖名单. 译林, 1983 (3): 265.

贺安芳, 后女性主义社会的女性自塑——从《心灵之罪》到《晚安母亲》再到《海蒂编年史》. 四川戏剧, 2007 (2): 25 – 29.

刘秀玉, 从《晚安, 妈妈》看玛莎·诺曼的女性主义戏剧创作. 辽宁大学学报，2008（3）：59－62.

刘岩，西方现代戏剧中的母亲身份研究．中国书籍出版社，2004年版。

石坚，论玛莎·诺曼的女主角的现实世界与幻想世界．戏剧，1998（4）：43－47.

汤立峰，"因为你已经死了"：玛夏·诺曼《母亲，晚安》一剧解读．戏剧，1997（1）：43－45.

陶家俊，创伤．外国文学，2011（4）：117－125.

吾文泉，跨文化对话与融会：当代美国戏剧在中国．中国社会科学出版社，2005年版。

左进，韩仲谦，死亡背后的深爱—《晚安，母亲》中呼语的语用解读．名作欣赏，2010（12）：129－131.

后　记

　　本书的完成得益于我的导师刘海平教授的悉心指导和帮助。在南京大学外国语学院读书期间，他严谨的治学态度以及在生活上对我的悉心关怀和帮助对我的学业产生了积极的影响，在此表示衷心的感谢。

　　在南京大学求学期间，我得到了朱刚教授、杨金才教授、王守仁教授、何成洲教授、江宁康教授、程爱民教授和赵文书教授等的教诲，对他们表示感谢。

　　我在南京大学求学期间以及后来重新回到曲阜师范大学外国语学院工作期间，在此书的撰写、修改和出版的过程中，有很多的同学、同事和朋友为我提供帮助和精神上的支持，没有他们的帮助，不会有这本书的问世。感谢课题组成员张生珍、张琳、兰海英对该书所付出的努力。

　　感谢我的挚友陈琳博士，她对我的信任、关爱和支持让我永生难忘。感谢好友胡静、王华、但汉松、麻晓蓉、罗媛对我在各方面的支持和帮助。

　　本书的出版得到了曲阜师范大学外国语学院出版基金的资助，感谢外国语学院领导的关心和帮助，督促我在学术研究的道路上前进。中国社会科学出版社的侯苗苗老师对本书的出版给予了大力支持，在此表示由衷的感谢。

　　我要感谢我的父母和公公婆婆，他们的朴实、善良和积极进取的人生态度让我受益终生。感谢一直支持我的爱人霍青，在我读书期间，他不仅要照看好女儿，更是我心灵的港湾。还要感谢我的女儿霍佳艺，她的乖巧懂事让我能够安心完成学业。他们对我的爱使我的思考和研究更有意义。

王莉

2014 年 4 月